Dear Diary, Book Series

Book 1

Dear Diary,

The Bullying Won't Stop

UNCUT

A Young Adult Novel

By: Delicia B. Davis

Precise Publishing Group
c/o Precise Production Group Inc.

Precise Publishing Group
c/o Precise Production Group Inc. 2013
New York

Precise Publishing Group:
Precise Production Group Inc.
233 Street Rosedale, NY 11422

Visit our website at www.ppgdreams.com

"Dear Diary, The Bullying Won't Stop"
First Edition: UNCUT

ISBN-13: 978-0-9892253-0-4

ISBN-10: 0989225305

"We all wanna be normal just like everybody else, but the truth is, we all have issues but no one ever tells…"

-Delicia B. Davis

UNLOCK YOUR SECRETS TO SET YOURSELF FREE

Dedication

~

I dedicate this book not only to my precious twin sons, Avery & Avion, who I am committed to standing up against bullying for; but also to *all* the youth who have encountered the act of force, intimidation, or violence used against them.

You are not alone.

My Inspiration

~

As an avid reader in my youth, I also grew very passionate about writing. So at an early age, I began recording some of my deepest thoughts in a collection of diaries. This has always helped me to let out my pain, anger, fears, and joys when I couldn't contain them anymore. This story is a recollection of the experiences seen, heard, and sensed.

In the time it took me to write this book, I continuously learned of incidents concerning bullying. It hurt me to know that similar situations I encountered in my own life as a child had become a growing epidemic in today's world; now ending in injury, mental illness, longstanding suffering, and even in death. I became discouraged at times, thinking I wouldn't be able to offer a resolve, but I, myself, have survived some painful and trying experiences and here I still stand. I had to share my story of triumph no matter how long it took. I continuously encourage my readers never to give up as they strive to achieve even the most difficult of dreams. Remember: You will only win if you **survive**.

Although I've seen some challenging times and even thought I had reached my breaking point, I learned to never give up and to always persevere. You just never know how close you are to a breakthrough unless you get through. My encounters with bullies have not only made me stronger but have forced me to grow. Through this story, I share with you my personal lessons of life and love. I truly hope the experiences portrayed in this fictional story evokes some **real** inspiration, strength, and change.

My Appreciation

~

I cannot stress enough how much I appreciate the loved ones who supported me throughout the making of this book. Those who believed in my vision and continued to encourage- and even pushed- me to complete it. In my darkest of days when I was not physically or emotionally strong enough to continue on, I had such great motivators to help me through.

First, I must give my thanks to **God**. I thank Him for my talents, my gifts, my creativity, my strength, my loving heart, and my sound mind. I thank Him for helping me turn every tragedy into a triumph and for allowing me to share my blessings with so many others.

I would like to thank my sons, **Avery and Avion**, who still have no idea how much of a role they played in my survival. Their smiles, their hugs, their kisses, and their various development stages have given me reason to persevere on the daily. Times when I didn't want to even get out of bed were quickly negated by their boisterous cries and most especially their newfound words such as, "Mommy", "I love you", "please", "thank you", and so many more. Their developing skills as artists, dancers, athletes, and strong little men have given me so much to look forward to in our present days and our futures. If ever I needed to find a reason to accomplish a goal in my life, they give me two.

To my parents, **Delroy and Donna**, who were extremely hard on me growing up, I thank you. Daddy and mommy set very high expectations for my siblings and I. They encouraged us to do a lot with a little, and so I did. They allowed me to do more with my mind and less with materials. As a result, I spent my entire life conjuring up creative thoughts, ideas, and visions. Most of all, they made me realize I had the power to bring them all to life. They've taught me to be strong in the midst of struggle, forgiving in the midst of pain, rich in the midst of squalor, independent in times of need, and faithful in times of doubt. There was so much value in the lessons they taught me. Although I didn't always see the benefit of their tough loving actions, I definitely do now and want to thank them for giving me such beneficial gifts that will continue to radiate through me for a lifetime and beyond.

To my younger sister, **Dawn**, who has always been my confidant & very best friend, thank you for your ongoing love and support. Even when we don't agree and our ideas conflicted, you always knew my heart and judged me solely on the love we shared. You've had my back when I least expected you to, supported me when no one else would, and gave me a helping hand in any and every way possible. Your maturity, independence, spirituality, strength, and will to do right has always inspired me. Even as my younger sister, I look up to you, literally (lol). And I will forever be grateful to you for being a sister, a supporter, a listener, a motivator, and best of all- a friend.

To my only brother, **Delroy Jr.**, I've watched you grow up to be a smart, handsome, talented young fella. I am proud to call myself your sister. When I lose all hope in the men of our generation, you continuously demonstrate what true chivalry, respect, love, and loyalty should be and most of all- that it still exists.

To my older sister, **Donel**, thank you for supporting my vision all the way through. You have always shared your knowledge, your gift of song, and voice of reason with me throughout my ever changing phases in this process. You've made yourself present for me whenever I needed you; whether to swing by the house or to show up at an event, and that to me is priceless.

To my ever-growing extended **family**, I thank you all. As a parent myself, I know it takes a whole village to raise a child. So I thank all my aunts, uncles, cousins, grandparents, friends of family, adopted grandparents, God family, and loved ones who were instrumental in my life. I appreciate all times spent with you, learning, growing, experiencing, and enjoying life. These memories are never forgotten.

To my God brother, **Clive Jr.,** who I've known a lifetime, thank you for pushing me, entertaining me, encouraging me, and acknowledging my creative gifts. You were one of the first to read the drafted pages of my book and gave me the thumbs up I needed to continue on and most importantly- to finish.

To the Godparents of my children, **Silvia**, **Travis**, **Kashmire**, and **Beth**, I've entrusted you all with the role of caring and loving for my kids for a reason. You've all given me an enormous amount of support and encouragement throughout many, many years. You've been there for me in times of joy and in times of struggle. You've given me strength, love, and wisdom. On top of all that, you have always provided me an ear to listen and a shoulder to lean on. Thank you for being more than my best friends, consistently loving me, and for understanding me when no one else would.

To my Goddaughter, **Skyy**, for coming into my life and showing me so much love from day one. Your beauty, your innocence, your talents, and your mind are all an inspiration to me as a parent. Your mother, **Andrea J**, one of my very best friends, has done a wonderful job raising you. I love and appreciate you for being such a profound reader and proving that literature in the lives of our youth, is still alive.

To my manager, **Glenmore Marshall**, who quickly became a new friend, I thank you for seeing greatness in me. I appreciate you sharing your many, many talents and gifts with me and in such a short time, changing my outlook and my life. I thank you for your time and your support and for aiding me in the completion and anticipated success of this book.

To my Writing Assistant, **Xavia Malcolm,** thank you for believing in my vision from the start. For giving me your honest opinions and ideas, and always being there for me in the midst of my constantly changing schedule. You are a smart, talented woman with so much foreseeable success in your future. I have been so blessed to have you by my side throughout the progression of this book and more.

To all my **Precise Production Group** staff who have each helped build upon this dream with me, I thank and appreciate you. You each possess such profound creative gifts that have touched so many lives. As we enter schools, organizations, youth groups, media outlets, homes, churches, and more; I know I can trust you all to deliver inspiration, motivation, and the vast creative skills that our company is built upon.

To **SUS**, my **first client ever**, I thank you for giving me an opportunity to work with you. For giving me my first chance to change lives, helping me build upon my dreams, and for the growth you've allowed me over our many years working together.

To all the **organizations** who have supported the anti-bullying movement from the start, thank you. You are allowing us to reach a wider range of youth much faster than I could've done on my own. Thanks for seeing my message, my vision, and my creative talents through.

To my **friends**, I love you! I cannot express how much you each have touched and affected my life thus far. I haven't always had such great friends around me so I appreciate you being in my life more than you'd ever know. I've spent countless nights out and many days in chatting, sharing, vacationing, dining, shopping, reflecting, experiencing, and living with you in my midst. I take my friendships very seriously so please know that anyone I call a friend, it is to my honor. Thank you for being there and answering every text, call, email, FB message, and more. Thanks for supporting my many events and limitless dreams. My life wouldn't be the same without you and I hope our friendship continues for life.

To my **coworkers** and **fellow parkies**, I love you for making work more than just a job to me. For keeping me busy, allowing me to learn and grow as a leader, meet great people, express my creativity, and experience new and wonderful things on the daily.

Share your thoughts

@

facebook.com/deardiarybooks

#deardiary #uncut

The bullying stops here...

"#DearDiary OMG I cant believe Patricia let
that happen during lunch! #volume2
#summerdaze #beatdown #stopthebullying"

Diary Log

Delicia B. Davis

VOLUME 1: IS THIS THE END?

Dear Diary,   *Monday June 19th*

I fuckin' hate my life!

And I've been keeping this old diary ever since my grandparents gave it to me 6 years ago on the Christmas before they died, so now's a better time than any other to start using it. Dammit, I'm fed up with this life of mine and there ain't no one to talk to about it but you.

People on the outside think I'm lucky enough to be living amongst the urban elite in one of the most affluent neighborhoods on Long Island. But Northfield Lane is more than just beautiful homes, manicured lawns, and fancy cars. It's also about keeping up with the Joneses and keeping your skeletons so deep in the closet that no one can see your struggle or your pain. You should never pout or complain because the way we live is how the rest of the world dreams of living. *Yea right!*

Our home may be comprised of sun-filled street views, high ceilings, and granite countertops but the curtains were often kept closed, the constant shouting was all that echoed through the halls, and my mother hardly ever cooked on those counters. Living the "good life" was not at all for me what it should've been.

I sometimes watched the kids next door play outside on their porch and I longed to have the genuine smile and laugh they did. Their mothers would come outside with a glass of fruit punch and share some quality time with them. Their fathers would join them for a basketball game or a swing on their swing set. That was not my reality. I didn't have a loving mother and I had no father period- at least

1

that's what my mother told me.

She said I was being ungrateful for even asking about him.

"You better be happy you finally got a lil money now and a working brain. Stop worrying about all that other stupid shit because none of that is gonna get you anywhere in life..." I guess she expected me to be materialistic and vain just because I live amongst people who were. But I'm different and I've always known it.

I mean, I appreciate my grandparents working their asses off when they were alive so that we could thrive off their wealth, but I also resent them a bit. They forgot to teach my mother how important it is to love. To them, it was much more important to portray the right image and keep up a good appearance. Well, I'm sick and tired of living the lie of bliss and perfection.

With everything I have to deal with amongst my peers, my mother pretends to be a supportive and comforting single parent when we were out in public; but behind our iron clad French doors, she was just as violent and mean as everyone else. And I can no longer keep up the facade.

It's time for me to find a way out of this awfully painted picture of a life I'm living or someone is gonna get brutally hurt- and I do mean that literally.

But I'm gonna need you to promise me you'll keep my secrets because I'm feigning to get some things off my chest. For the longest time, I've been letting all this eat me up inside. I haven't had any friends or family to share this with and it's finally time I let this shit out...

Dear Diary,   *Monday June 24th*

OMG! Today was officially the worst day of my life!

You wouldn't believe this, but just a few days before the school year ended, I was chased off the school bus today and left humiliated and scared. This beautiful spring day quickly turned gloomy when I became the target of a group of angry kids.

"Leave me alone!" I pleaded hoping the mean girls from my class would back down. But they were out to get me and they weren't giving up. So I just kept on running and had no plans of stopping.

This wasn't the first time I had to face torture from my peers but I damn sure hoped it was my last. It was humiliating being a loner and a punk. But that was me. I come from a beautiful but broken home and moreover, I was feeling a bit broken. Over the past 3 years of junior high, there was nothing I could do to shake the pitiful reputation I had at *Northfield Junior High.*

Even though the other students had my skin color and came from the same upper middle class neighborhood, they didn't understand my personal struggles. They didn't know what it was like to be a slightly introverted 8th grader. To be teased and mistreated on the regular was just an awful way to live. I don't dress as fly as them or get the kinks straightened out of my hair as often as they do. I have my share of issues at home and just try to focus on my grades when I'm at school. I've never had much of a social life and for that reason, I dread each day of school.

So there I was today, just making it through to the end of junior high and I was running for my damn life.

After all the teasing I'd dealt with these past few years from my peers, I thought I could stand up for myself, just this once, and end off the year with a win. It was my final chance to make a statement to the other kids before we all entered high school and I was labeled a punk forever.

So this time, when Dina and her crew tried to cut me on the bus line, I stopped them. I told Dina, "Hey! Wait your turn," as she pushed past me. She refused, so I put my hand out to stop her and she bumped into my arm.

"I know she did not just touch me!" Dina yelled, not realizing *she* actually touched *me*. But I knew she was too ignorant to argue with so I just stepped out the way and allowed her and the others to go ahead. Apparently it was too late, the whole crew was angry with me. They came at me demanding I show some "respect".

"This little bitch still don't know her place?!" someone yelled. "Let's teach her a lesson once and for all."

Dina pushed me out of the line and onto the bus shelter in the middle of the sidewalk. The whole group followed. I stumbled a bit as my head hit the cold hard glass. As I stood up and tried to back away, they were eagerly coming at me with clenched fists. I was afraid of what would happen next.

So I ran for my damn life, down the street, through a convenience store front, out through the back door, over someone's fence and onto an unfamiliar street. But the girls caught up to me and had me cornered. The boys who had followed behind gathered around to watch the beat down of the year.

All I remember was a tug of my shirt, a slap to my face, and a punch to my stomach. By then I was down and out.

As if they hadn't done enough damage, Dina signaled the crew to crowd closer around me. Some of the girls kicked me repeatedly while the others took my book bag and threw all my stuff to the ground. They were having a good ole time, at my expense.

I had actually hoped today would be the end of all the tormenting these kids had put me through over the years. But as I lay on the ground bruised and alone when my attackers ran away, I realized the bullying just won't stop. ☹

~

I lay there for what felt like at least an hour before a fine ass brother helped me up. I couldn't see clearly through my hazy vision but I do remember the touch of his smooth brown skin and those light brown eyes looking at me with such concern. I finally felt safe as I closed my eyes and passed out in his arms.

Dear Diary,   *Tuesday June 25ᵗʰ*

I woke up this morning in excruciating pain. I couldn't even turn to get out of bed. My stomach felt twisted inside, my face was burning, and I felt stabs of pain throughout my leg. As much as I tried to hold back tears, they came pouring down my face.

I probably needed to go to a hospital but after several visits to the emergency room over the past few years, I knew what I was in store for- long waits, a Band Aid, and a doctor's note. I was very familiar with the process.

My mother and I had our fights over the years so I was no stranger to the scuffs these stupid kids caused me. For some reason, I couldn't bring myself to tell her what happened though. The last time I cried about someone teasing me, she punished me for being *soft*. I couldn't imagine what she'd do to me now.

Coming from a single parent home, I know better than to complain to my mother about these things. She busts her tail working at *Northfield General Hospital*- the largest and highest rated health facility in our area- as a Nurse practitioner; so I have always appreciated the basic things she provides.

Love, style, and a peaceful life just weren't any one of them. So I knew I'd have to find those things elsewhere.

Of course it hurts me that I'm judged based on my appearance alone, but I know I'm a damn good person and one day people are gonna look deeper and realize that. Too bad today ain't that day.

And you know what, my grandmother prepared me for that rude awakening. She used to tell me to "always dress the part" and "look the way you want to be looked at". But my mother never allowed me to get the gear needed to carry out the right image. She actually prefers me suffering and enjoys witnessing my failure. It gave her the ammo she needed to put me down. It seemed like that's all that made her feel good. So I just deal with it.

Then at school, it's no better. My classmates have always made it clear how little they think of me and sometimes their awful words spoke louder than their cruel actions.

"Rat face! Twig legs! Flatty Patty!" the boys shout at me from time to time referring to my mouse-shaped ears, long skinny legs, and small boobs.

"Geek bitch! Plain Jane! Loser!" The girls would say referencing my rare intellect, my less than stylish clothing, and lack of social status.

These kids hated me for not having the values they had. They didn't like that I didn't focus on fashion, status, and beauty... probably because that was where all *their* power resided.

So as you know, this last week of school was pure torture. As ecstatic as I was about ending this awful chapter of my life-junior high- I couldn't enjoy it. There was always someone trying to mess with me.

But I tried to stay hopeful as I swallowed 2 of the painkillers I hid under my queen sized mattress.

I just can't wait for these pills to kick in so I could go to sleep and escape my pain. Because at this point, life can't get any worse.

Dear Diary,   *Wednesday June 26th*

What was I saying before? It couldn't get any worse? Well I for damn sure *lied*.

I decided not to go to school for the last few days. I mean, it's the last days of school and we're not learning anything anyhow. Well, my mother had a lesson waiting for *me* when she came home from work today.

Apparently the school called to let her know I hadn't picked up my report card today. *Dammit!* I completely forgot about that. The last day of school came quicker than I realized. So she was *pissed!*

As good as I got at keeping it a secret from her, it was time to tell my mother about my fight. I started to explain to her how wounded I was from this fight—matter of fact—the *beat down*, and all she could say was, "Your punk ass let those damn kids fight you?!" She wasn't the least bit concerned about the pain I was in or the torture I had endured.

"Ma, don't you care that them kids came running after me for no reason?" I pleaded for her to understand. "They caught up to me, stole my book bag, and beat me nearly to *death*!"

It was awful just thinking back about it. The punches, the kicking, and the embarrassment I faced as I lay on the dirty ground. It was the worst beating I had ever gotten, and that's saying a lot.

Until this moment, I had no one to confide in about this awful event. Telling my mother should have been a relief. But she didn't have even an ounce of empathy.

"You stay letting people come at you and you don't do nothing about it! That's your fuckin' fault! When's your weak ass gonna learn to defend yourself?!" My mother spoke to me with rage.

"How can you blame me for this, ma? They're always messin' with me and I don't know the first thing about defending myself." She looked back at me with both anger and disgrace then smacked me straight across my face with the back of her hand.

"Little girl, I done taught you everything you need to know."

I guess she expected that after years of taking her beatings, I would have learned to fight back. But instead, I was just beaten down and left defeated. All I wanted was a little peace in my life.

I stood there with both pain and shock. It had been a while since she hit me like that. Just as I was recovering, she came back and slapped me again, this time on my other cheek.

"That's for cutting school," she said. "You do that again , it's gon' be fire to your ass."

"But ma, I was hurt," I cried. But she didn't give a damn at all.

"Get over it!" She turned to leave the room. "Tomorrow you gon' have to go and get me that report card so you better dry up those tears from now."

I knew there was nothing more I could say. I had to obey her or *else*. I knew what was coming for me.

My mother had some anger so deeply rooted inside her that clouded her vision of any happiness. She didn't date and never really hung out with friends. She only enjoyed using me as a punching bag and I couldn't stop her. For a beautiful curvy woman, she sure knew how to display the ugly she had inside. I've always longed for her and I to get along. I mean, every girl wants a mother they could talk to. But I was shit outta luck on that. All she wanted to do with me is fight.

I've always tried to figure her out- but at 13, there's no reason I could come up with to explain the hatred she had for me. All I ever wanted was to be loved.

I'm her only child—her only family. Her only anything. I should be everything to my mom but she treated me like I was nothing. And at the end of a day like this—that's exactly how I felt.

Dear Diary,   *Thursday June 27th*

My mother drove me to school today and waited outside while I picked up my report card. As I was leaving her car, she hissed at me, "your smart ass *better* had got all A's."

And I knew that's exactly what she was expecting. But I was afraid I didn't get it this time. All year long, I sat in front of a boy in math that teased me. Tyrone always whispered weird mean things in my ear when I tried to raise my hand and ask a question.

"A smarty pants with all the stupidest questions," and "Only losers actually *want* to learn," he would say.

He pulled my hair and made itchy, scratchy noises whenever I touched my hair myself.

It was so intimidating and the teacher didn't give a damn about how I felt. I had been trying to get my seat changed the whole year and she insisted the seating chart was "strategically done to benefit the whole class and not just one person." *I mean, would it have been so hard to put all the troublemakers on one side of the room and those who wanted to learn at the other?*

I even told my mother about the issues I was having and she thought I was being petty complaining about a "stupid little boy who probably had a stupid little crush." But I knew well enough, Tyrone didn't like me one bit and neither did any of his friends.

Then in science, I had the popular girls threatening me not to get a perfect score and mess up the curve *"or else"*. It hurt my core daily. Tyrone and the others messed with my social life, my self-esteem, and even the one thing I thought no one could ever take away from me—my ability to learn.

So I didn't need to see my report card to know there would be at least one or two A's missing from it this time.

When I walked into the classroom, my homeroom teacher, Ms. Grimmer handed it to me with a look of disappointment in her eyes. I wasn't sure if it was because I'd cut a few days of school or because my report card was less than she expected of me, so I asked.

"Is something wrong, Ms. Grimmer?"

"Honestly, Patricia, I wanted to ask you the same," she looked at me with seriousness. "This was one of your worst reports ever. Is something happening at home?"

"Well Ms. Grimmer," I decided to tell her half the truth. "It's not so much home as it's been school, recess, and the bus rides home. All the other kids hate me. No one wants to be my friend. Everyone teases me," I expressed to her.

She seemed surprised at how honest I'd been.

"Well, I'm sure all you kids have your individual challenges. Some choose to deal with it by ignoring it and some of you take it out on others."

"That's not fair. Isn't that bullying?" I asked.

"I guess you can call it that," she replied. "But you can't blame anyone for your falling grades. You're the one who made these things affect your schoolwork and that's your fault. It's sad though, you had so much potential."

She was blaming me now! Did she not know what the teasing and threats did to a person? After opening up to her, I realized she didn't understand me one bit. She was basically telling me it was my fault for being affected by the constant torture. She sounded just like my mother.

How could they blame me for the awful way people treated me?! I didn't deserve this. It's simply human nature that I took my peers' awful words to heart.

They believed it was okay to allow my classmates to mistreat me this way? And that bullying was a simple little thing I had to just get over?

I heard enough. I took my report card from her and received my grades. I got three A's, two B's, and two C's. This certainly wasn't good enough for my mother or my teachers but after the tumultuous year I just had, it was good enough for *me*.

I forced a smile and just thanked Ms. Grimmer then wished her a great summer. There was no use hanging around her and her insensitivity any longer.

As I'm walking out she says, "Good luck in high school, Patricia. There are bigger problems and tougher kids. Better learn how to adapt now."

Her words stung me just to think about the next four years being any worse that the past three. I had to make a conscience decision to make things better. I couldn't let another person affect me the way Tyrone, Dina, and the others had this year.

As I walked outside to the car, I dreaded showing the report card and explaining it to my mother. I was afraid of what she would say and even worse... what she would *do*.

Dear Diary,   *Friday June 28th*

My mother didn't take the report card too well.

While in the car yesterday, she played it off cool. It was like it didn't even matter. I passed her my report card, she glanced at it briefly and threw it back at me. She had to rush off to work so she dropped me home with the quickness.

But when she got home this morning, it was a whole other story. She woke me up at two in the morning and asked me to show her the report card again.

I was deep in my slumber when she came in but I still conjured up the strength to obey my mother's wishes. She takes the paper from me and looks at my grades in awe as if it was her first time seeing it.

Then she made me read the grades aloud to her, although she had already seen it. But I knew what this was. She had a bad day and was trying to pick a fight.

"I just don't understand, Patricia. Why the hell you getting C's all of a sudden?"

"Well ma," if she really wanted to know, I decided to tell her. "I haven't been able to concentrate this year. The kids have been teasing me and threatening me and it's been a huge distraction." I tried to hold back tears because that would be the ultimate sign of weakness in the presence of my mom.

"You mean to tell me, you're letting them kids affect your grades now? Dammit Patricia! If you can't keep your grades on point, what the hell am I gonna do with you? " she yelled.

"Ma, I'm gonna start over. I know I can do better. Please give me a chance. I'm sorry." I begged for her forgiveness. As much as it hurt to hear her say it, it was true. All I have in my favor is getting good grades and I was letting that falter too.

My mother sat down on my bed shaking her head with disgrace. "You always so damn sorry. Your weak ass is always letting people get the best of you. First you let them kids chase you down and punk you on the bus, now you telling me they're threatening your schoolwork. You're hopeless."

"I'm sorry ma. Maybe if daddy was around..."

"Why the hell you bringing up your father?!" she interrupted angrily. "I done told you, you don't got one."

"Ma, I gotta have one. Why can't you tell me something about him? Anything?" I asked.

She turned around and swung her hands in my face. Yet another blow to my cheek for the week and it stung *bad*.

"Like I said, 'you don't got one'. And with the mess you be putting *me* through, you don't deserve one either." That wasn't the first time she dodged questions I asked about my dad. It was risky every time I tried. *But how could I not?*

She got up to leave my room but not before giving me her last and final order. "Tomorrow you better clean this house top to bottom. Better believe you ain't sitting on your ass all summer long doing nothin."

"Yes, ma'am," I obeyed.

VOLUME 2: SUMMER DAZE

Dear Diary,   *Saturday June 29th*

I did as my mother said of course and spent the entire first day of my summer vacation cleaning. It wasn't so bad having to do chores in an empty house. My mother wasn't there to harass me about what I was doing and how I was doing it. And best of all, I no longer had to face the kids at my school again or at least for the next few months. I was left alone in the house with just my thoughts.

My house was hardly a home to me with the dark dreary colors surrounding me. It was a large 2 story house with our bedrooms placed in two separate wings on the 2nd floor. We never had company and the stark smell that never escaped made the house feel more like a prison. Our furniture is expensive and covered with plastic since my grandparents suggested we preserve it that way. We never entertain so the plastic was never removed. We have one television in the untouchable living room and another kept in my mother's usually locked room. Watching television was rare for me because both TV's were difficult to share with someone like her.

She set parental controls on everything from the TV, to the internet, to the phone. She just had to keep her reigns on me even when she wasn't around. She never wanted to lose control of me.

Her parents passed away when I was 7 and that affects us both daily. Since then, my mother doesn't even speak of them or keep pictures of her mother and father in the living room anymore. It was as if a part of her died too. The loving, calm, seemingly happy part of her left and the angry, mean, abusive part of her moved in.

I've been longing to have some other family in my life for when times get tough. But my mother and I only had each other. And that really wasn't enough for me. I wanted a relationship with her. I needed love. I needed my father. Or I at least needed a friend.

How would I get it though? People don't even like me. How would I make friends? What would make people respect me?

I was constantly searching for answers.

I looked in the mirror and was disappointed with what I saw. I'm too thin, I have mousy ears, and my hair's too short. There was nothing likeable about me.

How are people gonna like me if I don't even like myself? I'm too smart to be cool. And too skinny to be cute. All I want to do is *fit in*. I want to be accepted for being me. Is that so much to ask?!

I want a father and a mother who truly loves me. I want to make friends who care. Overall, I just want to be loved. Is that too much to ask???????

I've taken enough beatings, now I'm left feeling weak and alone.

Enough is enough, how much more do I have to take?

I guess I don't deserve love or friendship *or* happiness because if I did, I would have it. Life simply isn't fair!!

I threw myself onto the bed and cried myself to sleep. Not knowing whether this life of mine was even worth living.

>:-(

Dear Diary,   *Friday July 7*[th]

Thankfully, my mind was quickly taken off my problems. My mother came home the other day with a brochure from a local day camp she signed me up for— Camp Cultivate.

Frankly, I was feeling a little too grown for camp but it was something to do that would keep me from the depressing summer days I was already having. Besides my mother wouldn't stop bragging about how expensive it was and how all the doctor's kids at her job go there. *Whatever!*

I started today and I think I was a little late registering because everyone had already made friends. It figures I would be the odd man out... like always.

The cliques had already formed and some of the teens already chose their pretend daughters—which are the cutest, coolest little kids who get adopted by the prettiest, coolest big kids for the duration of summer camp. They would give each other candy, do their hair, and basically have each other's back. And as usual, I had no one.

I wore my cutest outfit too, a jumpsuit shorts set covered with a colorful floral design. Apparently my version of it was the knock-off and a girl named Anastasia had the real thing. Of course she pointed it out and had her whole crew and their "daughters" laughing at me during lunchtime.

"What a coincidence," Anastasia said sounding like the snob she is. "You're wearing the imitation version of my outfit! I guess you couldn't afford the real thing." The surrounding crowd laughed at me in unison. I was so embarrassed. It was my first day at the day camp and I was already the laughingstock of all my peers.

It amazed me how much emphasis these girls put on labels and things in the first place. We all know to be living in Northfield, meant you had to have some standard of class and status. No one was broke and Anastasia knew it.

Well, I still couldn't take the embarrassment so I spent the rest of the break hiding in the bathroom. It was chicks like Ms. Anastasia why I could never be happy.

Dear Diary,   *Monday July 10th*

All I wanted was to make one friend at Camp Cultivate this week and things would be a lot easier for me. So I sought out any other loners at the camp and I noticed one chick that was sitting by herself in the play yard eating and playing with her phone. That had to be my new friend. I needed just one person to talk to. I just couldn't be alone.

I introduced myself and her name was Judy. She's an only child just like me, a little overweight, and was kind of a techno geek. I thought she was cool though.

She showed me a few games in her phone. She told me how she hacked into them and got the pricey ones for free. She amazed me with her fascination of technology; something I hardly knew anything about. She taught me a few things and even let me play with her phone.

I loved hanging with Judy because she either didn't know she was a loner or she didn't care. Her ability to be content with so little was impressive. I wish I could be more like that.

She was a little sloppy when she ate but I overlooked it. Judy was great, even though she was always stuffing her face with cheese curls and licked her cheesy fingers from time to time. I accepted her, mostly because she accepted me.

I was happy to have Judy by my side during our lunch break, in the yard, and even while the group was making crafts. Judy was full of great ideas- like how she would someday invent a phone that could beam food to us and create a digital cook that could prepare all her meals. Of course they were all great ideas for a big eater like herself and as I laughed, I still encouraged her to pursue her unique inventions.

I have never been one to rain on anyone's parade. Besides, now that I had a friend, I was determined to keep her.

Dear Diary,   *Tuesday July 11*[th]

Anastasia came up to me this morning and says "nice shoes" referring to the only pair of name brand loafers I used my birthday money to get last year. "A little outdated," she confirmed. "But cute."

This chick Anastasia was a real bitch. I could just tell she didn't mean anyone well, and I started to hate her.

She was one of those girls who tried so hard to be the prettiest and most popular that if anyone ever threatened her status, she would take them down. She probably had low self-esteem just like the rest of us but flaunted her money and status in everyone's face to gain power. I wasn't buying it.

Her attitude wasn't impressive to me at all. She wasn't even that cute either. Without her tightly pulled ponytail and perfectly curled bang, she would not be as attractive. And the expensive clothes she wore were not as appealing as she thought, I hated.

It was the fear of being ridiculed by Anastasia that drew everyone to her. It was her threatening demeanor that caused people to supposedly respect her. But I could tell by looking she was an evil, jealous little chick on the inside. She wanted everything she couldn't have and was eager to snatch it whenever she could.

I had to guard my friendship with Judy carefully because I knew Ms. Anastasia was on the pry.

Dear Diary,   *Wednesday July 12th*

Just as I figured, Anastasia was jealously observing the happiness I was experiencing with my newfound friend. For the first time in my life, I had someone to laugh with and talk to about my troubled life. I was just starting to open up about the bullying situation I'd been encountering thus far and asked if she could relate.

Judy stated, "Girl, nobody's ever gonna bully me! See how big *I* am?!" I joined her in laughter.

But when Anastasia noticed me Judy and I laughing together in the playground during lunch, she had to intervene. She couldn't accept the fact that two people were minding their business enjoying themselves without her.

"What are you doing with this *fatso*, Patty?" Anastasia said to me. I was surprised she knew my name and even more so, she nicknamed me.

"We're just hanging out," I replied. "My friend Judy doesn't care what designer I'm wearing nor where I got it from."

I didn't bother looking up from what Judy and I were doing. I just couldn't give Ms. Anastasia the satisfaction.

But she wasn't giving up so easily.

She stepped up closer and said, "Look, I'm wearing the outfit you had on the other day. But mine's from J. Crew. I wanted to invite you to come shopping with me and my mom this weekend. You'll see the stuff is so much cooler than..." she looked me up and down... "Wherever you usually shop."

Although she sparked my interest with this shopping invite, I couldn't leave my girl Judy hanging after Anastasia just insulted her. I wanted to know more about this invitation but that wasn't the time to ask. "I'll pass," was all I could say.

Anastasia shrugged her shoulders. "Your loss," she said and walked away.

"That girl has some nerve!" I exclaimed when Anastasia walked away. But Judy was scowling at *me*.

"Damn, that was a punk ass move!" she said angrily. I was so confused. "That girl just dissed me and you *let* her?"

"Uh, you were here too. You could have defended yourself." I said.

"She was talking to you. It wasn't exactly my place to jump in. It was yours!" Judy was pissed off and I was at a loss for words. "If you'd let people call me fat in front of my face. I wonder what you'd let them call me behind my back!" she continued.

"C'mon, Judy. I didn't think it was that serious. You just called yourself fat so what does that matter. Besides, people call me skinny all the time." I defended myself.

"I can say it about myself but I don't like anyone else saying it! And if you don't like people calling you names, then why do you let them?!" she questioned me. I didn't have an answer. She evil eyed me, "You're even weaker than you look."

I was sick and tired of being called "weak". I just didn't have the energy to fight over stupidity. Judy was bigger than me so she certainly couldn't understand how tough things were for me. I'm just not the aggressive type and my look isn't intimidating like hers at all.

At some point, I know I'd have to stoop to the level of ignorance and violence to prove I'm not just this weak little punk. That would be so out of my character but if that's what everyone was trying to beat out of me- I had to conjure up the balls someday.

Dear Diary,   *Saturday July 15th*

I'm so glad the weekend is here! Camp was starting to become a drag. Ever since the incident between Judy, Anastasia, and me I, it hasn't been the same.

Judy hasn't been hanging with me like she used to. She says hi and all but during game time, she makes it clear she'd rather be alone. Some people were content that way, I guess. But not me. I wanted friends. I needed them.

I couldn't stop thinking about something Judy asked me though. *Why did I let people call me names I didn't like to be called? Why isn't my first instance to defend and protect myself?*

It's not like I'm afraid of anyone. As many blows as I've taken, I damn sure ain't afraid of pain.

I'm probably so busy thinking about how I can make

peace with people, I don't even see when the war has begun. It's a blessing and a curse of mine I guess.

So I spent my weekend sulking as I dreaded another day in that awful camp. This whole summer would be wasted away with me in a lonely daze.

Dear Diary,   *Sunday July 16th*

My mother sometimes sends me to church on Sundays but today, she wanted me in the house slaving away.

She woke me up bright and early to let me know we were having company over next week. That was a first. So basically I had to get the house in order between now and then.

My cousin Erica is coming to stay with us from Maryland. She's my mother's brother's daughter. And her parents passed away five years ago in a bad car accident. She was in and out of foster care programs for about 3 years until a couple adopted her.

Why didn't my mother take custody? You ask. I'm guessing because she's too selfish, and as far as I know, Erica was lucky for that because my mom is no mother figure. Besides, our house is no more a happy home than any of her others.

I was starting to get fed up by my mother's demands today. It was "do this" "do that," "do it better," "that's not right" and "you're so stupid!" All day long. Even after vacuuming the living room, washing dishes, doing laundry and tidying my room; she wouldn't leave me alone.

Then she asked me to sweep the floor. "Okay, ma anything else?"

I said, picking up the broom with a bit of exhaustion.

"What you mean 'anything else'? You know damn well I'll let your dumbass know what else," she huffed.

"Ok, just asking," I said under my breath.

She gets up from where she was sitting on the couch and ran up on me angrily. "I'm tired of your rude ass. What did I tell you about answering back?"

I wasn't supposed to answer back this time, so I didn't. My mother got even more upset by that. She got in my face and smacked me. *Here we go!* I thought.

"A child supposedly as smart as you should know when *to* and when *not* to open your damn mouth!"

"That hurt!" I yelled.

"You think I care? Your foolish self deserves it!"

She snatched the broom out of my hand and started whipping me with it. Not by the straw bristles either, by the hard long stick.

My thighs were on fire as I jumped around to escape her blows. She chased me around as I jumped over our couch and almost bumped into our glass coffee table.

"Ma, stop! Please!" I begged. But she continued with her violent rage.

She caught me again and swung three hard hits to my legs, my thighs again, and then my ass. I fell to the ground and sobbed a loud cry.

My mother finally dropped the broom and sat down with

satisfaction. She was content as long as I was in pain. I don't understand why she hated me so much and why she wouldn't just kill me.

I guess if she did, then no one would be around to be her punching bag and her slave.

Dear Diary,   *Monday July 17th*

You wouldn't believe *this*! Today, *my* friend Judy was hanging out with Ms. Anastasia. I couldn't believe she- big boned Judy, was accepted in with Anastasia and her crew of "cool" chicks. And I wasn't? It just wasn't fair!

I was Judy's only friend all along and kept her company when no one else wanted to. Now she gets a chance to hang with the cool kids, she's treating *me* different.

Didn't Judy know Anastasia only wanted to be her friend so that Judy wouldn't be mine?

Either way, it hurt me so much because I was still alone and to make matters worse, Anastasia had turned her against me.

I was sitting by myself at the lunch table today and Anastasia approached me letting me know she and her little army wanted to sit at my table. So I told her they could all sit there with me.

"No we want the table without you on it," she said sternly while raising an eyebrow. I was astonished by her rude and demanding behavior. But I wasn't gonna be disrespected, not today in front of all her people.

"Well, I'm not going anywhere," I replied. "So you all might as well sit down with me." I tried to stand up for myself...

Anastasia laughed. "Not going anywhere? Really?" She signaled Judy who immediately rushed up to me and knocked me in my head. Yet again, I was taken for a joke.

"What about now?" some of the girls laughed. I was so embarrassed as I sat there in shock. When I didn't move, Judy actually pulled me from my seat and dropped me to the floor. The girls threw my food down on me and began kicking me.

I couldn't believe it was happening. Judy knew what I'd been going through. *Why couldn't she have my back?* I guess she was still angry at me for not having hers.

The kicks got harder. In my back. My stomach. And a thrust to my thigh. I was still throbbing there from my mother's blows this past weekend. "*Ahhh!*" I cried out in pain. But no one came to my defense.

Where were the counselors? Why didn't anyone try to stop them? Why were they doing this to me? I thought.

I lost all faith in my authorities today. There was no one to save me. No camp leaders, no counselors, no parents, and no teachers. I was alone here and alone in the world.

When my mother came to pick me up, I didn't bother telling her about the awful experience I had. I knew better than to tell her how I got punked out. She would punk me out double time. Just to punish me for being a punk in the first place. I just *couldn't*.

Dear Diary,   *Tuesday July 18th*

I decided to stop worrying about making friends. Clearly I wasn't meant to have any. And I was putting in way to much effort without the result.

I stayed home from camp today because my back and stomach ached badly from those mean girls kicks. I could hardly move to get out of bed. So I lied to my mother and told her I had a terrible headache, hoping she wouldn't fill my day with tedious chores... but of course, she did.

And just so I wouldn't make her suspicious of Monday's activities, I did them. Good thing she wasn't home all day to hear me scream out in pain as I walked around the house, mopped the floor, and washed those damn dishes.

Dear Diary,   *Wednesday July 19th*

I went back to camp today with a new focus in mind: boys! Since the girls around here wouldn't accept me, I'm sure a few of the guys would.

I went on *YouTube* last night and found a really cool hairstyle. I taught myself how to style my own hair by parting the front and giving myself a little side bang. I twisted the sides up then met them in the middle with a barrette, leaving some hair in the back to fall on my shoulders.

I borrowed some of my mother's earrings and bright pink nail polish. I even wore one of her pricey sun shades. When I looked in the mirror, for the first time, I felt kinda cute.

And the boys must have thought so too. It was as if they were seeing me for the first time when I walked on the yard. I was wearing a denim mini skirt and pink printed tee. Bright colors happened to be a good look!

I felt like a new person and I wanted all the boys to notice. Stephen, who was the object of my affection, was playing kickball. He was light brown, medium build, and taller than most the other boys. And I wanted him to be *mine*.

Unfortunately, he wasn't very focused on me. He was much more interested in the game they were playing when I walked over. So I decided to try something I'd seen in a movie. I came as close to the field as I could without interrupting. I dropped my book bag and some of its contents on purpose, just so I could bend down and expose my backside while picking them up.

"Get off the field!" One of the guys yelled.

"I can see her panties!" a younger girl yelled.

"Me too, and there's a stain!" another boy exclaimed.

"Yuck!" I heard.

There goes my moment of bliss. I was so embarrassed. I didn't know what they were talking about- a stain? I was suddenly very confused. My sunglasses fell down to the ground but this time I squatted down to pick it up. I took a peek between my legs and it was true!! I had a huge red blood stain on my underwear!

I gathered my things and ran to the bathroom. I was in awe at the timing. Of all the days, and weeks and months, I'd prayed my period would come, it decided to surprise me *and* the entire summer camp on *this* particular day. I didn't stay mad though. I was happy to officially be a woman and all they boys would know it now too.

Dear Diary,   *Thursday July 20*[th]

My mother found out all about me becoming a woman and she wasn't at all as thrilled about it as I was.

The camp counselor had to call her today and let her know I needed a change of clothes. This was a bittersweet moment for me. On one hand I was happy to be growing up. I would finally get the boobs and hips I'd been dying to have. But this bleeding on a monthly basis was so not cool.

My counselor came into the bathroom to explain to me that I would need to wear pads but in the meantime I should use a stack of tissues to prevent the staining of my clothes. She went on and on about being safe and protecting myself from getting pregnant. And about how this doesn't make me a woman. It means I'm just growing up but I'm not grown. *Whatever!*

I hardly knew what she was talking about. When my mother came to pick me up, she was pissed at me. For one, I hadn't told her I got my period yesterday. She came home very late that night and thankfully I was already half asleep.

This morning, I found stains on my sheets. I got up early to wash them and wasn't planning on facing my mother with this till days later. But it all came out today.

As we were in the car, she struck me in the face with her elbow.

I think she was upset about the shades and nail polish and jewelry I borrowed.

"What the hell, you think you're a big woman now?" I knew better than to answer as she continued on with her rant. "Wearing big woman things don't make you beautiful! You're a weak, stupid little girl and none of this junk is gonna change that!" she ripped the earrings out of my ears with one hand. I began to cry.

"Stop that pitiful sobbing, before I *give* you something to cry for," she hissed at me. I sucked up my tears.

At that moment, I certainly didn't feel like a woman, instead I felt a lot more like a worthless little girl.

Dear Diary,   *Friday July 21ˢᵗ*

Although my mother threatened me not to wear her things, I had to try my luck with it again if I was ever gonna get the attention I desired from the boys- Stephen to be exact.

These past few days, the guys been looking at me like I was brand new when I wore them. I still may not be beautiful as my mother pointed out but at least I would be noticed. And that's all I needed at this point— a little attention.

So I wore another miniskirt, borrowed my mom's razor to shave my legs, painted my toenails and wore open toes sandals. I was definitely becoming a woman so I had to start acting like it.

"Hey, boys!" I pulled together as much confidence as I could to get them to come over during craft time. "Look what I've got."

I knew it was a bold move of me but I was determined to get their attention. Besides, boys are much easier to win over than girl friends. They didn't care about labels. They didn't notice how often you switched up your hair. And they always responded to a little skin and women's underwear- a clean one of course! Lol

So I teased them a bit, pulling out a cute pair of drawers from my book bag. Lacy and red, they were all eyes. They huddled around me with curiosity.

"Whose is it? Where'd you get it?" they asked.

"It's mine," I lied. I actually found it with my mother's things. "And if you dare me to put it on, I will."

The boys looked at each other a little hesitant to dare me. We all knew this was risky. And believe me, I wasn't gonna do it for just anyone of them. I had my heart set on sharing some intimate time with Stephen but he didn't seem as interested in me. One of his boys dared me to try the sexy lingerie on, but I refused him. I was determined to get Stephen to notice my grown woman so I made an offer he couldn't refuse.

"Okay, Stephen. I'll show *you* during the break and you tell the boys if it's sexy or not," I said to my crush.

He shrugged his shoulders. "Okay." His boys high-fived him. I felt a rush of adrenaline- fear and affection I guess. All I wanted was some time alone with him.

When our break came, Stephen and I both excused ourselves for a bathroom break. I noticed Anastasia's eyes piercing into me when she saw us leave the yard together. I was hoping she wouldn't ruin this moment for me.

Once inside, I told Stephen flat out, "I think you're really cute. That's why I wanted you to see me in this. To get you alone."

"Thanks, but you don't have to put that on and show me," he said taking the lace panty away from my hand. "It's way too public here anyway."

"Oh, thank God! I really didn't want to!" I said with relief. "But you guys never noticed me before I started doing stupid things to get your attention."

"Oh yeah," he put his hand to his mouth and starting cracking up. "You're the girl who bent down the other day and –"

"Yes, I'm her," I interrupted, admitting my shame.

"Take this back then!" I don't want no stains getting on *me*!" he threw the underwear in my face and laughed. I wish he didn't see me as a joke, but instead as the growing young lady I am. So I had to make a move.

"I'm a woman now, that's all that means. And there's a whole lot of stuff I can do now, that I couldn't do before." I put my arms around him, poked out my moistened lips, and gave him a big kiss.

I started to give him some tongue, trying something completely new.

I noticed Stephen wasn't totally into my amateur moves, but he didn't stop me. He kissed me back and after just a few seconds, he took my hands and placed it on the hardened area in the center of his pants. That's when I drew the line. I jumped away, shocked and afraid.

"What was that?!" I exclaimed.

"That's what you did to me," he said a little taken back by my reaction.

"I thought you said you're a woman now. The women my dad messes with know what that is and what to do with it."

I was so embarrassed; I had gone too far and wasn't prepared for what I got myself into. And to make matters worse, I heard laughter.

Anastasia and her right hand, Cindy, were watching and

were amused by the whole ordeal.

"Patricia is no woman. She's just a little girl. See the little mosquito bites on her chest?" Cindy said with a chuckle.

Anastasia continued, "She just got her period a few days ago. While the rest of us got it like a year ago."

Stephen was uncomfortable as the girls neared us… "Ya'll talking about them stains?"

I threw the lace underwear in my bag and tried to escape the whole situation.

Cindy says, "We're talking about grown woman things. I can show you what I mean…" she went up close to Stephen as if to pick up where I left off, but Stephen wasn't having it.

"No thanks!" he said. "Y'all chicks is crazy trying to mess around at this place," Stephen said hurrying away.

As I was not too far away leaving the scene, the girls ran after me and pushed me down.

"Don't try to be grown if you ain't gonna be doing what grown girls do." Cindy stuck her tongue out at me and left the scene with Anastasia.

What a skank! I thought. And I, myself almost became one too. I was in waay over my head. All I wanted, was to get a little mindless attention, but I got a little too much more than I'd bargained for. I guess this is what my camp counselor meant about "growing up" but not being "grown". I still had a whole lot to learn.

Dear Diary,   *Saturday July 22nd*

After such a whirlwind of a week, the weekend was here. I was excited that my cousin was coming through to hang with me. I honestly needed the company. I really needed someone to talk to.

Erica is two years older than me. She has long thick hair and is extremely attractive with her caramel skin color covering her tall slender body. She's cool and confident and I've always looked up to her.

I missed her dearly. It had been a whole two years since I've seen her. I know she just finished repeating her freshman year of high school so there was a lot of catching up for us to do today.

My mother and I went to pick her up at the airport and I immediately noticed a difference in her appearance. She wore dark makeup, torn clothing, and had tousled hair. Not her usual style.

"Go get her bags!" my mother hissed at me as soon as she stopped the car at the arrival gate. I stepped out of the car happy to greet my cousin.

When I hugged her, I immediately felt the cold stiffness of her body and knew something was different about her.

"Erica, I've missed you sooo much!" I exclaimed.

"Me too, Patricia. How come you don't ever call me then?" she asked. The truth was, my mother doesn't let me use the phone much. So I don't really make an attempt. But for my cousins sake, I'd have to change that.

"Good question, cous'! I'm gon' make sure we stay in

contact from now on..." Erica was happy to hear that. She put her arm around my shoulder and walked us into my mother's car, a fairly new gray Lexus Coupe.

As I returned to my seat in the front, my mother snapped, "Let Erica sit up front! Get your bony butt in the back!" Erica and I looked at each other. She was astonished by my mother's attitude. I was used to it so I simply obeyed.

My mother took us all out to eat at a nearby BBQs. We caught up a bit about school and Erica quickly started venting about her new life. She began speaking about how much she hates living in Maryland because all the kids in her new neighborhood are so "uppity". Coming from Baltimore, where she lived with her parents and various foster families, it was an adjustment moving to Silver Springs.

She said she couldn't stand the other "spoiled kids with their two parent homes" and their "good grades". "I just don't understand how some people could have it all while the rest of us don't have shit..."

My mother chimed in. "If those spoiled brats be tryna throw that shit in your face, I hope you be shutting them down."

"Sometimes," Erica says with a laugh. She didn't know how serious my mother was about that. "The Springs just ain't my scene though. They be expecting everyone to be perfect. Life isn't all peachy for everybody though. Some of us have to go through some rough times just to get by. And those stuck up bitches don't even care!"

I've never been allowed to speak that way in front of my mother. I was very surprised Erica was. But my mother nodded in agreement and continued to let her vent.

"My family is cool though. They kinda let me be me. They

don't tell me how to dress or push me too hard to be like everyone else. Of course, there ain't nothing like having my real parents back in my life. Things were good back then. I don't know why they had to change," she said.

I decided to offer Erica a little encouragement. "Well, I can definitely relate. Those tough times are gonna make you stronger 'cous'. Just keep your head up though. I'm sure your joy will come again." I put my hand on her back to comfort her in whatever she was dealing with. A tear rolled down her cheek.

My mother blamed *me* for it. "Look what you did, you ignorant little brat! You don't know a damn thing about what she's talking about. Just keep your mouth shut!"

"Actually I do. Erica and I have a lot in common!" I couldn't hold back my own troubles.

"How can you say that?" Erica sobbed softly. "Your parents are alive. You weren't left to be alone. To have strangers take advantage- take care of you."

"That's what I'm saying!" my mother continued. "Patricia is so damn ungrateful. She has no idea how lucky she is. I'm busting my ass working hard to keep a roof over our heads and every chance she gets, she bashes me. I'm the one who has to bear this awful burden!"

There she was, making herself out to be a victim again, although *she* brought me into this world and had everything to do with why I'm so unhappy. "So I'm a burden now, ma?"

"I'm sure that's not what she meant, Patricia," Erica defended my mother. "She wants you to appreciate that she's here. Through the good and the bad, you should just be grateful you have a mother."

"But you had a mother *and* a father—and you can at least carry the memory of them both in your heart," I replied. "I never had a chance to know the other half of who I am. She robbed me of that!"

"Your father doesn't want you!" my mother exclaimed with anger in her eyes. "You're lucky I didn't leave you for dead like he did."

Erica wiped her tears. "You're lucky for real, Patricia. If your father couldn't step up and be a man, you aren't missing anything. You should be happy he's not running in and out of your life disappointing you all the damn time. You know what it is with him and you gotta accept it. The men I've come across in my life recently only came around to take from me—you don't even know the half. Just consider yourself *lucky*."

It got very quiet after that. My mother was pissed at me for mentioning my father again- I could see it on her face. I tried to let Erica's words wallow in my head instead of continuing to argue. But I didn't believe I was at all lucky to live the life I live.

Erica might have had her trials but I had mine too. No one could tell me one's problems were worse than the other unless they had to experience both for themselves.

I wanted to be empathetic towards my cousin's situation but I was in pain too. She lost both her parents and that has *got* to hurt but I never knew my dad. I've never seen his face, or even heard his voice. And that hurt too. Every time he's brought up, my mother finds a way to hurt me just for thinking about him.

A girl deserves a dad, or at least to know of him. There was definitely more to the story of my father and someday, I had to find it out.

At that moment, I hugged my cousin and gave her as much comfort as she needed. My problems could wait. Hers were clearly eating her up inside and it was affecting her attitude and her appearance.

I wanted to know more about her dealings but with my mother sitting at the table with us, I knew it wasn't the time or place to discuss it.

Dear Diary,   *Sunday July 23rd*

My mother sent us to church today. We sat through a sermon about forgiveness. Forgiving those who did you wrong and allowing yourself to be freed of the pain they caused.

Pastor Clark's voice boomed from the church's speakers and into my ears. "There is no *growth* in holding on to your pain. There's no *lesson* in wallowing in your pity. There's no *joy* in staying angry. So for your own blessings to come showering down, you must *forgive*! Let it go, my people. Free yourself and *forgive*!"

Dammit, I've tried that with my mother, my colleagues, and even my father. *But if the pain is still there, how could I just let it go?*

I don't know if my mother and cousin received that sermon the way I did and tried to apply it, because while I felt a little freed and forgiving, they left the church with that same chip on their shoulders.

I never did understand why my mother even attended church anyway. She was always angry and bitter and no amount of church visits has ever reformed her. She put on such a facade when attending and it pissed me off.

But I was still happy to hear this sermon that softened my heart a bit. It was like a healing came over me.

As we were in the car heading home, Erica spoke up about what the pastor had said. "How the hell is forgiveness supposed to help us heal? Doesn't that just let the other person off the hook?" I thought it was a good question.

My mother responded with a decent answer too. "It helps because you don't go walking around with all that hate anymore. You can just be happy, and free."

"So, mom, can you *please* forgive me for whatever I've done to make you so angry? Why can't *you* be happier and free."

I saw her glare at me from her rear view mirror. She wanted to contain the anger my question brought on but she couldn't. "That ain't happening! Because every time I look in your face, I see weakness and failure. And it pisses me the hell off!"

Erica and I looked at each other, both wondering what in the hell I could have possibly done to cause the change of tone in my mother's voice. But we both knew better than to open our mouths and ask. Hopefully we would get a moment alone to talk like we did way back in the day.

Even after that long drawn out sermon, we both knew forgiveness was easier said than done. And it's something all three of us had to work on in our own time...

VOLUME 3: AN UNLIKELY COMPETITOR

Dear Diary,   *Monday July 24th*

I was so happy to have Erica join me this week at camp. But I soon realized we wouldn't be the power team I expected us to be. I was hoping we could do art projects together, share lunches, play together during our break, and maybe even get boy crazy together. But Erica was different from me and everyone knew it. She wasn't shy and corny like me nor was she bony and plain like me. People respected her and accepted her in a way I'd never experienced. Even with her dark clothing and messy hair, people around her still noticed how cool she was. It made me a little jealous.

Erica was getting so much attention from the guys in this camp that she and I never got a chance to have that intimate talk I needed us to have.

Stephen was one of the first guys to approach her today.

He acknowledged me with a short, "hello", but his eyes were glued to my cousin. "Who's this?" he asked.

"This is my cousin, Erica. She's only here for a week," I specified. But that didn't matter to the group of boys that were surrounding us.

"Well, I guess we have one week to get it poppin'!" a perverted campgoer says to Stephen, hardly being discrete with his words.

Erica spoke up, "Y'all are funny. None of y'all little boys getting it poppin' with me. I only deal with men, believe that."

I didn't know she was "dealing" with anyone at all.

Stephen seemed to be feeling her sassy attitude and took it as a challenge. "Girl, that's exactly why you and I need to be hanging out later. I'm a man and you seem to be the only woman up in here. What do you say..."

My heart was slowly breaking. It was bad enough to throw yourself at a boy, mess up, and get rejected- but to see him groveling over someone else, it kinda hurt.

"Patricia and I have to go home together and we have plans," Erica flirtatiously continued entertaining Stephen's advances. I guess she was a bit interested. I hadn't gotten a chance to tell her that Stephen was off limits so I couldn't even be mad.

Stephen was not giving up. "Me and Patricia are cool, ain't we?" He looked at me and winked. "She wouldn't mind hanging out with me, you, and one of my boys at the crib lata. Right?" They both looked my way with a smile.

I couldn't refuse his oh so sexy smile. Although he wasn't tryna woo *me*, I was wooed nonetheless.

So when I said, "yes," it excited the both of them. I felt good inside too. At least if the 2 people I cared about most would be happy, I would get over my crush at some other point.

~

By the end of the camp day, Erica and I started walking home. Stephen and his boy, James, quickly interrupted us. James was a lot shorter than Stephen. He had crooked teeth and a little acne. But he was there to entertain me so I just rolled with it.

I couldn't help but glance over at Erica and Stephen a few times throughout our journey. Erica was busy smiling in his face as he had his arm over her shoulders. I guess the two of them were really feeling each other.

It was time for me to forget about our lousy kiss and that surprise touch we shared. Stephen simply wasn't interested in me.

When we arrived at Stephen's huge 3 story crib, we settled in his colonial style kitchen and had a bite of the afternoon snack waiting on the counter for us. He pressed one button on his *Bose* remote control and instantly, had some Nicki Minaj track blasting through his surround sound speakers. Apparently he also had a chef and even cooler, he had lots of freedom in that big empty house. After chiilin' in there for a while, they moved into another room upstairs while I sat in the living room with James watching TV. I peeped how Stephen touched Erica's butt as they left the room and it was turning me on. But Erica had him all to herself.

I decided to make the most of that sudden heat in my pants as James got close to me on the couch. I didn't like the smell of his breath as he came close but I let him French kiss me anyway. He was at least a good kisser.

He sucked on my bottom lip and ran his tongue in circles around mine. *Where did he learn that?!* This intimate affection felt so good. I was warming up inside and to my surprise, down below.

He put his hands inside my shirt and went straight for my chest.

I felt a little guilty for allowing this boy I hardly knew to touch on me like that. He had his hands all over me and it felt so right when I knew for sure this was wrong.

But Erica was in the room with Stephen doing similar things I'm sure. And it was things like this that made her a woman. I needed to know what that was all about.

James started kissing my neck and it felt soooo good! I didn't know exactly what was happening but I liked it! He had one hand on my ear and the other softly caressing my jaw. He worked his tongue like magic across my collarbone and I enjoyed every minute of this bliss.

I didn't mind his hands in my shirt either but when he started tryna take it off, I stopped him. We were in an open living room for goodness sake! Then, when he tried to put his hands down my pants, I decided I had enough.

I was enjoying his every kiss and touch but after the hard bulge I felt in Stephen's pants last week, I knew *for sure* I didn't want anything happening below the belt.

"What's wrong?" James asked me.

"Nothing," I said fixing my clothes and sitting up in the couch. "Whatever you just did was all good. But I gotta get Erica. If we don't leave now, we could get in a whole lot of trouble with my mom."

"Aight, aight. Cool, so we gonna finish this up some other time then?"

"No doubt," I agreed.

I called for Erica and when I didn't hear a response, I ran up into Stephen's room. My cousin was passed out in the bed. I was in shock.

"What did you do to my cousin?!" I screamed out to Stephen.

He stared back fearfully. "I promise I didn't do anything to her! She just took a pill. We had a little fun and you don't have to panic, she's still breathing."

I was in awe. My cousin was laying there in Stephen's bed looking lifeless and exposed in her unbuttoned shirt and this guy didn't even have the courtesy to let me *know*!

"I'm calling the police!" I exclaimed, mad as hell. "I need your phone."

James and Stephen looked at each other, with no intention of giving up their phones. Luckily, she began coughing and rolled over.

"That was some good shit! Stephen, you wanna try?" Stephen backed away with fear, not willing to try whatever she had tried. I was just glad she was okay.

"Can you at least get me some water?" Erica said while fanning herself. James ran out to get her a tall glass of water from the kitchen.

Though she was high as ever off of some kinda drug, she was conscious and full of energy. I was stunned by the whole ordeal. I hurried up getting my cousin dressed and pulled her out of that boy's house. Stephen didn't give a damn about Erica's wellbeing at all, as long as they had their little fun. Guys... SMH!

Dear Diary,   *Tuesday July 25th*

Yesterday was a real scare for me. I mean, Erica had me thinking for a moment that I had lost her. And the thought of my mother finding out we stopped at some boy's house instead of going straight home, it was all too much for me.

I had to have a serious talk with my cousin. Something was wrong with her and I had to find out what. So on the way to camp today, I asked her straight up, "what's up with you cous'? I know you've been through a whole lot these past few years, how've you been holding up?"

"Why is everyone always asking me that?! How do you think?!" she snapped at me.

"Hey, I don't know about anyone else but I'm asking because I -honest to God- care about you. You're just about the only fam I've got and the only person I can really talk to. I don't want to lose you to no dudes or no drugs," I opened up my heart to her.

She softened her tone with me a bit. "Girl, I appreciate that. But my life has been a damn roller coaster. I'm so happy one moment then instantly unhappy the next. And it sucks because I finally got a good family again but I really do miss my old one."

"I definitely understand you, girl. You're always gonna miss them. But don't let that take your joy away from the new fam," I offered my advice.

As we were passing a park, we sat down on a wooden bench to talk.

"I just can't get over some of that past shit, Pat. I been through a lot when I was in and out of foster family homes. Here I am, just recovering from the tragic death of my loving parents- two people who struggled to give me their best. Then all of a sudden, I'm dumped in the homes of strangers. It was terrible. I lived in the midst of everything from drug use, getting molested, getting beat, and even left for days without food. You wouldn't believe some of the sorry motherfuckers they had taking care of people's kids. Those low lives pretty much took us in just to get a check from the government and it was a win win for them cause they didn't actually have to do anything for us wit it."

I was shocked out my mind! "Are you serious?! Couldn't you report those people? Run away? You could've called me!"

"Please, if you try to report that shit, they want evidence. How could I prove that? Especially when it would just take me from one bad situation to another. And where could I run away to? The streets, where it's the same thing ten times worse? I just dealt with it. And ever since I moved in with the Maxwell's, things have calmed down. They kinda remind me of my moms and pops, then those moments when I realize it ain't them, and my parents are never coming back- I start buggin' out! I'm telling you, Patricia, you're so lucky you don't have to deal with that. They got me going to therapy and I'm on prescription drugs too. It's awful!"

I had no idea my cousin was dealing with all that. It was pretty bad what she'd been through and I wish there was something I could have done to help. But all I could do was offer my empathy. "I had no idea this was going on. I would have definitely fought for you to come live with us."

"I done tried that. Your mother denied the request. She told 'em she's a single mother and she couldn't handle another child being in the house on her income. So foster care is where it left me until the Maxwell's adopted me."

All this stunned me. Erica had been living a nightmare these past few years. From losing both her parents, to abuse in the foster care system leading to some kinda mental issues. My mother had the power to help her in her ultimate time of need but she refused. She'd rather Erica suffer just like she did me. Not that our home would've been perfect for Erica, but at least we would have been together. I grew angry at my mother as I thought about it.

"Well girl I'm glad you made it out of the system and you got a good family now. Honestly, I wish sometimes I could get a new family, a new start because some days my mother is an absolute monster. She literally hates me and doesn't miss a chance to show it."

"Yea, I noticed your mother has a few anger issues. What's that about?" she asked.

"Girl, I dunno. I just hope one day I could find out and help us both get past it. Cause she flips out on me sometimes for no reason at all. I mean throwing stuff at me, beating me down, it gets crazy," I explained.

"What brings her to that point?"

"Usually when I ask her about my dad. But she will never tell me anything about him. Could you imagine not knowing who your parents are?" I asked.

"No," she softened up with the thought of her parents. I saw tears filling up in her eyes. "You gotta find out what's the story with your pops. There's something there and your mother is keeping it from you. Don't give up, Patricia. Because honestly I don't know what's worse, knowing and loving your parents then losing them, or not knowing them at all."

We both followed her statement with silence. For the first time since she'd been there, we understood each other's pain. There was no need for words.❤

Dear Diary,   *Friday July 28ᵗʰ*

This week at camp was the best I had. Erica and I really got to bond. I had someone to enjoy camp with- or anything with- for the first time in my life. I had a friend. It was so sad she had to leave this weekend.

I didn't get picked on this week, I didn't worry about getting attention from the boys, and I didn't care that Ms. Anastasia, Judy, or Cindy didn't wanna be my friend.

But apparently Anastasia didn't like any of this. The girl just had to be in control and if she wasn't, she'd fight to be. But she picked the wrong person and the wrong day because Erica didn't let people get over on her as easily as I did.

Anastasia comes up to us during our meal break while we were sitting there minding our business. Of course she brings her little army to back her up.

"I see we have another loser up in here now. I thought we had taken care of the one but I see our work isn't done," Anastasia says.

"Who are you calling a loser?" Erica stood up showing no signs of intimidation.

47

"Who do you think? Oh, I bet you'd prefer to be called a whore or a Molly poppin' drug addict? That's how *Stephen* described you..." the girls all laughed. Erica was a bit embarrassed and searched the room for Stephen angrily.

"Erica, don't let these girls get to you. They have no life that's why they're trying to mess with ours. Who cares what they have to say?" I tried to calm her down.

"I need to teach them a lesson either way!" Erica got up and threw one hard punch at Anastasia's face. Her fist went straight to the side of Anastasia head. No one expected that my cousin would be the one to set Ms. Anastasia straight.

I, myself, was stunned at her boldness. Apparently Anastasia was too! That lesson was learned! Erica whispered to me, "I did happen to learn a few things back at those homes."

The group of girls huddled around Anastasia to make sure she was alright but no one dared fight back. Judy made eye contact with me for the first time in weeks. I know she had the strength to fight us both but she didn't dare. I think she even smiled a bit. I'm sure she finally learned that being Anastasia's little pet had its flaws. She was probably happy someone finally gave that chick a taste of her own medicine.

Dear Diary,   *Saturday July 29ᵗʰ*

My mother took us to the mall today. We couldn't send Erica back home without some new clothing. So we shopped 'til my mom dropped. We ate dinner in the food court. My mother snapped at me when I carried her food to the table but got the wrong sauce. *Oops! Damn.*

Of course she made a big scene. In the middle of the food court, she started spitting out all kinds of mean things about me. "I swear your dumbass can't do nothing right! You'd think you had the common sense to get the right sauce. On top of that, you took long enough to get it! With your slow ass!"

I tried to explain they didn't have the one she always gets so I got something similar. But she hardly listened. I just apologized and tried to enjoy the rest of the day.

We went to the arcades and I beat Erica's ass in a Nascar race game. I teased her playfully about my victory. Then she beat mine in a horse race. We had an amazing time! And a little while later, the best friend I've ever had, was gone.

It wasn't a long day but I made the most of my last with my cousin. There was no telling when we'd see each other again.

Back to reality.

VOLUME 4: BROKEN

Dear Diary,　　　　　*Monday August 5th*

With Erica gone a few days, I missed her. At home my mother was back on my back about everything from chores to manners to me being me. It was a relief to go to camp these days.

With Anastasia and her crew finally off my back, I got to enjoy the summer camp a bit. It was my last year doing crafts and games and sports and stuff at this time of year. I know next year I'll probably have to get a job or take some summer intensive courses. So I made the most of my last few summer camp days- and even got to know my new friend James a little better.

Dear Diary,　　　　　*Thursday August 8th*

Today, while sitting out of the yard games, I was thinking about what Erica said. At the back of my mind, I knew she was right. I had to find out something about my father. Or I would never feel complete.

And just as I thought about that, Stephen's friend, James came and sat next to me. I guess we did have a lil connection the other afternoon at Stephen's house. So we chilled some more that day.

My crush on Stephen was completely gone. He was still on my bad side since leaving my cousin all passed out in his room. Then had the nerve to spread rumors about her to the other kids at camp? I could never respect him.

Dear Diary,　　　　　*Friday August 9th*

I enjoyed most of my breaks at camp with James. We found a private spot under the staircase where we could mess around.

He kissed me softly and touched my chest. Even though my titties were slightly bigger than mosquito bites, the affect his touch had on me was out of this world! I was tingling all over. I let him get to 2nd base with me, and during the later part of the day, we got to 3rd.

I mean, after he'd touched every part of me from my neck, to my chest, to my legs, I wanted more. He put his finger in my pants and found a wet spot between my legs. Whatever he did with that finger made me so hot. I loved the way it felt. He stroked it in and out of my private part which I never knew could feel so good til I got even wetter.

Then he took my hand and placed it in his pants. This time, I learned what to do with that long hard piece. I stroked it good and well. We were both in ecstasy.

In some way, that kissing and touching made me feel complete for the moment.

But that moment wasn't long because a junior counselor caught us messing around in the hallway. They heard some kids were hanging out doing scandalous things so there were all kinda spies lurking around and we didn't even notice. No one was around when I was getting my ass kicked around during the lunch hour but when I was finally experiencing a blissful moment, they had to interrupt. *To hell with them!*

They went hard too, called up my mother and everything. The *nerve* of them to report us!

~

When my mother came to pick me up, she punished me right in front of everyone. She yelled at me, screamed all kinds of evil things. Even pushed me by "accident". So much for her keeping up a facade in the public eye. Today, she held nothing back.

She said outright in front of my group of campgoers, "stupid little slut! If you not letting these girls get over on you, you're getting under some horny little boy. What the hell am I gonna do with you?"

I was utterly disappointed in myself. And even more embarrassed. There was no way I could go back there.

Dear Diary,   *Sunday August 11*[th]

The summer went much slower as I spent most of it cooped up in the house. I was disappointed in myself for getting so carried away with James. This week at camp was trip week and I was gonna miss it. More than that though, I was missing the way James made me feel. I craved more of that attention and didn't know how I was gonna get it.

Dear Diary,   *Tuesday August 13*[th]

My mother hadn't finished punishing me for what happened in the staircase at camp. She gave me so many damn chores to do, inside and outside of the house. If I didn't finish everything she asked me to do, it was *hell* to pay.

Tonight when she was pulling up to the house after work, she caught me outside on the steps with my neighbor, Diesel. He was just riding his bike past my house as I was sweeping our pavement and waved at me. I waved back so he stopped through for a chat. His beautiful brown eyes seemed all too familiar but I couldn't place why.

"I haven't seen you outside in years," he said. "You stay in the house even on the hottest days."

He knew what he was talking about because my mother didn't allow me to hang out on the streets. I was always doing either schoolwork or housework.

"That's for damn sure," I replied. "My mother keeps me on lock." We laughed. It was good to know a guy like him even noticed me. He was kind of the cool kid on the block.

"You getting older though, she can't keep you on that leash forever." he said with a wink.

He had no idea *what* my mother is capable of, and when I saw her pull up, I did not want him to find out. "Here she comes," I jumped up off the stoop. "You gotta go!"

It was too late. My mother's glare was enough for me to know I was in trouble. She walked in the house without saying a word. She inspected each room for cleanliness. I didn't think I had anything to worry about being that I spent my entire day tidying up. But of course she would still find reason to punish me.

She stopped by our 1st floor bathroom which I cleaned, but it wasn't clean enough for *her* so she passed me the mop.

I started to do something with it but apparently I wasn't doing it fast enough for her. "Ma, hold on," I said as she rushed me to do this spot then another. But I figured her impatience was not because she wanted the house clean but because she needed to let out her anger. I wish she would let it out some other way; talk to me, scream, yell, whatever.

But no, instead she took the mop from me and hit me with it.

"Lazy child! You can't do nothing right!" It stung as she struck me with the long metal stick. I crouched down to protect myself. "And you have the nerve to be hanging out with some *boy* on my front step!"

She continued to yell at me, accusing me of all kinds of obscene things. You'd think I was making out with this boy on the step when we were just talking. Isn't that what she wanted from me- to be social and make friends?

Apparently not, I thought. My mother pulled my hair with one hand and held me down to the floor as she beat me down. One throw after another, she kept on hitting me.

"Ma! Please! I'm sorry!" I screamed out in pain begging for her to stop but she wouldn't stop until the damn thing was broken- both the stick *and* my back.

I was in extreme pain. The bones in my back did not feel quite right. As I tried to fall asleep tonight, I realized something was terribly wrong. This time, I think we might actually have to take another trip to the hospital.

Dear Diary, *Tuesday August 20th*

So yea we missed a few days. But I'll catch you up...

Could you believe it's taking this long to recover from my mother's last beating?

I actually had to spend a week in the hospital. I fractured two bones in my back so I've been on painkillers, had to undergo an operation, I was in and out of x-rays, and getting tests done all day everyday. And still, my back is throbbing. ☹

Dear Diary, *Thursday August 22nd*

When they finally sent me home, I was no happier here than I was in there. Life just sucks!

Being in bed without good care and attention gave me a lot of time to think though. About how awful my life is. I couldn't go out at all, I was left on bed rest, and the summer just floated by with me in agonizing pain.

I hate my life!!!

While I was drugged up on pain pills, I ranted on about how they should have left me in the hospital. And how I wouldn't have minded if I just died in there. The visiting nurse must've documented the way I'm feeling as depression when she realized how much pain I was in *emotionally*.

Now she's sending me to a therapist. SMH! I'll let you know how *that* goes.

Dear Diary,   *Saturday August 24th*

At first, that therapy stuff was such a joke to me. I didn't see how being there was supposed to ease my pain but since I was forced to go, it was worth finding out.

Being in the neatly decorated room as I lay on a smooth leather couch and she, the therapist, in her brown leather chair, was weird for me. There were plants all over, awards on the wall, and it was eerily silent. It felt like being in a doctor's office but without the needles and stuff. I kinda felt like a lab patient and just couldn't get comfortable.

Dr. Graham, my therapist, started out with a calm, laid back demeanor. She asked, "So tell me, what makes you happy? I mean, truly fulfilled?" I searched my mind for an answer and couldn't think of one. It had been a long time since I had experienced any kind of joy. Even as I was discovering new things about myself, my body, my desires, and attractions... I could not honestly say I was in any way happy and by no means fulfilled.

Her next question got me talking though. "So what are the things that make you unhappy?"

It was easy to share the "rejection, fear, hate, and loneliness" I felt. "I'm just misunderstood," I shared without being too specific about the who's and why's.

But my therapist started going *in*! She asked me a whole lot of questions about my life. Things I didn't even remember from way back when. She said it was good to "reflect on the past to help me refresh the future. When I think back, I only remember a past filled with emptiness and disarray.

I don't recall any exceptionally *happy* moments. Everything before my grandparents passing, became a blur. I remember my mother growing angrier and more violent as the years went by. And I always remembered missing something- or someone rather. My father. I missed having someone to love and someone who loved me. It wasn't fair how my mother robbed me of that.

Thinking about all this made me even more depressed...

And Dr. Graham had the nerve to ask me, "How does this all make you feel?"

If she wanted an honest answer, I *feel* like killing myself. Of course I don't have the balls to tell her I'm thinking about it. But seriously, no one would miss me. No one would grieve or care. I could just imagine the kids from my school and the camp shrugging their shoulders when they heard of my passing. They wouldn't bat an eye with remorse.

I have no impact on anyone in my life. I'm worthless, just like my mother always says. Life isn't really worth living for me.

With all her prying, I came pretty close to letting the therapist know what was really going through my head about my mother's abuse and my thoughts of suicide, but I decided it was best to hold back. What I blabbered to the visiting nurse already landed me in this strange office, where would they send me next?

So I kept my contemplation to myself. Instead I called Erica, the only person I know who could ever relate.

Dear Diary,   *Monday August 26th*

I managed to blurt out my feelings of suicide today. Erica said I was safe telling my therapist all about how I felt inside. She said it helps to vent instead of letting it eat you up inside. And I'm glad I did. Apparently therapists are sworn to secrecy.

And the doctor was very understanding. I revealed to her how unhappy I am and that I want to end my life. "There isn't one good reason I have to live, Doctor. You have no idea."

She let me speak today and listened with open ears.

She wanted to know why. So I told her about my 8th grade year, coming close to flunking and getting jumped at the end of the school year. I told her more about my camp experiences and even about my cousin. After sharing the experience I had with the kids at camp, she wanted to know everything I knew about my father but it really wasn't much. And then she asked more about my mother. I told the doctor as much as I could without revealing the abuse I've been encountering with her.

I didn't think telling on my mother would be the right thing. Many times, my mother threatened me that if I ever reported her, I'd end up with no mother *or* father. I didn't wanna live that way. I heard all about the awful life of being a parentless child from Erica.

As bad as things were between my mother and I, I think it is unspoken, that I still need her and she still needs me. We both would be worse off alone.

Besides I didn't have it as bad as Erica. I had to start appreciating the little bit of "family" I have.

Dear Diary,   *Saturday August 31ˢᵗ*

Today is my 14th birthday. *Happy Birthday to me!*

Of course there was no real celebration. My mother let me straighten my hair out for the first time though. And I got a few dollars to go down the street and buy myself some ice cream. My mother gave me ride there, which I appreciated. We didn't fight today which was cool.

I got to see some of the neighborhood kids hanging out, which included my boy Diesel. He was so fine sitting amidst his crew. I waved at him as I took my ice cream sundae from the store clerk. He smiled back and licked his sexy pink lips. I blushed a little as I left the store.

He's someone I really wanted to get to know better. Someday I suppose.

Dear Diary,   *Sunday September 1ˢᵗ*

The whole therapy thing finally started to make sense. I'm starting to understand things about myself that I never realized before.

Dr. Graham helped me understand that I am a victim of bullying because I have always allowed myself to be. I never even saw myself as a victim. I've always thought- and been told- that the things happening to me is my fault. I thought this is all a part of who I am and I've got to just accept it. But she said I didn't have to accept the way things were all the time and that I *could* make a change.

"Honestly doctor, I don't see why *I* have to change anyway. I'm not the problem. They are," I said.

Dr. Graham replied, "We can't do much to change other people. But we can do everything to change ourselves. Since you're here, we are going to do whatever we can to make *you* a better you." I continued to hear her out. "You have been mistreated a lot, you say. And if there's no strenuous violence in your home, we have to explore your social relationships."

As much as I wanted to start by correcting her on the 'no strenuous violence in your home' statement, I couldn't go there. I couldn't tell her about how my mother treats me. I had already told her too much. So I let her believe it was just my peers.

"The kids in my class have never liked me. They've always teased me because I'm too smart or because they think I'm ugly. Or because I'm too skinny or don't dress the way they do. I just don't fit in. They think I'm too different so they reject me in every way they can."

"You say a lot about what *people* think of you, Patricia. But how do you feel about yourself?"

Good question. I had never really thought about that. How I feel about myself never seemed relevant before. No one ever asked me how I feel about anything! It just never mattered.

"I don't really know, doctor," was all I could say. "But I do believe I'm a good person."

Dr. Graham started recording notes. "That's a good start!" she exclaimed. "Knowing that there's some good in you takes you steps away from negative thinking. I challenge you to express all the good in you that you can. Stop worrying so much about everyone else's opinion of you and work on building your own."

I guess she gave me one thing- a little hope. But loving myself was a lot easier said than done. Especially when I'm surrounded by so much hate.

Before we ended our session, Dr. Graham suggested I get a new social and academic start. She wrote me a recommendation to attend a high school in a new district. She highlighted that I'd be *required* to take up an extracurricular activity: Doctor's orders. Hopefully this would be good for me.

I'd finally get a chance to experience life in a new neighborhood. Compared to what I've been through in Northfield, I can't wait for a fresh start elsewhere! :-D

VOLUME 5: A NEW BEGINNING

Dear Diary,   *Thursday September 5th*

The expectation of change was refreshing. I would get to start all over and that was just what I needed. I was getting a second chance to be liked and accepted. I could use the advice Dr. Graham gave me and make some amends. I would worry less about what everyone else thought of me and more about how I can be good old me. *Right*?

Wrong! I knew everything the doctor said I could do, would be much easier said than done. I tried to open up, I really did. But the kids in this uppity neighborhood were a whole new breed of mean! They're much more materialistic and vain. They all have money- lots more money than I'm used to- and I would never be able to keep up.

Middlebrook was the real deal, they weren't just well off like us folks in Northfield, they are extremely wealthy. They were not like us who fought for their status in the world; they were born with it and were bound to die with it. In Middlebrook, the grass was certainly greener, the houses were larger, and the cars were much pricier. The kids around here didn't take the bus- they were driven to and from school. Not by their parents either - but instead by their drivers. That's *if* they didn't already have a car of their own.

Instead of me worrying about how to be cuter, cooler, and more sophisticated; I was also now competing with chicks that are richer, more fashionable, more talented, and more powerful. I entered a whole new ballpark. And I damn sure wasn't ready to play their game.

For one, I had to travel pretty far to get to Middlebrook and it was out my mother's way for her to give me a ride. So I had to take the bus. Surprisingly, my mother loosened her reigns on me a little and allowed me to ride public transportation. Which *would* have been exciting if I had a friend or two to ride with. But you already know the deal, I was alone.

However, this school year, I had my mind made up- new school, new friends, and new life.

The kids at *Middlebrook High* are extremely competitive which meant I had to make some serious changes in my looks, my gear, and my attitude if I'm ever gonna fit in. Some new clothes, new shoes, fine jewelry, and a confidence boost was definitely necessary.

After my first day of school, I begged my mother to take me shopping. She just threw a few hundred bucks at me and told me to take myself.

I don't have much style but I tried my luck at the *BeBe* store, *Guess*, and *Express* where I knew I couldn't really go wrong. This was just a start for me to get on the level my new peers were on.

I didn't spend it all either, I wanted to make these dollars stretch so I'd have a little bit of change for a rainy day. Who knew when my mother would be so generous again.

Dear Diary,   *Friday September 6th*

I instantly tried to step up my gear game and hoped my peers would notice.

So when I ran into my neighborhood friend, Diesel, coming off the bus today, I was happy he caught me looking my best. As he walked down the road with me, I told him about the new school I got transferred into. He was much more interested in how my back was doing though. He was sorry to hear about me having to go to the hospital and being on bed-rest for a while. I assured him I was fine, I mean its been a month since. Either the streets were talking or I was on his radar. ;-)

For the first time, I got a chance to gaze into his deep light eyes, which seemed all too familiar.

"Diesel, are you the one who got me home that day I got jumped?"

"Oh yea," he smiled. "You ain't know that?!"

"No, I was really out of it at the time," I whispered. "But, thank you." Knowing the smooth skin and strong arms that rescued me were his, had me feelin' him for real. But he was humble and chill about it as he walked me home.

"No doubt, boo. So what's poppin'? You don't go to Northfield High? What you taking that bus for?"

"You don't even wanna know," I replied, a little hestitant to let him in on my struggles with the kids in our town. "I just needed a change. And Middlebrook is definitely a change but I can't say whether it's for better or worse."

"What you mean?" he asked.

As I began to share my new school troubles with him, he listened. I told about how different it is and how difficult it would be for me to fit in.

"Oh, please. Girl, you got this," he encouraged me. "You just need to relax..."

"I think it's gonna take more than that," I giggled.

"Not at all, ma. Matta fact, I know exactly you need."

I was curious what. But Diesel got a phone call and immediately had to go. So we're meeting up after my mother leaves for work tomorrow to talk some more.

Dear Diary,   *Saturday September 7th*

Diesel and I met up at the Checkers down the street from where we live. As I thought about our date- I mean, meeting- I felt tingles.

When I spotted him in the crowd, I was in awe at his confident demeanor, chiseled jawline, and dreamy eyes. He's 16 years old, tall, and dark brown skin, just the way I like 'em. He's a little hood and rough around the edges but I appreciated him that way. He said he always knew me as the "little skinny chick down the block" from him but he was noticing that I'm "growing up nicely".

When we met up, he was just leaving the register with his chicken sandwich and fries. He motioned me toward his table and gave me a hug. It felt good to be in his embrace even if just for that second. He dressed well in a hooded vest, a t-shirt, and some dark blue jeans. He wore the new Jordan's on his feet, the ones everyone at my school was rockin', and he smelled good. Diesel had swag.

"So what's up, Patricia?" he asked as we sat down. "What you been dealing wit?"

"Same ole shit, school and home, that's pretty much my damn life."

"What more do you want?" he asked offering me some of his fries.

"I dunno. *More*," I pondered. "Happiness I guess. Friends. Fam. Love."

"Word, you don't think you got none of that? Probably 'cause you be thinking so hard about it. You just need to chill, P."

"Yea, you right. I probably do. Cause I don't know how else I'm gon' make it through. Things are so tough for me. I can't even concentrate in my classes. I just don't feel comfortable up in there..."

He put out his hand to stop me. He knew I needed a moment of ease and said he sells something that could help me with that. I wanted to try whatever he was selling.

Just because he lived in our high priced neighborhood, he affirmed that, there were some corrupt things he had to do to get here and stay here. Selling drugs seemed to be one of them and although he wasn't proud sharing that, he was confident in doing so because he was the sole provider of his family.

"Girl, you too cute to be worrying 'bout all that though. I bet you take one pull of this, you gon' stop giving a damn about what people think, and just do you."

I hoped he was right about that. I really needed to let loose and feel as carefree as he described. "Well, if your stuff is so good, let me try it."

"Aight, let's go. But I betta get you a snack of your own." He ordered some more food and we left the restaurant.

~

We went to his house where I had to be sure no one was watching me. I could not risk my mother, or someone my mother knows, seeing me walk into a guy's house.

Diesel made me feel real safe and protected though. He took me through the back door and into his living room. He took out a huge chunk of dried green leaves from a brown paper bag. This was the first time I saw weed up close. It smelled good, like exotic mint or something. I was excited to try it.

He had to break it up into tiny pieces, gut a cigar, and roll the greens into a blunt. The whole process was pretty cool. I was living on the edge for once and was anticipating how this stuff would make me feel.

He sparked it up and the smell instantly filled the room. I was catching my high on contact. Diesel demonstrated for me what to do, "Just put it in your mouth and inhale slowly." I did just that. It was smooth as I breathed in but I started coughing uncontrollably. I guess I did it wrong. But Diesel told me that's how it is sometimes.

I wanted more. So I took another pull, longer this time. My head was spinning and my mind was racing. The effects of this stuff had already hit me.

He was quiet for a while, took his deep long pulls and passed the blunt to me. I didn't feel like I was doing it right, but he assured me I was. He had me feeling so at ease. As we sat on the couch, smoking through the joint, he got up and turned on some music. *Ahh... Usher, my favorite.* I started rocking to the beat.

"Oh you like this, huh?" Diesel said, smiling at me. He was amused by me trying to dance.

"Hell yea. Usher always puts me in a good mood," I said. I felt so good. Nothing mattered at all to me at that moment but me, Diesel, the blunt, the comfy couch, and the sound of Usher's voice blasting through the speakers.

"You sure it's Usher putting you in that good mood?" he smiled again with those oh so sexy lips. "It could be the green. Or is it me?"

"I think it's all the above," I flirted back. For the next few minutes I was experiencing nothing but bliss. I was sitting next to the most handsome dude ever and smoking that good stuff that eased my mind. Everything around me seemed amazing. The music was pure perfection. The couch was extra soft. And I couldn't help but move closer to Diesel to feel his body. I needed to be closer to his fine ass. And he didn't mind at all.

He pulled the scrunchie out of my hair and told me how cute I looked with my hair down. He touched my face so I touched his stomach. "You be working out?" I asked.

"I try," he blushed a little while putting his hands on his own chest. "But most of this is all natural." We smiled at each other.

Diesel touched my cheek and said, "You mad cute too, ma!" I couldn't believe what I was hearing. As hot as I was getting by his gentle words and hard, smooth body next to me, I didn't want to move too fast with Diesel. I wanted to get into his head and heart more than anything. Of course I missed the touch of a guy on my body, but it was too soon. Besides, I wanted more than just that this time. I wanted his love.

"Diesel, why can't anyone else see me the way you do?

"Look, P. You just gotta tell yourself you're the shit and believe it. Nothing else matters but what you want and what you think," he said.

"It's so hard to believe that though. Especially when you got everyone around you telling you the opposite." I opened up.

"The sooner you start believing in yourself, everybody else will too. It's that simple."

I couldn't even argue with him. That's just what Dr. Graham said. I had to get that confidence and things could be so much easier for me.

We smoked the joint down to the end and I was definitely high. The more Diesel and I spoke, life did seem simple. I felt good about the changes I was gonna make. I enjoyed the moment and was excited to live my life.

Starting with a soft but intimate kiss between Diesel and I. I thrust my body onto his and fell deep into his arms. He returned the kiss and left me feeling hot and wet inside my pants.

He held me tight in his arms and the kiss seemed to last forever. When my lips began to dry up, finally we stopped to get a drink. That was as far as things went. Which was good enough for me!

Dear Diary,   *Monday September 9th*

I was called into the guidance counselor's office today. According to my records, I needed to sign up for an extracurricular activity if I was gonna stay in this school. The counselor ran down a list of things I could participate in, from Chess Club to Drama Club, Volleyball to Basketball, and poetry to Mathletes. Lol. *What do I look like?*

The only thing that actually caught my attention was cheerleading. I had a bit of experience with that having taken acrobatic classes when I was 9 and 10. Hopefully the dips and turns I learned back then could help me get on the squad.

I know cheerleaders are reserved for the prettiest and most popular girls in the school but hopefully they would let me in based on my talent and ability. Tryouts are coming soon so I've got a lot to prove and fast.

Dear Diary,   *Thursday September 12th*

My mother's rage has officially become unbearable. And I'm not gon' take it anymore!

It all started while waiting for her to give me a ride to school. She was off today so I begged her for a ride. Boy, was it *not* worth it!

The woman started picking on me for no reason. It's like everyday, she finds a new reason to attack me and I needed a break from it all. She still doesn't understand that I'm growing up. I'm a teenager for *God sakes!*

I'm old enough to have sex, get a job, and learn how to drive and though I haven't gotten to any of that yet, I could, soon as I damn well pleased- yet my mother still treats me like I'm a child. Freedom for me was so close, I could taste it! But dammit, it wasn't close enough.

This morning, my mother started with me again. Telling me my clothes were slutty and that the boys in high school were gonna think I'm easy. When did skinny jeans and a Bebe tank top become "slutty"? And what mother would say that to her daughter anyway? It's not like she was there to help pick out these clothes with me.

Well, I was through dealing with the foolishness. I wanted out. I even told her loud and clear, "I hate you, mom! You don't deserve a daughter like me no ways!"

When she responded, "A weak little nerd who wants so badly to fit in, she'll run the streets looking like a whore?!" I had enough.

I was a smart girl, and I knew that being smart wasn't cool. So I had to do a few other things to fit in. Especially if I was gonna make it onto the cheerleading squad.

I needed a fresh start in high school, and that requires me dressing like the other girls do! Why would she use that against me. I still worked hard, I respected people, and I respected *my damn self*.

"Whatever, ma. I'm not dealing with you right now. I'll just take the bus."

I'm nothing like the violent and destructive person she is and that was something I was proud of. She had beat me down so much over the years and I didn't want to fight anymore. But my mother insisted she would continuously challenge me. So, when she charged at me with the hair brush sitting on my dresser, I pushed her into my che drawer and ran for my escape. That was the first time I'd ever done anything to defend myself from her.

I was proud of myself for a moment. I actually thought I might win this one. But boy was I wrong!

My mother was filled with embarrassment and rage. She got up quickly and pushed me hard and far into a hallway door. "Who do you think you are? You think you're grown? I'll remind you who got the power in this damn house!"

My shoulder was throbbing by the intense pound into the door. I rubbed it and tried to get up. My mother was quick though. She had me cornered and grabbed my neck. She repeatedly knocked my head into the wall. Then she smacked me in the face and said, "Don't ever try to get big on me again. I will teach you a lesson every damn time!"

Her threat rang in my ears, and in my soul. I was in so much pain. *How much longer would I have to succumb to her abuse?*

When she finally left me alone, I could hardly get up off floor. But I was determined to get out of the house. I picked up my bag for school, packed some extra clothes, took the $200 I saved from my shopping money, and ran away from home hoping I never had to return.

VOLUME 6: FIRST TIME

Dear Diary,   *Friday September 13th*

After that awful incident with my mom and being away from home, I went to Diesel's crib after school today because he was the only one I could turn to. He welcomed me with open arms and allowed me to stay with him and his mom.

His mother, who is a known alcoholic, didn't mind me being there at all. She offered me a glass of Southern Comfort, a liquor I've never tasted. But when she brought it close enough to my nose for a whiff, it was too strong for me so I refused. *Didn't she know I'm way underage anyway?*

"She don't want none of that, ma!" Diesel answered for me. "I got something for her anyway." He took out a huge stash of green.

"How much she got on it, D?" his mother asked. "

"Ma, chill," he said.

"You better not be smoking up these chicks for free."

"'These chicks,' ma? We done known Patricia as long as we been living on this block? She my homegirl."

"I don't give a damn. You need to stop smoking up your profits, boy. Don't be stupid, Diesel."

They started talking like I wasn't in the living room with them.

"Ma, who's holding us down around here? You or me?" he challenged her boldly.

"Boy, don't even go there. You know I'm just going through a rough time."

"So don't question my moves, ma. I'm only 16 and I'm taking care of most the bills, ain't I? You can't start telling me how to handle *my* money. Like you can do any better."

As they continued to go back and forth, I looked around his house at the rugged decor. It was apparent that he and his mother didn't pay attention to the details within their 1 story mid-century ranch home. I didn't judge them for the unkempt carpets and furniture that surrounded us. I actually appreciated them for being themselves amidst such a neighborhood of such stuck up people. They've been living here for about 4 years and I'm sure they came from the 'hood and wasn't gonna change who they were just because they changed their locale.

I began to grow uncomfortable with their argument though so I decided to cut in. "Diesel, it's cool. I got $20 on it. Your mom is right. I don't wanna be taking nothing from you." I pulled out a twenty dollar bill from my stash.

"Cool," Diesel eyed me. I know he didn't want to take the money from me but with his mother still in the room, he figured it would help diffuse an argument.

His mother, Babs, kept on drinking and waiting around for Diesel to roll up.

As we started the cypher, I told Diesel about the fight I got into with my mother and he was so understanding. He told me I could stay with them as long as I needed. But I knew sometime soon I'd have to go home and face my awful reality with her.

As we smoked, my mind was racing. Being under the influence was definitely different this time.

I thought sadly about school, home, and my father. I had no control of the awful thoughts I was having. I felt a tinge of loneliness and even some pain. I didn't like the negative places my mind was going. I was feeling trapped in a whirlpool of dark, hurtful reflections and couldn't find my way out.

Diesel noticed I was in deep thought and came close to embrace me. He knew what I was going through and comforted me the best way he could.

"Let's do a shotty." He put the butt end of the blunt in his mouth and blew the smoke from the other end into my mouth. "This way, we both get high at the same time." That was a new way to do it.

After we both exhaled, he kissed me softly on the lips. That warm feeling came over me again. I was tingling all over. I wanted Diesel and I wanted him *bad*. Only because his mother was sitting right across from us, I kept myself from tonguing him down again.

But Babs peeped the tension. "Y'all need to get a room!"

"Ma, yo! We just chillin." Diesel backed up away from me. Him and his mother are close but he was still respectful of her presence.

He put on the TV and we started watching *Hearts & Hip Hop* together, a guilty pleasure we all shared. Babs was hood as hell but she was cool to hang with. And this was one show we could all find something relate to. I didn't understand everything but I knew a little something about having drama with the girls, fighting to fulfill a goal, absentee dads, looking for love, and certainly, hip hop.

I never understood why these lovely looking ladies got so violent sometimes but I guess that was how they dealt with their pain. We all had our outlets so I didn't wanna judge.

Anyhow, I'm getting ready to take a shower now. And boy do I need one bad! BRB

Dear Diary,   *Saturday September 14th*

After the warm soothing shower Diesel and Babs allowed me to take in their house last night, I dried off in Diesel's bedroom. I was still high and feeling out of my element. I tried to let go of all those painful thoughts I was having and decided to relax on Diesel's bed. It was neatly spread and smelled good.

He knocked on the door. "Come in!" I said inviting him to join me before I had a chance to put back on my clothes. "Can I borrow a shirt, please?"

"Sure, you can," he took one out his dresser and threw it on the bed. "But I don't think you really need it."

He climbed in the bed with me and put his strong hands on my shoulders. He caressed me gently, allowing my towel to fall onto the bed. I felt so uncertain for a moment with my body all exposed.

But again, Diesel brought me to the highest level of comfort. As he saw me shy away trying to cover up, he moved my hands, cupped my breasts and said, "They're a perfect fit in my hands. So what you all nervous about?"

Uhhh, maybe it was the drugs in my system, or my own insecurity, or the paranoia in my mind. But I quickly let my guard down for Diesel. "Nothing, babe. This is just a first for me."

"Well, there's a first time for everything love." He continued to move his hands around my naked body, following it with soft kisses.

Down below he fingered me, giving me the ultimate pleasurable experience. I cupped his man piece and stroked it gently.

Diesel gently laid me down on his bed. I stared into his beautiful eyes and allowed him to make his move. I trusted him as he tongued me slowly. His lips were juicy and tasted oh so damn good. I kissed back and was instantly aroused as he bit my lip gently. He tongued me down intensely and I was in absolute bliss. I closed my eyes and enjoyed every minute of this.

His lips went from my lips to my neck, to my breasts and it all felt amazing. I held his head still for a moment. The more he sucked on my nipples, the more powerful my body shook. I was getting so moist down there and I didn't know what exactly was happening throughout my body, but it all felt too good.

Next thing I knew, he was putting on a condom and then his man piece was in my most intimate place. There was a moment of pain. I yelled "Owww!" as he made his entrance into my body.

"Relax, baby girl," he insisted so I obeyed him. I shook and tensed up a bit, but the more wet I got, the more ease this magical moment gave me. As he went in and out of me, the pain went away. All I felt was a bursting sensation.

"Ahhh... Ohhh...!" I shrieked out in ecstasy. It was amazing. He put his hands to my mouth to quiet me down. I couldn't contain myself. The way he made me feel was out of this world! I was loving this feeling and craved him more and more.

But when I saw him shake and tighten his arms around me, I realized he'd reached his peak. "Ooo!" We both exploded after reaching a powerful orgasm. He laid next to me and kissed my neck. I smiled at him and closed my eyes.

I had become a woman. And that's when Diesel asked to be my man.

Dear Diary,   Monday September 16th

I got the info about the cheerleading tryouts today! And I actually think I can make it in. I started working on my gymnastic routines, I'm working on the confidence, and I definitely have the energy. Hopefully nothing else will stand in my way.

Dear Diary,   *Tuesday September 17th*

It's been almost a week since I left home. And quite a few days since I'd been staying with Diesel and Babs.

Diesel met me at the bus stop and was a little upset that I was running late.

"Today was the orientation for cheerleading tryouts," I told him excitedly. But he didn't share my joy.

"That's cool," was all he said. "But I been waiting here over an hour for yo ass."

"I'm sorry, babe. How can I make it up to you?" I put my hands around him.

"I know at least one way," Diesel kissed my neck playfully then pulled me toward him by the waist.

"I got you, babe. I'll race you home!" I teased. But he didn't wanna go home just yet. He said his mother was chillin' with some friends at the crib.

So we went to the North Fields Mall and he led me straight to *Fredericks of Hollywood* to pick me up something sexy. He bought me a silky nightgown and some lacy underwear. *I finally had a pair of my own!*

We went to pick up some CD's and DVDs from the electronics store. Next thing I know, we were locked inside a huge dressing room in Nordstrom. He pulled out the items from Fredericks and said, "Try this on." Diesel was so daring and spontaneous.

"Really?" I asked him sarcastically as he started lifting up my shirt. "Someone could be right there!" I pointed to the next dressing room over.

"You know *I* don't give a fuck. Do you?"

"I don't if you don't," I said. But I knew he truly didn't want that lingerie on me or anything at all. So we started getting it on right then and there. It was hard to keep quiet with the tantalizing ways he made me feel. He held nothing back as he kissed my body, rubbed my back, and stroked himself anxiously inside of me.

"I love your smooth, sexy body," he would say kissing my belly button and heading further down below. "You taste so sweet..." and I believed his every word. He made me feel so special and so loved.

We came on one accord as if we were made to love and make love to only each other. I felt so alive, so complete, and so fulfilled being in his presence. Every touch gave me tingles. Every word he spoke made me feel loved. *This* made life worth living. I wished every moment with Diesel could last forever...

Dear Diary,   *Monday September 23rd*

Today, Diesel and I really bonded. We watched a classic flick we both used to love, "Love & Basketball". We spent some intimate time together before his mother came back from running her errands. Some of the love scenes in the movie inspired our own throughout the film.

At the end, he affirmed, "See, when something's meant to be, it'll be. You can't rush nothing or push it into existence. Challenges come but that don't disrupt what's in the cards for you. Don't you forget that, babe."

I didn't know what he meant at first or why that was relevant at all. But I guess he was telling me in his own way, everything will be alright in time. And I truly hoped so.

Dear Diary,   *Wednesday September 25th*

I came straight to Diesel's house after school today and was greeted by an unfamiliar man outside by their back door. He was big and tall, wearing worn clothing, and was smoking a cigarette by the door.

"Who are you?" I asked.

"I'm Drew, Diesel's father," he said. I had assumed Diesel's father was out of the picture. I hadn't actually asked about him but there was no evidence that he had any presence in their lives. I guess *everyone* had a father but me.

"Oh," I said. "Well where's Diesel?"

"You asking a lot questions little girl. Who are you? And what you doing about to walk up in my house?"

"I'm Diesel's... girlfriend, Patricia. I've been staying here. I thought he would've told you." I was a little fearful giving this man all that information.

"Well he ain't mention you. And if you his girlfriend, who's the red boned chick he's had over the house all day?" Drew questioned me.

His words crushed me. And I felt really stupid. *Was Diesel really with someone else? Were the past few nights just that to him- A few good nights? Was it over between us? Where would I stay? And where was I gonna get my high?*

As I stood there frozen with questions running through my mind, Drew put out his cigarette and inched closer to me.

"Can I talk to him?" I asked.

"He don't want no visitors today. But don't worry girl, if you need someone to lay with tonight, I'm sure my lady Babs wouldn't mind you joining *us*." He touched my waist and I instantly backed away disgusted. I couldn't believe what I was hearing. I wanted so badly to rush up in the house and demand answers from Diesel but his father was freaking me the hell out. I had to get away. Far, far away.

I ran away and toward my house where my mother spotted me running frantically. I know she hadn't reported me missing or anything so I wondered how she really felt seeing me for the first time in weeks.

All she could say was, "I knew your weak ass would be back sooner or later." She laughed at me and continued making her way in the house. Still, I was happy to be home.

I realized, Diesel didn't love me. I was just an easy, vulnerable target to him, just like I was to everyone else. It hurt bad to think I fell for his top notch G and was still alone.

As I walked up the steps to my door, nowhere else felt safer. But when I thought about losing Diesel, and possibly never having him back, I couldn't help but cry.

Dear Diary,   *Thursday September 26th*

High school sucks! But anything was better than hanging around the house being my mother' slave. Or sitting around depressed because Diesel played me. *Why did he have to come into my life and bring me such joy, just to snatch it away so quickly? Didn't he feel the same passion for me that I felt for him?* I was really starting to fall for him. Now, how would I ever trust again? I needed to escape the thoughts and feelings of my heartbreak.

But nothing changed since my return home. So I tried to focus on my schoolwork and my activities- things I could kinda control. Being at school was the only disruption I had from the awful nights I had with my mother. Her yelling, us fighting, her beatings, my pain. It was nice to get away a few hours out of the day.

There were soooo many people in my school so I was easily getting lost in the crowd. I know it wasn't my plan to go another year unnoticed but at least, I didn't have to deal with getting teased and picked on like I did in junior high. This time around, it had to be different. I was gonna feel good about being smart. I was gonna have to make friends. I had to be noticed for all the right things. And I had to do it quick.

I was determined to get my spot on the cheerleading squad. But I could tell by the orientation that it wouldn't be easy. The girls there all seemed to fit a mold. They were all about the same waist size, they wore expensive shoes, and had on the trendiest clothes. I had a lot of work to do if I was ever gonna fit the bill. So I convinced myself I wouldn't even waste my time.

Then coming home, my mother made me feel even worse about it all. I was glad I made it through the first few days of high school but she must have known I was still unhappy. And I'm sure she wanted to get back at me for running away from home after her attack the other day, so she pointed it out.

"Guess high school got the best of you already," she said one evening. "I can see it on your pitiful face."

"Huh? What are you talking about. Everything's going fine," I answered.

"Yea right. You made any friends? I bet you ain't make no friends. You just a lonely little girl and you're gonna stay that way."

Her words stung me because she always said stuff I was already in fear of. Stuff I had to deal with without her blatant negativity. So I walked out of the kitchen with defeat and head to my room.

As I was leaving, she threw a fork into my back. The 3 pointed prongs dug lightly into my skin.

"Ow!" I stiffened in pain. "What was that for?!"

"For being a damn failure," she said.

I looked at her with disgust. How could I respond? She was convinced that I am every bit of the daughter she never wanted. No amount of passing grades or kind words was gonna convince her otherwise. So I'm going to bed a failure tonight, but tomorrow things have got to change.

VOLUME 7: FRENEMIES

Dear Diary,   *Friday September 27th*

I made up my mind and I'm trying out for the cheerleading squad!

How else am I gonna get in with the right crowd? Or convince my mother I'm not always gonna be a failure? Mathletes and chess club damn sure wasn't gonna do it.

Today, all the applicants met up in the gym after school. Tammy, who seems to be in the running for "most popular freshman girl", was like, "Hey, what's your name again?"

"Patricia," I said. "Tammy right?"

"Yup, and you're the girl they're betting won't make the squad."

"Who's 'they'? Our jealous, anorexic opponents, " I joked trying to make light of the insult.

"Is that what you have to say about my friends?" Tammy said with a slight attitude.

"I don't know who your friends are but I'm pretty certain I'm the girl that *will* make the squad," I answered confidently. I couldn't punk out at that point, no matter what I truly believed.

"Well, I hope so," Tammy smiled. "Sometimes you have to prove people wrong to shut them up. Morgan and Tiffany have been my besties since junior high, they are always trying to prove they're better than everyone."

I knew exactly the "Morgan and Tiffany" type. Even before meeting them, I figured they were insecure girls just like the rest of us who tried so hard to hide it- they ended up making others feel insecure. But Tammy came off different. She clearly knew she was the shit and expected everyone around her to realize it too. I was so relieved Tammy didn't already staple me a bitch and a loser. She was someone I needed to be hangin' with.

"Well, that's not my style. I'm sure there's room for all of us to shine on the squad."

"Exactly, 'cause I know I'm gon' shine for sure. I'm not worried about anyone else." Tammy's confidence was so genuine. I only hoped someday I could possess that quality. "Let me introduce you to the girls," she said with a smile.

So I met Morgan who was beautiful and probably was truly anorexic, then Tiffany who seemed like she needed to be. Tiffany was a little big boned and didn't quite look like she was meant to be on the squad. But hey, they probably thought the same about me.

Me and my petite frame, no hips and small boobs, with little to no fashion sense to complement it. I have a slight overbite and pretty short hair. My ears are slightly pointed and have previously been compared to that of a mouse. But I already decided, I wouldn't let any of that stop me. This time around, I was gonna woman up and seize the day. *If these hating ass bitches would only let me.*

Upon meeting them, Morgan immediately mentioned how unlikely a choice I'd be for the squad. "Oh Patricia, nice to meet ya! I hope that even if you don't make it, we can still be friends."

"Why wouldn't I make it?" I asked.

"Well," Morgan didn't hold back. "They expect cheerleaders to represent the school all over town. We have to have beauty, style, and confidence. Do you really think *you* have all that?"

Funny thing was, I didn't. She had me shut down at 'beauty'. Although I'd taken gymnastics for 2 years, I wasn't ready to rumble with the big girls. But I had to at least try.

"I was thinking, you girls could probably help me step my game up a notch." I snuck in a complement, "Y'all seem to have it all worked out. Maybe you can help *me* out!"

Tiffany jumped in. "That *would* be a great experiment! What do you think, Tammy?"

"Hell yeah!"

I was so glad they bought it. And that's how I got in good with the popular freshman girls. Hopefully, I would soon be considered one too.

Dear Diary,   *Tuesday October 1st*

I couldn't help but notice the "friends" I made were a little cold to me at practice today. They agreed to help me get my moves together for the final auditions but they were way more focused on helping each other.

Tammy was having a hard time getting her triple cartwheel straight so they spotted her for like an hour. Meanwhile, I needed just a moment of their time to get the step count and they weren't interested in helping me at all.

"Weren't you paying attention when Julie showed it to us," Morgan hissed at me when I requested her assistance.

"Yes," I said. "But I think I missed something."

"Well, figure it out." Tiffany replied. "We gotta make sure Tammy got the cartwheel. That's way more important."

I got the picture after that. I was kind of on my own here. I watched them all up under Tammy the whole practice.

Anything I said was meaningless. Even when I suggested we take a quick break to get a bite to eat.

Tammy says, "Look, making the squad is the most crucial thing right now! Some of us can't afford to stuff our faces until we're reached perfection."

I thought that was so funny. "Perfection? Really?" I laughed.

Tiffany didn't think it was funny at all. "Yes. And that may not be attainable for you, but it is for us."

"Okay, Tiffany. I get it. But seriously, are you telling me you're not the least bit hungry?" I asked.

"Do I look hungry to you?" she answered.

"Do you want me to answer that," I asked jokingly of course. But she was instantly insulted. Maybe she was a little insecure about her weight.

"You think you're funny, huh? You got some nerve. Your boney ass ain't funny. And if you wanna keep hanging with us, you better tone down that sense of humor you think you got. "

Was that a threat?

"And that's a threat," Morgan confirmed.

I had to lighten the mood. "C'mon guys. We're friends, I didn't mean to hurt you. Can we just drop it and practice?"

Tiffany came up in my face, "Let's get one thing straight. I'm Tammy's friend. And you're supposedly Tammy's friend too. But we are *not* friends with each other. So don't think you can make jokes like that with me, got it?"

"Understood." I wasn't about to go back and forth with her so I got back to practicing.

Tammy interrupts me. "I think it's time for you to go. How 'bout you pick up where you left off tomorrow."

I didn't like that Tammy was dismissing me but it seems like she runs the damn show around here. "Okay, whatever." I picked up my things and left. I was really hungry anyway and I was growing very impatient with these girls.

As I left, I overheard Morgan say, "Where did you find that loser anyway, Tammy?"

Tammy replied, "I think she's cool and c'mon that *was* funny, Tiff."

I smiled hearing her defend me. At least I made one friend. But sadly, I'd made 2 enemies.

VOLUME 8: CUTTING DEEP

Dear Diary,   *Friday October 4ᵗʰ*

I tried to sit down with my mother for dinner tonight and thought I could share my joy of trying out for the cheerleading squad with her.

"You really think you're cut out to be a cheerleader. Who you fooling?"

"I figured I could at least try," I said.

"Well, you're wasting your time. Stick to what you're good at- hiding away in a book!" she laughed to herself barely looking my way.

"Whatever, mom. I have other skills. You'll see..."

"'Whatever?' You better watch your mouth when you're talking to me before I pop you!"

I couldn't win with my mother so I just rolled my eyes at her and excused myself.

"Hey," she stopped me. "Clean up this kitchen before you go anywhere."

I wasn't in the mood to stick around for another minute. "I barely made any mess."

"Girl, don't you talk back to me! I said clean this shit up!"

I didn't respond again and just emptied my plate. As I was coming back to take hers, she got up with anger. Her plate came flying at me and I ducked. It hit the cabinet and cracked into a million pieces on the floor.

"Look what you made me do! Clean that up you disrespectful little bitch!" my mother had truly lost it. I wanted to tell her I was coming to clean her plate next before she went crazy but what sense would it make? She had to win every time. Even if it meant she was the loudest and angriest, or got the last word, she just had to beat me. So I let her.

I spent the rest of my evening in the kitchen cleaning up every bit of the ceramic plate that was splattered around the kitchen floor. And my mother stood in the doorway watching. She loved to see me struggling and I couldn't understand why.

I wished I could just sit down and ask her why she hated me so much but every time I considered it, I punk out in fear that she'll get angry again. And with her, there is no telling how far she'll go in the heat of her rage.

Dear Diary,   *Saturday October 5th*

The weekend finally came and to most teens, its what you look forward to. But for me, to be home from school while my mother is also home from work, it's dreadful.

I finished my chores early this afternoon and just wanted to stop at the mall down the road. Tammy said she and the girls were headed there later and she wanted me to come too. I was excited to embark on this new thing- a social life. But my mother gave me hell as usual.

First she screamed at me to vacuum the living room because she was having company later today. While I was doing that, she asked me to re-scrub the bathroom toilet. She said it still smelled like shit. And rightfully so, lol.

So I did as she asked. While I was getting dressed, she decided to take interest in my whereabouts for a change.

"Where the hell you getting all dolled up to go?"

Although I was just wearing a pair of skinny jeans and a v-neck tee, she was probably taken aback by the neat ponytail I carefully put in place as I was getting ready to roll a sock in it for my bun. I guess that was over the top for me. "I'm meeting some friends at the mall."

"Oh, you got friends now?" she asked. "When since you got people to hang with?"

"I tried to tell you about the girls I met at school. At the cheerleading try-outs."

"Don't tell me what you told me. I'm asking you now!"

I just wasn't in the mood for another argument, but when am I ever? I replied, "I met them last week."

"Oh, so you just met these girls and you're calling them friends?" she hissed. "How ignorant of you."

"Well I know we aren't besties or anything but Tammy and I are friends. And she's extremely popular so I'd like to stay close to her."

"Ohhh, that's what this is about. You're trying to be popular?" my mother asked but didn't expect an answer. "Well don't waste your time, you ain't never gonna be."

I was furious at how far my mother was going to press my buttons. She didn't give a damn about my feelings or my happiness. She knows how hard a time I had at my last school and she was determined to not let me forget about it.

"Mom, I'm really getting tired of you putting me down. Why do you hate me so damn much?!" I screamed.

"And who are you raising your voice at little girl?"

"I'm angry mommy! You are always hurting my feelings. *Why do you keep doing this to me?*"

"Because it's your goddamn fault I'm so unhappy. Why *shouldn't* I let you feel my wrath?!" she said.

This was news to me. *How could I be the reason she was so displeased?* I used to love my mother with all my heart. I used to appreciate her and value all her hard work for me. But she'd become bitter and abusive and I don't have it in me to love that anymore. So I asked for an explanation.

"Mom, how could *I* be the reason for your unhappiness? What have I done to you?"

She stopped what she was doing and stared at me with evil eyes. She couldn't believe I asked her that question. But I was determined to get an answer. "You wanna know how you ruined my life? How you messed up my chances of being a doctor like I always wanted? You were born, that's how!"

"*What?*" I didn't understand how that was my fault and I started to cry.

"Why did you have me then?!"

"Your father wanted you. And I wanted him. So I kept you. But when he left, what the *hell* did I need you for?" her eyes started to water.

"Wow, mom." I was hurt as hell. It was like everything I was living for went to the dirt. Every ounce of my body got weak with pain. How was I supposed to feel knowing my mother had me only to keep her man. And that he didn't care enough for me so neither did she. *Why was I so worthless and unimportant that my own parents didn't want me?*

"You asked for the truth. So there it is, Patricia," she said holding back tears. "But I knew your *weak ass* couldn't handle it."

I broke down in tears and ran out the door. But I no longer wanted to go to the mall. I felt so empty inside. Nothing could ease the pain I was feeling inside. I wasn't worth anything to my mother *nor* my father. No wonder I wasn't worth anything to anyone else.

So I sat down on the steps of my back door and allowed the tears to fall down my face. I found me a piece of metal from the recycling bin outside the house and dug it into my skin. I kept pressing it into my arm until I saw the richness of my blood oozing out. I cut deep into myself hoping this stupid act would ease the pain in my heart.

As I felt the painful sting of the blade digging into my skin, it hurt like hell on the outside but at least it distracted me from the ache I was feeling inside.

VOLUME 9: REJECTION

Dear Diary,   *Monday October 7ᵗʰ*

After such an awful weekend home, I was excited to see Tammy and the girls at school. I was hoping I could tell them what I'd learned from my mother and that they'd be able to relate or console me in some way. I was sure they each would have some home life stories of their own to share.

But Tammy was pissed that I didn't show up to the mall on Saturday. And her little army made it very clear that wasn't acceptable.

As I walked up to their lunch table, where groups of the popular kids sit, I was greeted by Tiffany's scowl.

"You think you could stand us up at the mall and still expect to be a part of the clique? Sorry, sweetie, that's not how we roll. Goodbye," she waved me away.

I stepped up to Tammy and said, "I'm so sorry Tammy but I've got to tell you about the drama I had on Saturday. It was awful. Can we chat?"

"If you wanted to chat, you should've called me on Saturday and told me what's up. It's too late now," she replied barely looking my way. I didn't know why she was being so damn mean to me.

"Are you guys serious?" I asked.

"Serious as cancer," Morgan chimed in. "You had your chance to hang with us and you blew it. So get to stepping."

The girls were being heartless. I really, *really* needed a friend.

"Speaking of stepping, good luck at the final cheerleader auditions on Friday!" Tiffany said. As I took a step back and starting walking away, I heard the girls laugh in unison.

"And that's how you show these chicks who runs things around here!" someone said.

I was so embarrassed. I felt lonelier than ever with no one else to talk to. I just wanted to die. So I went into an empty bathroom stall and cut through my skin again with a sharp piece of glass.

When the warm red blood started pouring through my skin, I cringed with pain. But it felt good to be in control of the pain myself instead of allowing everyone else to be.

Dear Diary,   *Friday October 11th*

As much as I wanted to be a part of this group of friends, I'd lost all my fight. Within the past few days, I found out the father I never really hear about couldn't give two shits about me, the mother I sought to love truly regretted my existence, my boyfriend lied to me, and the girls I thought would enhance the outcome of my next 4 years in high school, were only set out to humiliate me. *Life sucks!*

Today at the tryouts, Morgan and Tiffany literally sabotaged everything I'd been working towards these past few weeks. They even told the captains of the squad I was disloyal and slow. Making up lies that they had been working on the routines with me all week and I still couldn't get it.

They were pure evil. Tammy, who I thought had a little dignity, didn't say a word to defend me. She stayed focused on her steps, her routines, and the cartwheel she had mastered. And me- I didn't come close to the "perfection" I was striving for and didn't think I ever would. So when they read off the list of names for girls who made the squad, I wasn't surprised mine wasn't on it.

Nonetheless, Tiffany wanted to throw in a little extra evil and asks in front of everyone, "What about Patricia Thomas? Did she make it?"

Captain Shelly looks at me and replied, "No, sorry. You're not quite cheerleader material."

I was soooo embarrassed. As if it wasn't obvious enough, the captain of the squad had publicly announced that I wasn't talented enough. Not pretty enough. And certainly not good enough.

I was already being rejected and this was just the beginning of the school year, the first few weeks. How the hell was I gonna make it through the year, or better yet, the next four??

VOLUME 10: THE BIG BAD BULLY

Dear Diary,   *Monday October 14ᵗʰ*

I came to terms with the fact that I wasn't good enough to be on the cheerleading squad. And that I wasn't worthy of true friends. It was even difficult thinking about the love I shared with Diesel and losing him to some next chick. SMDH. But having to accept that my mother and father didn't want me was soooo much worse. And I had to understand why.

I mean why would you bring someone into the world that has every bit of your blood and soul running through them, and not want to be a part of their life? What kind of person wouldn't want to share themselves with the very being that will live on their legacy? How could my father just disappear from my life before even giving me a chance? And my mother who did know me, why couldn't she appreciate me the way I needed her to?

I wanted to change things. Because there was too much agony buried in my heart. I didn't want to have to keep finding ways to stop the emotional pain by creating some physically. Cutting myself last week was a mistake. It didn't help at all. I was left with these scars on my arm and the ones in my heart certainly hadn't gone away.

As my mom came down the stairs, she noticed me rubbing my wound. She startled me by asking, "Something wrong with you?" *As if she really cared.*

"No, my arm's just sore from all the exercising I did for the squad tryouts," I lied. I was sure to keep these wounds covered.

"Oh, how was it? Did they *actually* pick you?" she asked in shock.

I was planning on telling the truth but I was not sure I could handle any more of her negativity this morning.

"Yes. Surprised?"

"Damn right, I am!" she exclaimed. "You finally giving your mother something to be proud of."

I smiled. It was the first time she'd ever said she'd been proud of me. But the joy I felt was a little bittersweet. She was proud of me for accomplishing something I didn't even accomplish. I guess it would take a few more lies for my mother to love me.

And if a few lies was all it took, I would definitely swing a few.

Dear Diary,   *Friday October 18th*

Ever since I told my mother I made the squad, I had to spend a few late nights hanging out before coming home, just so she'd actually believe I was at practices. I needed her to buy it because it made her respect me. It made her proud.

But today, it all came crashing down.

I was hanging out at school sitting in on one of the practices when a group of guys came in to check out the squad girls too. They saw me sitting alone in my jeans jacket, matching pants, and floral turtleneck. As they approached me, I wasn't sure if they had any interest in getting to know me, or if just to make fun of me. But I straightened my back up like the confident girls do, ran my fingers through my hair like the pretty girls do, and smiled like the popular girls do. I hoped they would consider me at least *one* of the above.

One of the upperclassmen guys from our basketball team, Kendrick, spoke up first. "So which of the girls are you here checking out?"

I was extremely confused. "What?"

Kendrick continued. "We know *you* ain't on the squad." He and his friends laughed. "So you must be trying to get with one of the girls who is. We know how some of y'all get down."

His friend, Christian says chiming in, "Word, she gotta be a dike!"

They thought I was gay!

"You guys are sadly mistaken. I'm into guys." I defended myself. I even took it a step further to say, "I'll prove it."

"Oh really," Kendrick raised his eyebrows. "So prove it then. Take one of my boys into the locker room and give him the best proof you got."

The guys slapped fives with excitement. I desperately wanted to prove that I was all woman. I wanted them to know I could hang like the other girls. So I pulled Christian by the hand and took him into the boy's locker room like I was asked.

When we were finally alone behind the last row of lockers, I said to him, "Would a dike do this..." and I did something I've hadn't done in a long time. I tongue kissed him. He put his hands behind my head and returned the affection.

It had been a while since I was touched by a dude so I was happy to be experiencing this with one of the cutest, most popular guys at our school.

Christian smelled good and his lips were wet and smooth. I ran my tongue across those lips and felt a rush of heat move through me then. He grabbed hold of my breasts. I felt a little violated doing this so publicly, but I wasn't gonna miss the chance to prove I was all woman to this dude who was all man.

"Any dike could kiss like that," he said. "But a real woman knows how to go down."

He started zipping down his pants and I got scared. I didn't know what he wanted me to do down there, nor was I prepared to find out.

But he aided me by bringing his hands back to my head and pushing it right down to his crotch.

I stuck out the tip of my tongue just to experiment and was frozen in this compromising position, not sure exactly what I was expected to do next. In an instant, I heard a camera click, followed by a heap of laughter.

The guys in his crew were hiding behind a row of lockers and were taking *pictures*! OMG!

I was sooooo embarrassed. I ran into the restroom of the locker room and checked myself out in the mirror before making my getaway. I had to fix my hair from when Christian had tousled it trying to get me to go down on him.

As I was finally heading out, the guys were still discussing the incident loudly and even congratulating him for it.

As if that experience wasn't horrifying enough, one of the upperclassmen squad girls came bursting through the locker room door with her group of friends screaming, "Christian, who is this skanky little bitch!"

Christian was as shocked as I was to see this chick who I figured was his girlfriend, an "it" girl I'd seen on the squad, standing there with her midriff shirt and her hands in the pockets of her cut up jeans. Her friends stood beside her looking ready for war.

One of them had the picture of me with my tongue way too close to Christian's crotch in her phone. Word- or *image* rather- travelled fast! I was *extremely* mortified!

One of the girls pushed me aside and I fell into a locker. I could tell Christian was scared as he stuttered, "I don't even know her name. She told me she wanted to show me something, and all of a sudden she's zipping down my pants."

His girlfriend stared me down with rage. I couldn't believe she bought Christian's little lie. She must be one of those stupid chicks who lets her man get away with anything and he knew it.

The girlfriend quickly directed her anger at me. "Oh really, you wanna show my man something, huh?" she said to me. "Well I have something to show you." She took her hand out of her pocket and threw it at my face. I managed to block her hit and rolled away from the commotion.

As I attempted to protect myself, I was almost free until one of her friends got close enough to my hair and pulled on the neatly rolled bun I had placed back on my head. *I just couldn't win.*

At that moment, Tammy and Morgan walked in the locker room from cheerleading practice. Although they didn't seem to like me, they had come to my defense. Apparently everyone had heard, or seen, the details of Christian and I's escapade. The locker room was full of both guys and girls.

"Hey!" Morgan screamed as she saw the girlfriend's friend grab my head, about to bang it into a locker. "Leave Patricia alone! What the hell did she do to you?"

The girlfriend replied, "Oh, this your friend? She was trying to give my man a blowjob. You freshmen sluts better watch who you messing with, especially if y'all wanna keep your spot on the squad."

Tammy stepped up to the girlfriend without an ounce of fear. "C'mon Gina, why you tryna threaten us? You know we ain't scared of nobody."

"Well, if I catch any of you this close to my boyfriend again, I'll give you a good reason to be," she said firmly.

I appreciated Tammy having my back but I had to put a word in for myself. "Uh, hello! Your man was the creep trying to get *me* in *his* pants!"

But the girlfriend and her friends had turned their backs and laughed at my statement. "*Whatever!* Like Christian would be interested your scrawny little ass when he has a bad ass bitch like me!"

This girl actually thought that mattered to a scumbag like Christian? Please, even *I* knew better than that. Dudes like him would go after every and any type of girl they could get. But she didn't know the first thing about her own boyfriend's distrustful ways. Someday she'll learn, I suppose. It didn't take me so long at all.

VOLUME 11: RESPECT

Dear Diary,   *Monday October 21ˢᵗ*

I was extremely shocked that the girls were there for me when I'd least expected it. I couldn't understand why they went from out casting me from their crew to welcoming me back in- but for the first time, I felt like I belonged.

Just a few moments before they came to my defense, I was feeling devalued and pressured. I wanted to make an impression on the guys that stood around me but not exactly in that way. I wanted them to notice me, not for being a whore and a pushover, but instead for being bold and in control of my sexuality.

That incident with Christian was not at all what I had in mind. It was almost a relief to hear that camera click. It snapped me back into realty to experience that moment of shame. *What was I thinking?*

Then when my Tammy and Morgan came through to prevent that huge fight, I couldn't have appreciated them more. I owed them everything for turning that awkward and embarrassing moment into a triumphant one.

"Girl, you gon' have to stop getting yourself in trouble. We ain't always gon' be around to save you," Tammy said as the group of us fixed our hair in the bathroom mirror.

"Oh, you don't have to worry," I replied. "After you checked them chicks, I'm sure they won't be a problem anymore. So neither will I."

They nodded with a side eye, "Hope not..."

Tiffany asked, "How did you end up in that position with Christian anyway?"

"He accused me of being a lesbian while I was waiting for you guys at cheerleading practice. So I told him, I'd prove I wasn't."

"Are you serious?!" Morgan said. "Go Patricia!"

Tammy asks, "How exactly were you gonna prove it though? Especially with his girlfriend and her minions watching him as closely as they do?"

"Well, I didn't even know he had a girlfriend. I just wanted to give him the best French kiss of his life! Then he starts pulling out his dick on me!" I said with disgust. "And I know I'm a whole lot of things to people but I ain't no hoe!"

"That may be so," Tammy said. "But you just got a reputation you are *not* gonna be able to shake. Those girls are the big bad bullies around here and they're brutal with revenge."

"Yeah, you definitely messed with the wrong woman's man. Gina don't play," Morgan said. "And that picture of you ain't just gonna disappear." She took out her phone proving to me that it had already made its way to her phone and most likely others.

Fear came rushing back to me. But I was determined to keep it hidden. "Whatever! She needs to worry less about me and more about keeping her man's perverted ass away from freshman girls like me. We can take her on if we needed to. Right, ladies?" Although I spoke words of confidence, I hoped they would reassure me.

"We're just hoping she won't be a problem for any of us, like you said Patricia."

"Yea, 'cause even Tammy wanted a piece of Christian but she knew better than to try and push up to him. You happen to have a lot more balls than we thought. Good for you," Tiffany says.

I was pleased to hear them say that. *Me having balls?* That was new. I guess it was true, pretending to believe in yourself was worth more than not believing at all. My friends finally gained a little respect for me. Of course there was a little price to pay, but at least I finally got what I was looking for.

Dear Diary,   *Tuesday October 22nd*

My days of waiting for the girls after cheerleading practice were over. As you know, I had gotten into enough trouble in doing so. And besides, I still hadn't found a club that would accept me so the guidance counselor took it upon herself to sign me up for the poetry club.

I was a little hesitant to attend my first poetry club meeting because I thought it would cramp my style. I was finally fitting in at Middlebrook. I had friends who kinda respected me and I was successfully keeping my grades up- and keeping *that* on the low. I was no longer an outcast because I hung out with the coolest crew of girls in our freshman class. Life was starting to have its highs.

To my surprise though, when I walked into the room of poetry geeks, I actually fit in. (Does that mean I'm a geek too?)

I was amongst a group of people who gave a damn about their education and were actually here because they wanted to be. There was no strenuous audition to get in and no one judged you for being there. I was right at home here. This was a mix of overachievers who just loved to write and chilled out folks who used poetry in raps and rhymes.

I felt comfortable as I sat down with a group of guys and one girl that looked like they had the urban bohemian vibe going.

"What's up guys, I'm Patricia," I introduced myself. "Is this the hip hop crew?"

"Nah, it's the poetry gang. You down?" one of the brown skin guys with dreads answered.

"Ain't that kinda the same thing?" I asked jokingly.

"Guess so," he smiled back at me and extended his hand. "I'm Don, by the way."

"Yes, you are!" I flirted a little. I thought he was a little cute but when he smiled, his stunning straight white smile was even more captivating. "I'd love to hear some of the poetry you got going on."

"Uh, Donald, stop tryna be cute," the girl sitting at the table interrupted. "You know we gotta deadline."

"That's Sandra, the hater," Don chuckled. "She's referring to the poetry slam we're performing at in two weeks. You rhyme?"

I acknowledged Sandra the hater with a genuine smile. "Nice to meet you guys. I'm actually new to this poetry thing so rhyme and rhythm may not come so natural for me. I'd love to sit in and listen to y'all though. Maybe some of your skills will rub off on me."

Sandra the hater replied, "We actually need to make some real progress and if you don't already got the skills, you ain't gonna get it no time soon." I quickly understood why she was called, "the hater."

"Okayyy..." I replied, a bit stunned by her rudeness. I was ready to turn around and walk away.

"Hey, Sandra chill." Don ushered me back to my seat. "Patricia, please stay put. As a new member of the poetry club, we should be welcoming you. I apologize for her disrespect. We'd love to show you our stuff."

Don started tapping the table while Sandra and the other guy joined in with a beat coming from his mouth. "Che- Che- Che- Check this out homie. You don't even know me. But you got your guard up cause you think you are a trophy. You ain't win a thing and you ain't got no bling. But that ain't what I mean, you need to check the scene. We got skills and we got style. We ain't rich but we survive. We make beats, we bring the heat. We are live and we live high. We don't mean to cross the line but we are flyy and we can't hide!"

"That was amazing!" I exclaimed. It truly was. They made music with their hands and mouths that sounded like music on a track.

As I tried to get myself comfortable at their table, I couldn't help but notice the hateration coming from Sandra and the other dude sitting there staring at me.

When he finally spoke up, I was embarrassed by what he said. "Yo, you look madd familiar. You ever been in the boys locker room?"

I couldn't believe that awful occurrence had come back to haunt me so soon. "What are you talking about?" I pretended to be oblivious.

"I seen a picture of a girl doing some nasty things in the boys locker room. I swear it was you!" he insisted.

"Nah, I don't think so." I tried to lie my way out of this but it was evident the rumors had started circulating and the pictures were too.

"Stop lying. I can prove it," he said. I couldn't even look at Don to see what he thought of this. I was too ashamed to find out.

There was nothing left for me to say. It was time for me to run.

Only problem was, I couldn't. I would be pulled out of this school in just a matter of time if I didn't commit to one of these clubs.

"I don't know what you heard, but I ain't that girl," I insisted. I just hoped he wouldn't pull out that evidence and humiliate me anymore than I already was. I couldn't run this time and I couldn't hide. So instead I said, "I'm not gonna stick around and be judged like this. Please excuse me." Then I got up and walked away to another table.

The next group was a focused group of writers. Most of them wore glasses and barely looked up when I walked over. They each were working on something intense and I wanted to take part.

"Can I join you guys?" I asked as I sat in.

The group leader, Joan, introduced herself. She was a senior and was editor at large of the school's poetry magazine.

"Sure ," she said.

"How can I contribute?" I asked.

"Just give us the words that speak straight from your heart and soul. Whatever you're feeling, whatever you're thinking, write it down and try to make it rhythmic," Joan challenged me.

I was excited with this task. I had gotten very used to writing my thoughts out on paper since I starting writing in this diary. I could definitely do this. If only I could keep thoughts of that awful rumor from distracting me. On the contrary, I tried to use it to inspire me...

Hidden
By Patricia Thomas

Alone all the time, but still looking for a place to hide
Being me ain't easy when I'm on the outside
Always been an outcast but searching to get in
Even when I'm surrounded, I'm so lonely within
I could stand around waiting, shouting for attention
But no one ever hears me or even makes a mention
Even when I'm noticed, they don't really see who I am
There's a distorted view of what I'm about & where I stand
Although I sit before you, showing you my honest face
I'm still hidden and can't find my way out this place

Not bad for my first poem, right? ☺

Dear Diary,   *Wednesday October 23ʳᵈ*

After days trying to take my mind off silly boys, I got weak. I couldn't get thoughts of Don or Diesel out of my mind. As I lay in my bed tonight, I thought about them joining me. I craved the intimate touch of a strong sexy man in my company and I couldn't help but close my eyes and dream.

I imagined Diesel cupping my breasts as Don massaged me from head to toe. The two of them kissing each of my shoulders and making me feel whole again. I pictured them heading down to my stomach and to my navel, as I shook with pleasure. Each of them caressing my legs and tickling the bottoms of my feet, as I lay down with ease to enjoy this bliss. The passion each of them had me feeling as they kissed their way to my most sensitive spots made me crave their touch with such eagerness.

I had no plans on stopping these intimate thoughts. But the feelings were so real, I had to find my way to true pleasure. Diesel had become one with my body and Don with my soul. I couldn't let the thought of that go. I was getting too turnt up by this fantasy I created in my head. I needed to achieve real satisfaction.

So I started to explore my own body and the personal places my ex had previously found. Today, I invented something I call, finger lickin' love. It was my lil secret to using my own hands to love me. I discovered some pretty good tricks, I only hope I can remember them all. **;-)**

As I lay down into my plush pillows with satisfaction, I felt so refreshed. Someday soon, I had to have my man back in my life so he could love me the way I dreamed.

Dear Diary,   *Thursday October 24th*

The worst thing happened to me today! This breakout started forming on my forehead and had me looking crazy. *Puberty sucked!*

Tammy, Morgan, and Tiffany laughed so hard at me when we met up in the schoolyard this morning.

"That's embarrassing!" Morgan said as if I didn't already know. "It must be your time of the month again."

"Girl you gonna have to start controlling your skin. Ever heard of Neutrogena?" Tammy said. "If you use it everyday, when your skin gets oily during period time, you won't get those huge nasty bumps on your face." The girls laughed again.

"Now, you're gonna have to put a dot of toothpaste on those bumps and hope to God they dry up overnight," says Morgan.

"Really?" I asked in the midst of both wonderment and humiliation.

"Duh!" Tiffany exclaimed. "Ain't you got a mother to teach you that?"

Morgan adds, "And by the looks of the outfit you're wearing, she hasn't taught you anything about style ether."

These girls sure were reading me. I had never gotten a chance to let them in my troubled home life but they saw that something was lacking. I felt a little vulnerable to the situation and so I wasn't gonna share at that moment.

"We gonna have to give you a mini makeover girl!" Morgan cut in.

"Y'all would do that?" I asked.

"What are friends for?" Morgan said.

Tammy looked at me and said, "And if you gonna be hanging with us, you need to look the part. Greasy skin and tacky clothes may have worked over in Northfield but it ain't cutting it here in Middlebrook."

She was almost right about that. But even back in Northfield, there was hell to pay for my lack of image game. I was not trying to go through that again. Or any worse.

"Go inside and wash your face before your skin problem becomes contagious!" she exclaimed.

I couldn't believe the disrespect I was putting up with. Tammy had some nerve! With her big forehead and long neck. Calling herself my friend, but using me as punching bag and a project was just *wrong*. Just like Dina at my old school, and Ms. Anastasia at the day camp, Tammy was only powerful if she could find someone weaker than herself to boss around. And as much as I needed this group to get by, I don't think I could withstand another overbearing bully in my life.

"Well, Patricia," Tammy said, interrupting my thoughts. "Go!"

Morgan even pushed me. But I just didn't have the balls to defend myself today. I knew if bad got to worse, they'd all have each other's backs and no one would have mine. They had already proved that's how it worked. So I just obeyed.

"She needed that trip to the mall much more than we thought," Tiffany said as I turned to leave.

I knew I was selling myself short by hanging with these girls who were always tearing me down. But I had to milk the experience for what it was worth. Certainly they would help me revamp my reputation and hopefully, fit in.

~

Afterschool, the girls introduced me to some skin care remedies to help me get rid of my acne. Ugh! It was such a tedious process but apparently, it worked. "A girls gotta do what a girls gotta do!" they said.

Dear Diary,   *Friday October 25*[th]

On our way home today, Tammy invited me to her house for a girl's night slumber party. I was ecstatic!

I really wanted to take a deeper step into their world, especially the beautiful, confident- Tammy. I admired her for her great talent and the ability to gain friends and maintain power over others. She was sassy and told me like it is, even though she hurt my feelings oftentimes. I needed someone who would help me step my game up.

Today I asked Tammy, "Do you think I'm pretty?"

She hesitated for a moment and said, "You look like a... Patricia."

What was that supposed to mean?

"Is that a good thing or a bad thing?" I asked.

"It means, you look as good as you feel. How do you feel?"

"Not that good," I answered honestly.

"Well, it shows. You put like zero effort into looking and feeling good, Pat. You're kinda clueless." Tammy was back to the blatant – and hurtful- honesty.

"Well, give me a clue, girl. I ain't got no one else to do it."

She stared at me for a moment. "First, you're gonna need some extensions in your hair. That tired bob makes you look like a child. And you need to start wearing a little lip gloss. Here, try mine…" She took out some of her soft pink MAC lip glass and applied it to my lips. "Pucker up!"

I felt better already. "Thanks, Tammy."

I never would have thought in a million years, I would get to hang with someone like Tammy who's pretty and popular and seems to have all the answers.

She's actually been treating me pretty well lately and at times like this, I feel guilty about the things I said and thought about her.

When we're on the phone and outside of school, she could actually be pretty cool. But when we're with the other girls and even between classes, she could be a real bitch and it's extremely hurtful. I guess I should just be happy she even let's me hang with her crew, though.

It's the downside to being the outcast who finally made it in good with the cool kids. You get no true respect. But if this is what friendship and popularity is all about, I have no choice but to put up with it for a little while.

Dear Diary,   *Monday October 28th*

OMG! Today Tammy told me she got a new phone, an Iphone at that. She's so freakin' lucky. Tammy seems to get everything she could ever want—beauty, popularity, lots of friends, and all the other material things. It's like a genie watches over her and grants her every wish. Hopefully the more we hang out, that good luck she has will rub off on me!

All I have to do is ask my mother permission to attend the sleepover party she's gonna host at her house. Maybe I can learn some of her secrets to good living. This girl obviously had it all!

Dear Diary,   *Wednesday October 30th*

My mother had a new man in her life. And that meant I could have a little peace in mine.

This was a first, my mother having company on the regular and actually staying the hell off *my* case. We hadn't fought at all since he came around. But I had never actually met him. My mother actually forbid me from coming out my room when *he* was around.

I pondered about whether or not this man could be my father. I hadn't actually asked her though. When I finally got a chance to talk to her, I'll try. But I was too focused on getting her permission to attend Tammy's party.

Thank goodness, her main goal was to get me out of her hair so she instantly said "yes".

Yes! I thought. *It's party time!*

VOLUME 12: VIOLATED

Dear Diary,   *Saturday November 2nd*

When I arrived at Tammy's 4 story mansion on Middlebrook Grove, it was quite a spectacular arrival. The gate opened up for my mother to drive on up the circular driveway leading up to her front door. Beautiful flowers and an assortment of decoratively trimmed plants, stone statues, and garden animals greeted me at the brick lined pavement of their front step. It was a warm and inviting welcome. No wonder Tammy had the confident demeanor she possessed. She truly did have it all.

"Well ain't this some fancy shit!" my mother exclaimed sarcastically. But she wasn't genuinely impressed.

"Wow," was all I could say as I stared at this humble abode.

"I hope you not hatin' on this shit like you don't got a house of your own to be proud of!"

Oh believe me, I wasn't. I know I had it 'good' and that was as good as it gets for me. Besides, there was no use dreaming.

"Live in the wake of reality not in no damn dreams!" my mother would always say.

I just nodded in agreement as I unlocked the car door.

A doorman greeted me out on the front step and had the door standing open to walk me inside.

"I'll pick you up in the morning." My mother let me out and drove off.

I walked inside their gorgeous home. Tammy came down the spiral staircase and greeted me. She was being so nice today. She was dressed in her Sunday best, a pleated plaid skirt and a ribbed neck blouse. *How much fun could she have wearing that?* I thought.

"Hey, Patricia! You're the first one here!" she said excitedly. "And I bought some extensions you can put in your hair."

She worked on my new and improved do. And while we were up in her sparkling pink decorated room, a butler of some sort came in and out offering us snacks and drinks. Then, he gave us the agenda.

"Manicures and pedicures in an hour in the spa. Dinner on the patio at 5pm and a movie showing at 7pm." They had this all planned out. I'd never been in such an extravagant home and been treated so well.

By the time mani-pedi time came around, Tiffany and Morgan still hadn't arrived. I didn't mind them not being there but it certainly was strange. The three of them did everything together.

"Where's the girls?" I asked.

"Uh, um," Tammy stalled. "They're not coming. Tiffany's on punishment and I think she was Morgan's ride."

I nodded, not thinking much of it.

I enjoyed the four course meal we had for dinner. It was a typical American meal, complete with baked chicken, mash potatoes, and beans with a custard pie for dessert; but it was laid on the plate so fancifully.

During the movie playing in her home theater, we sat beside each other and Tammy interrupted a love scene from *Twilight* to chat.

"You ever had a boyfriend, Patricia?"

My mind immediately went to Diesel, the first guy I ever loved or made love to. "Unfortunately, yes" I replied.

"Why, unfortunately? Having a boyfriend is like a dream come true for most girls."

"Not for me," I expressed thinking back to the good- and bad- times with Diesel. "You get so excited when it's new and he's all into you. Every word he says is special, every touch, every kiss. But that relationship stuff never lasts. It just sets you up for disappointment. Especially if you fall in love with them."

"You were in *love*? Really?" she continued to question me.

"I was. With this neighborhood kid from around my way." I had never opened up about my love thing with Diesel to anyone before. But I felt comfortable talking to Tammy. And I'm sure she wasn't expecting me to have such a story to tell. "He was tall, dark, and oh so sexy! We used to spend days together just talking and chillin', getting high at his crib. I met his mother and even lost my virginity to him! Then I find out he was entertaining another girl. In just a matter of weeks, he won my heart then broke it."

"Wow," Tammy said in shock. "That's a helluva lot. You've gotten high? *And* you're not a virgin? I guess it's true, we shouldn't judge a book by its cover."

"No, you damn sure shouldn't. But people been doing that to me all my life, I don't think it's even possible to have it any other way," I said.

"Pat, if you put out a certain look and energy, you can't be mad when people read you the way they do," Tammy said. I guess it *was* partially my fault I get judged the way I do.

"I feel you, Tammy. But I don't have the big house, the money, or the parents you have to keep me on point. I have no one. You don't even know..." I put my head down with sadness.

"No, *you* don't know the half. I don't have no 'parents' either. It's just me, my father, and all the help. My mother left us for her pilates instructor 3 years ago. She up and had a kid with him and everything. I've only met my half brother once. My father has been depressed and stressed out ever since. He puts all his time into work and has like no time for me- ever! But it's whatever," Tammy strengthened up after her quick rant. "That's why I have friends like you, Tiffany, and Morgan. Who needs family, anyway?"

I, of all people, knew how important family would be *if* we had them. "Tammy, that's awful of you to say. We need our families. Trust me, I know. I have a mother who's mean and unsupportive and I don't have a dad at all. That shit kills me everyday."

"Well, if you *never* had a dad, I would think you'd be used to it by now. I've only had 3 years to adjust to not having a mom. And as you can see, my father hardly exists around here either," she said. "Lucky for you, having a boyfriend and having sex and all. At least you found some damn good ways to keep your mind off the problems. All I have is more money than I could ever spend and hardly anyone to spend it with. My every move is planned out and monitored around here. The only freedom I get is at school and at cheerleading practice. My friends are pretty much all I've got."

"Well, if you got friends- true friends- you got a hell of a lot," I affirmed for her. But her attention was back on the theater screen.

She sat on the leather theater chair in silence. People sure did perceive their problems awfully different than I could ever imagine. Thinking back to my cousin, my camp friend Judy, and now Tammy; they each were fighting a silent struggle despite what the outside appearance may lead you to see. I sooo wish I could help them. But I had my own problems that still had no resolution.

Dear Diary,   *Sunday November 3rd*

Waking up in Tammy's huge bed was quite a dream. Her bed was softer and her blankets were cozier than mine. The beautifully painted walls gave an alluring feel as the light gently lit every corner of the room. She was up staring at me awkwardly as I stretched and yawned.

"Wanna play a game of truth and dare, Patricia?"

It was an odd question so early in the morning. I doubted this game was on the agenda. But hey, whatever Tammy wanted to do was cool with me.

"Sure," I said quickly coming out of my slumber.

Tammy jumped out of the bed in her pink camisole pajama set and locked her room door. Then slightly dimmed the blinds that the bright sun was cascading through.

"Okay," she started. "Truth or dare?"

"Truth."

"That's wack, Patricia. We already got all that truth out last night. You afraid of a dare?"

"Okay, dare," I said.

"This is gonna sound crazy, but I dare you to make love to my stuffed animal, the way you did with your ex. What's his name, Darryl-?" She pointed to a huge stuffed dog she had lying in a heap on the floor.

"Diesel." I thought this dare was way strange but I've heard about how freaky *Truth or Dare* can get. I shook my head at her.

"I've done it before, Patricia. It's really not that serious..." she convinced me.

Usually *boys* had to play for it to get freaky but apparently Tammy was gonna take it there with just us two. "That stuffed animal is missing a whole lot of the parts Diesel has. But I guess I can try."

I had actually been yearning for some intimacy. Not that I thought a stuffed dog would do me any good but if it would satisfy Tammy to watch me do it, it just might satisfy me.

I took the dog off the floor and jumped into the bed and under the covers. I was nervous to do this but I did it for Tammy. It seemed harmless enough to help satisfy her curiosity.

Tammy peeped under the cover and I could see she was entertained.

"Isn't it so cool?" Tammy asked. But I felt strange. It was weird that a stuffed dog would take any part in my sexual pleasure. It felt very off.

"It was something- weird maybe," I answered.

"That's how I felt the first time. But you get used to it when you don't have a boyfriend," Tammy laughed. "It's your turn. I'll take a dare."

I couldn't think of anything nearly as daring, so I challenged her to do the same thing. I wanted to know why she made me do that and I was curious to know how freaky she got with her stuffed pals when I *wasn't* around.

Without hesitation, she picked up a stuffed bear from her collection and got right under those covers to do the dare, indeed.

She held the bear tight as she caressed her chest with the its soft exterior. She readily started thrusting and moaning, really giving it to that damn bear. She definitely needed a man, cause this shit was awfully strange.

I couldn't believe what was going down. But for Tammy, this was normal and she wanted to continue this freaky little game.

"I got a dare for you, Patricia. You ready for it?"

"Not sure," I answered truthfully.

"I dare you to lay down and let me lick your right titty," she insisted with a smile.

"I'm not into girls though, Tammy. That would be violating," I said.

"No it won't. It would be fun. Believe me, I'm no lesbian myself, but I can't deny how good it feels…"

"I'm not interested," I remained.

Her smile quickly turned to anger, "Don't be stupid. If you don't play the game by the rules, there are consequences, you know…"

"Consequences," I asked. "Like what?"

"Do you really wanna find out?" she threatened. "Or would you rather just lay down and let me show you how to have a little fun?"

I can't lie, her threat put fear in me. I wasn't prepared for Tammy's revenge and didn't wanna feel her wrath. I was finally in a good place with her and the girls and wanted to stay there. I wasn't willing to face the unknown consequences Tammy spoke of.

So I laid down to appease her.

She didn't waste time in getting my training bra off. She sat with her legs around me and started to touch my chest with both her hands. She gave me a short kiss on my nipple and opened her mouth wide to suck my entire breast. I had to admit to myself, it didn't feel bad but it felt *very* wrong. I couldn't understand why a girl like Tammy who could get anything and anyone she wanted- wanted me. It was all too damn uncomfortable.

I guess she knew she'd easily obtain the power and control she wanted. But it was too strange a feeling for me. I felt so forced and intimidated.

As Tammy continued, I started to feel *extremely* violated. She was slowly taking an innocence away from me that I wasn't at all willing to give up. I've never wanted to feel this way from another girl but here I was succumbing to my first homosexual experience and I didn't have the strength to stop her.

Luckily, her housekeeper knocked on the door in that moment. "Breakfast girls!"

Tammy jumped up and off me in an instant. She got up to unlock her room door. *Thank God!*

I thought I wouldn't ever want to leave. But when my mother came to pick me up later in the afternoon, I couldn't have been more happy to see her.

I was disappointed in myself yet again for allowing someone to use me the way Tammy did. I needed to gain some sort of control in my life. I don't know how, but I was gonna have to figure it out quick.

VOLUME 13: TAKING CONTROL

Dear Diary,   *Monday November 4th*

Monday morning at school was extremely awkward. I was greeted by the girls in the school yard but felt a strange aura as I approached them. I could barely look Tammy in the eye after our experience this weekend but she was eyeballin' the hell outta me.

"What's up, girls?" I asked casually and cool.

"You tell us," Tiffany started. "I hear you have a girl crush on Tammy!"

I looked at Tammy and saw her devious smirk. I don't know what story she had told them but I was growing furious with whatever lies she was spreading.

"No way! Who said that?" I exclaimed. "Tammy, what are they talking about?"

Tammy replies, "I told them about the sleepover. About how you came the wrong weekend just so you can have me all to yourself."

"Huh? But you invited me to come. You said Tiffany and Morgan were gonna be there."

Tammy continued to lie her ass off. "Clearly, the girls know our party is this weekend. But I'm used to it Patricia. Sometimes I have that affect on my friends," she laughed. "I didn't know you were into chicks though but it certainly is flattering."

I couldn't believe my ears. Tiffany and Morgan started calling me names. "I could've told you she was gay. Look at the way she walks."

As I tried to tune out their negative words, all I could do was defend myself with details about my past sexual encounters.

"Hello, ladies. I'm probably the only one who isn't a virgin around here. I've been with a guy and I liked it. Matter a fact, I *loved* it! Have any of you even sucked a dick? The whole damn basketball team *and* cheerleading squad knows how I get down. It's a shame my own 'friends' would accuse me of being a dike after that damn locker room show!"

I know, it was a terrible defense. I hated that I had indicted myself for being a sexual deviant and damn near a hoe, just to savor my reputation from stupid "gay" rumors. But it's all I had. And if these girls were my friends, maybe this conversation wouldn't have to go any further.

"You're right about that. We know you're willing to go down on a guy but according to Tammy, you'd do it to a girl too!" Morgan chimed in.

"Whatever," I said turning to Tammy. "You know that's not true."

"Are you calling Tammy a liar?!" Tiffany defended her.

I continued to speak to Tammy. "Tell them what really went down."

"You want me to tell them the details?!" she exclaimed. "I'm traumatized enough that you tried to kiss me!"

I could not believe the charade she was keeping up. I had heard enough. Tammy was nuts. Even after the bonding we'd done and good times we had before she absolutely *violated* me, she was using me as a scapegoat to protect herself from her own questionable sexuality.

Whatever, I figured it was easier to let her have her way. As long as they would let me have mine. "You guys better keep this to yourself. I'm trying to get a date with this guy I met from the poetry club and I don't want anymore of these rumors crossing his path."

"We'll keep your lil secret, Patricia. What are friends for!?!" Morgan giggled and the others joined her.

That was a damn good question. But I sure as hell couldn't answer it. To this day, I hadn't had the pleasure of having any *true* ones.

Dear Diary,   *Friday November 8th*

Today was the Poetry Slam competition that Don from the poetry club invited me to. I was so excited to support. The entire poetry club would be there.

So when Tammy invited me to sit in and watch the home game she and the crew were cheering for today, I instantly refused. I was much more interested in getting to know Don a little better than I was in spending time with these lying, intimidating, controlling girls. I was happy to spend as little time with Tammy as possible since that incident at her house and those rumors she started anyway.

After what she'd done and how she made me feel, I knew I needed to keep a distance. God knows what else she will pressure me into that I couldn't find my way out of.

Besides, when I invited them to the poetry slam, Tammy stated "I don't do the whole 'losers meets rap' thang. Have fun though."

It was offensive and I knew it. But I didn't have the balls to respond back. I just wanted to be far away from the girls and closer to a guy that can bring those hot and warm feelings from my fantasy to the forefront of my reality. Tammy's pressure left a bitter taste in my mouth and I needed someone to leave a savory one. I hoped Don would be the one.

After school today, a group of us from the poetry club walked to the local café where the performances would be held, *The Cave*.

As we all settled into *the Cave*, I sat as close to Don as possible. He was the only one I'd made a connection with here and I truly enjoyed being near him. He hadn't been treating me any different even with his friend's allegation about the locker room incident. So maybe, just maybe, I would have a chance to get with him the way I did in my dreams.

"Hey, Patricia, what's up," he approached me with a hug.

"Nothing much, I'm so happy to be here. I've never been to anything like this before."

"You're gonna love it! This is where you gonna see poetry and rhyme at its best," he displayed so much passion for his craft. "You want me to get you anything to drink?"

"Iced tea would be great," I replied.

"No doubt, I got you."

When he got back with my drink, he said, "Joan said you been working on some pretty cool poetry, you mind that I put you on the agenda?"

"You what?!" I yelled in shock. "My work is personal."

"You afraid to share? I thought you were about building and growing as an artist. It starts here. Next time, you may even be able to perform with us in the competition."

He was right. It was time for me to start facing some fears and gaining an ounce of genuine confidence. So I agreed.

I opened up my notebook trying to figure which one I was gonna share with this crowded room of teenagers.

After rummaging through my notebook, I found the perfect piece. It was titled, "Invisible."

When I got up on the small stage to perform it, I felt a rush of adrenaline like I never felt before. For the first time ever, I had everyone's attention all at once. This attention wasn't negative, intimidating, or judgmental either. They were supportive and encouraging as they all cheered me on and awaited a chance to hold on to my every word. Being up there had me on a new kind of high.

Invisible

Fighting for a chance to be seen, to be heard
Tryna be first place winner, not second nor third
Wanting to prove I'm made of more than what you see
Needing someone to notice the skill and grace in me
In a world so greedy, where people steal your shine
I push, I scream, I fight for a little airtime
No matter how hard I try, I feel a bit pushed around
The higher I seem to climb, I feel stunted right back down
Can't you hear my voice, don't you feel my pain?
Like walking in a crowd and no one knows your name
I see them look my way but no one says a word
I must be invisible 'cause when I spoke, no one heard
When they look at me, they hate on whatever skills I possess
With all the jealous stares, I persevere, I still progress
Although the world won't see me, or even look my way
They ignore my presence but my passion will always stay
Soon they will figure out what they're up against
A fighter, a survivor who won't settle for no nonsense
Today they may look through me, pretend I'm not there
But the day will come when they all can't help but stare
There's too much hope inside me, dreams that do not die
Love that goes on loving, no matter how much I cry
With all the steps I've taken, on this journey along the way
I paid my dues, been patient, now I await my better day
I wanna show the world exactly what I've got
The multitude of talents that go on living, never stop
No vanity, no fear, no conceit or cockiness here

Just me, a longing soul, filled with passion I wanna share
Open your eyes, take a good look at me
Don't let invisibility be all that you see
Check out my body, the way I move so gracefully
My hips, my lips, my eyes, more than blatant sexuality
Listen to my words, speaking louder than any shout!
Appreciate my curves, it's what womanhood's all about
Feel the gentleness of my touch, even if we never meet
Cause when I pen my thoughts, it's to the world I speak
If you still haven't noticed the view that I speak of
Grasp the words of my poem, 'Invisible', you just may fall in
love...

As the silent room erupted with applause at my poems conclusion, I felt powerful and in control for a change. Capturing the hearts and minds of this huge crowd was a priceless experience. Someone was listening to me for a change and were finally hearing what I had to say.

As the applaud simmered, I knew my moment on that high was over and I wanted more. I realized in that moment how much I loved the stage. That performance gave me the power to impact so many people with the words within my heart and soul.

My thoughts were interrupted as Don and his group hit the stage in my place. I was lusting after him more than ever. They beat boxed, they rhymed, and they flowed. Music and poetry swam out their mouth and through the speakers as the audience cheered and yelled in awe.

They rhymed about love and lovemaking. All I could think was, *I had to have Don* and I had to have him tonight. I made eye contact with him throughout his performance. I peeped him from head to toe. His rugged dreads, his skater boy t-shirt and fine pressed jeans with new Converses. He wasn't quite my type but I was feeling his whole swag anyway. I needed something new in my life anyway.

So after the poetry slam ended and all his fans finally stopped coming up in his face to congratulate him on another great performance and that awesome win, I approached him to ask if he'd walk me halfway home.

"No doubt, girl," he agreed. "Lemme get my stuff."

He lived in the Middlebrook area and asked if I'd like us stop by his house and get his brothers car. After all, Don is 16 and already knew how to drive. So I agreed to do that. No point taking the bus home when I didn't have to.

As we walked on a dark street lined with trees, I noticed Don on his phone texting away. I was starting to get used to that with this crowd. Everyone had a cell phone but me and I only hoped I would someday get with the program.

He interrupted my thoughts and said, "Hey, my boy lives around the corner and is having an afterparty. Wanna stop through?"

Without much hesitation, I answered excitedly, "Sure, why not?"

He smiled back at me as we walked and talked toward the friend's crib.

"So, where's your friends at?" Don asked me.

"They're cheerleaders. They had a game today," I replied.

"So you ditched your friends and a home game to be with *me?*"

"You and the entire poetry crew. Yea, why you so surprised? I like chillin' with y'all."

"Just funny. Most girls travel in packs. It's so strange that you would be heading home alone. But I like your independence. It's very attractive."

Don had me all blushing by now. *He thought I was independent and attractive?* Those were firsts for me. I was becoming a new woman I suppose. And thankfully, he noticed it.

"Thanks, Don. There's a few things I like about you too." I smiled back at him.

"Really? Like what?" He stopped to look me in my eyes.

"I like your smile and your cool dreads," I touched his hair softly. "And the fact that you write rhymes. That's maad sexy. I feel like I'm walking with a rap star right now!" I knew I was gassing him. But I didn't care. He was all that and more. He had me all open. I was prepared to give him whatever he wanted to make him feel like a man.

"Girl, you gassin' the kid. I'm wanting you so bad right now."

And I wanted him. He put his hands on my ass and squeezed it with excitement.

"Don't tease me now!" I exclaimed.

"I don't tease girl," he replied. "I please!"

As we neared his friend's house, he stopped by a line of huge bushes in front and gave me a hard, passionate kiss. I was shocked at this. I knew we had been flirting with each other for a while but it was very rare a girl like me ever got what she wanted. Don was a stunning looking guy with just enough swag to turn me on. And it had been a long time since I was turned on and fulfilled emotionally, physically, or sexually. I needed this. I needed the touch of a dude to erase that awful encounter with Tammy from my mind. I needed to feel wanted, appreciated, and loved.

He tasted my bottom lip then I tasted his. I began to feel butterflies in my stomach. All my fantasies were beginning to come true. I didn't even notice at the time, that the front yard we creeped into was quiet and completely vacant. No trace of an after party there at all.

As we lay on the cold grass hidden behind these tall bushes, I felt risky and submissive. His strength and eagerness was sexy to me.

It wasn't often that I had a dude so turned up he couldn't even wait to get behind closed doors to rush in on me. I felt so good at that moment, until his kisses got more and more aggressive. He threw me down onto what I believed was his friend's front lawn, ripped off my shirt, and rolled over to get on top of me.

He wasted no time putting more and more force on me as we were hidden behind the huge bush.

He bit into my lips and sucked it deeply as if he was gonna take my lips off. It hurt a little but I didn't complain.

He licked my face and bit into my neck. It started getting painful as he sucked hard and long on my skin. It was on some vampire shit. I didn't know whether to stop him and risk losing this moment or to keep quiet and just succumb to the pain.

I tried to lead the moment with passion and held on tight to the back of his head.

But he took over once again. With anxious moves, he ran his rough hands through my bra and grabbed hold of my boobs. He squeezed and twisted them as if he wanted to grab them off my body. As much as it hurt, I didn't ask him to stop. I just wanted to feel him inside me. That couldn't possible be any worse than this.

Don pulled my pants down a bit and forced his fingers hard and fast inside of me. It started to hurt again and I didn't know how much more I could bear. He was moving wildly and thrusting much too hard into my pelvic bones. I tried to slow him down by grabbing hold of his hands to slow his flow down, but he had his own agenda. And I just wanted to scream.

It hurt like *hell*! I was finally ready to push his ass off me as this initially pleasurable moment was filled with too much pain.

"Don, chill," I said.

"You don't like it, girl?"

"You're being too rough. Slow it down."

"Bitch, please. I'mma do this shit my way." he ignored me. "Just lay your ass right there and be quiet."

I was ready to obey him as his aggressive words put fear in me. But when he pulled his pants down and hung his huge dick in my face, I had *enough*!

"Oh hell no!" I tried to push him off of me once and for all.

"What? Don't act like you ain't never done this before," he cupped his piece and tried to position it in my mouth.

"Get the fuck outta here, Don." I pushed, smacked, and fumbled my way out of his hold.

"The whole basketball team talking bout the mouthwork you do and you ain't gonna give your boy, Don, a taste?!"

I couldn't believe what I was hearing. That one mis-understood incident in the boys locker room had gone too far.

"I didn't suck anybody's dick!" I screamed. "And I damn sure ain't sucking yours!"

Don looked angry as I tried to make a run for it. He quickly came after me and caught my arm. He threw me down in the hidden patch of bushes again and said, "That's what you think. I'm gon' get mine someway..."

He pushed his already exposed penis into me and I yelled out in pain.

"Stop! I don't wanna do this!" And not just because I didn't want him anymore, but also because he was being too aggressive with me, and he wasn't even wearing a condom.

But Don did not respect my wishes. He continued to move into me against my will. His thrusts were so hard that it hit my bones and shook my insides. Not in a good way either.

"Owwww!!" I couldn't hold in the pain so I screamed out.

But as loud as I was, no one came to my aide. Not that anyone ever did. You'd think on a busy night like this, someone would be around town hearing my howls of pain.

It wasn't until I conjured up enough saliva in my mouth to spit in his face that he lost his strength for a moment. I started to kick and push again. Right in the crotch, I found his weak spot.

He loosened his grip on my arms and I rolled away into the night.

I pulled my pants up and tried to cover myself after he ruined my shirt. I was ashamed to get on a bus looking like this so I sobbed my way home. I had no one to talk to and no one who'd understand how hurt I was.

I truly thought Don was different from the basketball players. But I was terribly wrong about every guy I've cared about thus far. I didn't know a damn thing about boys. And it figures because I didn't have a father to teach me.

VOLUME 14: REBELLION

Dear Diary,   *Wednesday November 13th*

I couldn't go to school for a few days. I was still scarred from that awful encounter with Don. My mother wasn't paying any attention to me anyhow. She was still so caught up entertaining her man friend. So I spent my day cleaning my room and simply stayed out of her way.

I just thought if I saw Don again, I wouldn't know how to react. Would I go up to him and straight up punch him in the face, find some goons to fuck him up, or should I find some way to just shoot him myself? Many aggressive acts of violence crossed my mind. So to be on the safe side, I stayed home.

I wondered why this even happened. Why did I have to like someone who was cold hearted enough to take advantage of me this way? What was wrong with me that I couldn't see through the violent evil that was within him? I trusted his smile and his kindness and once again, I got burned.

Why did guys even go through the trouble of being pleasant to a girl just to use and abuse her? Do guys actually get pleasure and pride from that? If so, that's just *sick*!

How many more guys like this was I gonna have to deal with? Why was it so hard to find someone who would love me the way I deserved to be loved? Or a friend who cared about me the way I cared about them? Is there something sooo wrong with me that I will never find the happiness I seek?

None of this made sense. I don't even anticipate the meanness and evil shit that these people are putting me through- but still, I'm a victim of it every time. So much hate lives around me, I only hope someday I could move on out and find a place of true bliss.

I decided to write some poetry. It was the only way I could express the pain I felt inside.

Stolen

You grabbed, you pushed, you stole me away
My love, my innocence, you replaced it with heartache
You took my affection and turned it to fear
You could've had my heart but instead you left me bare
You didn't have any self control
You left me for dead out in the cold
You robbed me of my pride and joy
You played me like a fiddle, a toy
You broke me down, you made me cringe
You gave me reason to not wanna live
I opened up my heart to you
But in return, I got abused
I begged you to see me for who I am
I'm not invisible nor am I a tramp
I wanted you to love me for my mind
To see my wisdom, to peep my grind
But you looked past all that and more
And hurt me to my tender loving core
You used your force to snatch what you lacked
You stole my joy and I only hope I get it back

Dear Diary,   *Thursday November 14th*

On my third day home from school, my mother came home from work for the first time in a while without her man.

When I heard our front doors slam shut, and her racing through the house calling my name, I knew it was bad news for me.

"Patricia!! Get your ashy ass down here right now!"

Uh oh! I thought. This definitely meant trouble for me.

"Yes, ma?" I made my way down the stairs.

As I stood before her, she wasted no time in expressing her anger toward me. She greeted me with a smack to the face.

Wham! Her backhand went straight across my cheek. I rubbed my face gently and asked, "What was that for?"

"Don't play stupid little girl! Why you ain't been going to school?"

Oh, damn, they called her. It was time for me to explain, if only she would listen. I sat down around the dining room table, hoping to lead my mother to a calmer place.

"I'm sorry, Ma. I went through something really terrible at school the other day and I'm terrified of going back."

"Oh really? Why don't I know about this? Why don't the teachers know?"

"It's kinda hard to talk about, ma. It didn't exactly happen at school either." I was ready to lay it all out on the table. "I met someone in the poetry club and he invited me to his poetry jam showcase. I performed some of my poetry and everything..."

"Poetry?" she looked puzzled. "When since you write poetry?" I realized then that she didn't know anything about me being in the poetry club. I'd been keeping up with my lie about being on the cheerleading squad for so long, I'd forgotten about the rest.

"I started a week or two ago," I tried to keep my lies in place. "Yea, I kinda found it to be a better fit for me."

"So you're telling me, you gave up cheerleading to write poetry? What a freakin loser! I thought you had a little more sense than that, Patricia."

Her insults were meant to cut deep but after the severe pain Don caused, I wasn't nearly as affected by my mom's words now.

"Just listen!" I exclaimed. She hadn't even let me get to the part I really needed to share. With my soft shout, she kept quiet.

"Anyway, I was offered a ride home by one of the guys in the club. I really thought I knew him. He's been so sweet to me since day one. But after the show, he took me to some abandoned house and-"

"Lemme guess... he took advantage of your weak ass? He realized you were a dummy when you decided to walk out with him alone so he did what any man would do?"

My mother had obviously known what was up. She knew exactly what happened. But right when I thought she would have given me a little comfort after such an awful encounter, she only made me feel worse.

"How did you know?" I asked.

"Because that's what little boys do. Even grown men. They don't want nothing to do with no little girl unless they can take something from her. And you- you're the perfect target." My mother got up and casually headed to the kitchen. "I guess that'll teach you once and for all not to mess with boys till you're grown and ready enough to handle the damn consequences."

"I guess so," I said lowering my head with shame. *How could I have believed this guy actually liked me and wanted me for me?* I knew well enough I wasn't the kinda girl these guys liked. It was my fault this happened, like my mother confirmed. I was Patricia Thomas, the outsider, the loser, the outcast that nobody respected.

There was no use going to school trying to build up my reputation when it would be shot down every time. I wanted out of this. I just wished somebody would've warned me. I could've just stayed focused on my schoolwork, taken my ass home, and this never would've happened. But I so badly wanted to fit in, and feel wanted, now I'm left feeling like shit. Broken, robbed, and abused.

But I refuse to feel this way for long. I've had enough! I had to do something drastic, something to make people see me a new way. I wasn't going back to school without a plan of revenge.

VOLUME 15: CYBER SHOTS

Dear Diary,   *Friday November 15ᵗʰ*

I called my cousin up today. While cutting school, I sneaked into my mom's room to use her cordless house phone. Yes, it was purposely hidden from me and used to control me. But I needed to talk to someone so I wasn't the least bit concerned about the repercussions.

It was rare for Erica and me to see each other, and even more rare when we would speak. She proved to be the only one in my entire life who understood pain as I knew it.

Luckily, I knew she had a cell phone and I was sure she would answer if she could.

"Hey Erica!"

"Patricia? About damn time you gave me a call!"

"I know, I know. I miss you cous'. But you know the deal. I don't have a cell to call you at any ole time."

"That's true. It's alright, girl. So what's goin' on with you?" she asked.

"Not much, same ole stuff. High school is kicking my ass! Literally..." I started.

"What you mean? Didn't I show you what you gotta do to handle those bullies? Next time a chick wanna step to you, you gotta shove 'em outta your way. And if that don't work, you sock 'em one time in the jaw!"

I laughed. "I definitely remember what you taught me cous'... But the bullies in high school are different. They're coming at me in different ways. It's like they found a way to hurt me without even touching me..."

"Really? So what's the problem? You can handle yourself then. Sticks and stones, Patricia. You can't let words hurt you."

"What about pictures, though?"

"What do you mean?" Erica asked me.

So I told her about how the locker room incident with Christian led to rumors, threats, and a whole lot of messy nonsense.

"I seriously don't feel safe at my school. I waltz through this beautiful neighborhood to get there and gotta deal with some really ugly characters. The girls I hang with are always taking advantage of me but I feel like I need them because they're all I got. And the guys don't respect me. They treat me as nice as they can before they get a chance to take what they want."

"That's crazy, Patricia. You don't need nobody if they ain't gonna treat you right. And what you mean, the guys *take* what they want though?"

I knew Erica knew what I meant. I didn't wanna spell it out for her. "You know..." was all I could say.

"No, Patricia. Tell me what happened."

"Well," I started. "First there was this guy I thought was my man, Diesel, the sexiest, finest guy in town. We were hanging out, chillin, and I was even living with him for a minute when my mom ran me out. I eventually gave him my virginity-"

"What?!! Lemme find out my lil cous' is a woman!" she exclaimed excitedly.

"Barely," was all I could say to that. "We had some good times too but all of sudden I stopped hearing from him and then I heard he moved on to someone else."

"Aww, Patricia. I'm sorry. Sounds like you really liked him too."

"I did."

"But that's how guys do. They're only around for a season. Don't expect much more from them and you won't be disappointed..."

"That's what I'm starting to see," I said with true belief in her statement.

"Matter fact, don't expect *anything* to last forever. Life is a roller coaster. Ups, downs, twists, and turns. You might enjoy the thrill but at some point, its over and done." Her tone softened as I knew her mind was on her parents.

"You might be right, Erica. But one thing's for sure, true love, like what our grandparents had and your parents had for you- that shit lasts forever. It even outlasts the pain, don't you think?"

She was silent for a moment but eventually said, "Yea, I guess you're right. That's probably all that keeps me going some days."

"I hear you." I was happy to give us both a tinge of encouragement. I had to continue venting though. "There was another thing that happened too... Something worse."

"Worse than *heartache*? Damn, girl. What?"

"Well, this guy I was really feeling from the poetry club I'm in- I- he- he offered to take me home and stopped by a friends house on the way and... he raped me."

"What??!!" she shrieked. "Oh hell no, Patricia! What's his name? I'm coming back up there! What the-"

"Erica, it's alright. If I can't fight my own battles, I don't want anyone else fighting them for me."

"When did this happen, Pat?"

"Last week. And I haven't been to school since. I haven't even left the house. I'm so afraid of what I'll do or how I'll feel when I see him."

"What's his name?" Erica asked again.

"Why? You gonna call the police?" I asked back.

"No, that's what *you* should do. But I know what I gotta do to cause him real damage."

"What?" I was curious.

"I know you're not up on this but I'm going online to his *SocialFace* page to hit him where it hurts."

"How do you know he has a page?"

"No offense, Patricia. But anyone who's anyone has one. Gimme his name. I'll prove it."

I told her his full name and she quickly searched him. She was able to find out his school, his neighborhood, his hobbies, his friends, even his family members, and that he was a lyricist who performs at *The Cave* regularly. All that info before she even joined his social network. The internet was very informative, who knew?! Lol.

She promised me she would handle the situation once he accepted her into his network and although I had no idea what she would do or *could* do, I trusted her to handle it.

Dear Diary,   *Saturday November 16th*

After talking to Erica yesterday, I felt a lot better. She knew every bit of the pain I felt because she had been there and done that. She was the one person that understood me. And she helped me realize that I didn't experience such

139

hardships just because I'm me. It could happen to anyone, no matter how smart or beautiful or talented or nice you are. Life sometimes has to kick your ass to make you a little stronger. I guess she was living proof of that.

It amazed me when she spoke about her troubled experiences because looking at her, you'd think she was good. On the contrary, she spent most her life feeling like she had it so bad. It was like that day at Tammy's. The girl literally had it all and was silently leading a troubled life. One in which she had to use and deceive me to get what she wanted. A smile sure does hide loads of pain.

It made me wonder what Don's issue was. He had to have a pretty damn big one to hurt me the way he did. It was all too confusing for me. *Why did everyone have to take their pain out on others?*

Dear Diary,　　　　*Sunday November 17ᵗʰ*

I actually spent my day in my mother's room watching TV. After sneaking in for the phone the other day, I pushed my luck to watch reruns of the show, *Baller's Wives*.

What a bunch of ratchet women!! Grown ass people bickering and bullying each other for ratings. These women had no jobs, some of 'em had no men, and their main concern was confronting other women about their opinions of each other at high profile events. I didn't understand how the title even applied.

As a young lady myself, I was ashamed at them- dressing up, looking good, and behaving like some of the kids in my school. And that's low. I thought, *it's so pointless to be around women who don't like you, support you, and can't bring value to your life.*

But that's when I realized, I had more in common with these chicks than I thought. They probably had their own bucket of issues to iron out so who was I to judge?

Dear Diary,   *Monday November 18ᵗʰ Day*

When Tammy called me today, I was astonished and confused. I rarely got calls on my house phone. But with me being out of school so long, it was nice of her to check on me.

"Patricia, where you been girl?" she asked, seemingly out of concern.

"Home. Something terrible happened to me and I'm not ready to face anyone right now," I explained.

"Well, girl. You need to get to a computer. Because you might have to face it a lot sooner than you think..."

Huh? "What are you talking about?"

"Haven't you been on *SocialFace* lately? There are lots of rumors going around about you. And being your only friend, I thought it was only right that I let you know."

"I'm confused." Wasn't Erica supposed to handle things on *SocialFace* for me? How could things have gotten any worse within a day? How could new rumors be surfaced when I was staying out of school, off the streets, outta trouble, and in the comfort of my home?

"Girl, you need to get to a library or something. This shit is no joke!"

So that's what I did. I got dressed, headed to the *Queens Library* a little ways outside my town, and went online. Internet access was free there and I wouldn't run into anyone I knew. I just needed to see the garbage that was being posted on there. I typed in Don's full name and immediately saw the attack my cousin Erica had made on him in my defense.

141

I was fearful to find out how bad any of this could be. I mean, it was just words and if no one told me about it, would I ever have known or even cared?

It started with my cousin ranting about Don and the awful things he did...

"Who the hell is Donald Quinn?? Some of y'all think he's a poet, a lyricist, a dread, a sexy brown fella, maybe even a Socialface friend... But I know the truth- he's a fake ass rapper wannabe and a dirty lying Rapist!! if u put ur trust in him, you're gonna be disappointed. Yea I said it- and I ain't afraid to blast out the losers, because how would any of us know what kind of greasy, grimey, piece of shit dudes are among us if chicks like my cousin Patricia don't let us know. I'll always protect you cous! Ladies, protect yourselves!!"

Oh no! Was all I could think. My cousin thought *this* was the way to deal with Don? Putting him on blast while also putting me out there too. OMG. This obviously wouldn't end well.

I clicked on the next post that came up. It was a photo. The very photo that had been haunting me for months. I hadn't seen it since. But there it was in front of me, live and in color for all the world to see with just one click.

It was me, with my mouth open wide and my tongue stuck halfway out pointed toward Christian's penis. It was the picture they snapped in the locker room and although I knew it was a huge misconception, I could only imagine what all the spectators thought when they saw me in such a compromising position. I couldn't even bring myself to read the comments attached. But it was apparent that the rumors circulating at school had finally hit cyberspace.

I looked skanky, easy, and fast. And that sooo wasn't who I am. But in that moment when the picture was taken, I was so anxious to fit in and now, I stood out in the worst way.

VOLUME 16: LOSING CONTROL

Dear Diary,   *Monday November 18th Night*

The school contacted my mother today about me not showing up again. The guidance counselor is putting me on probation. They've got on record that I haven't been consistent with my extracurricular activities. *Dammit!* There was just no way to win with these folks. With the shit I've been dealing with, how the hell could I concentrate in school, moreover, stay afterschool and get involved in somebody's club? These days were getting way too difficult... Especially after what I saw online about me earlier.

But after my mother punished me for cutting classes, I agreed I'd go back.

Dear Diary,   *Tuesday November 19th*

Today, I had to meet with my therapist. She was all ears when I told her about the awful encounters with both Tammy and Don and tried to offer me encouragement.

"Patricia, I hope you know it's not your fault this happened to you. Your peers each have a problem. They're both lacking something in their lives and thought taking it from you would help. But no one wins," she said. "The only way you get through is to find an outlet to let out the pain and become stronger. Be more aware and help others who have been through the same to help avoid similar encounters."

I hoped her words would help heal my soul. But at that moment, I didn't feel I could overcome the pain without revenge.

So when the doctor asks me, "How do you feel?" I lost all control.

"I feel... Like I've had *enough*!" I got up angrily out of the leather couch then stormed out of the doctor's office. I had enough of people trying to force me into uncomfortable sexual acts and violence. I had enough of everyone taking advantage and trying to control me. "From now on, I'm just gonna do me! Right or wrong, good or bad!"

No one gives a damn when I do the right thing anyhow. It's like you have to do something stupid to get people's attention. Look what it took for my friends to finally show me some respect, and to get a little attention from my mother. Lies. Deceit. Sexcapades. Embarrassment. Pain. No one credited or acknowledged me when I was getting good grades and walking that straight line. If even my mother gave me props for being me, maybe it would be worth it. But no, she went right along with the rest of them and shunned me for being a skinny little nerd. Well those days are over.

If ratchetness is what everyone wanted and expected of me, ratchet I would be.

Dear Diary,   Wednesday November 20th

I woke up with a vengeance today. There'd be no more nice Patricia. If I kept doing the right thing and was being shut out and misunderstood for doing so, it was time to do something different.

So today, I walked up into my school for the first time in over a week. I had my head held high and my chest pressed out. I put on all the make-up I had, from the concealer to the mascara, to the blush to the lip glass. I was feeling confident today all because I had a plan. No one was gonna stop me now. Not even Tammy and the gang who insisted, I was overdoing it with my dolled up look and scandalous one-piece cat suit pants set.
I focused a little more in my classes today. I took notes and raised my hand. When the kids around me snickered and whispered about me, my *Socialface* pic, my hairstyle, or my

outfit; I didn't even hear them. I was too busy doing me. And anyway, I was gonna give them something way more interesting to talk about today.

During my lunch hour, I knew it was time. I went to the basketball team's lunch table where they would sit everyday. I was never invited over but today I didn't need an invitation.

"Hey, Christian," I said walking up to the crew with all the boldness I could conjure up. "I gotta show you something."

"You mean something else?" one of his boys snickered.

"No, Christian didn't really get a piece of me before. But this time he will."

What everyone thought they saw in that "sext" was all wrong. It was nothing. I was determined to give everyone some facts to talk about, *if* they were gonna continue talking. Doing this was the only way I could justify the way they had me feeling about myself.

Christian was more than eager to find out what I had in store. My appearance had greatly improved since that day he tried to play me and call me a dike. I was a seriously becoming the woman I wanted to be and with this next little trick I had up my sleeve, I could prove I was.

I led Christian into a private stall and finally made those rumors true.

Dear Diary,   *Thursday November 21ˢᵗ*

Today was mad chill. After what I did yesterday, I felt confident and in control for a change. If anyone tried to bash me or look at me sideways in school, it didn't bother me one bit. I deserved it now. I knew what people were saying was true now and after that awful thing I did with Christian in the bathroom, the backlash was valid.

I stopped by Diesels house on the way home, bold as ever, trying to buy. But of course he wasn't home and to my surprise, his mother gave me her stash for free.

"Diesel been saving some for you," she said. "But he ain't coming home no time soon to give it to you. So take this."

It wasn't long before she shut the back door on me. There was not even a moment to ask questions.

My mother was working late today so I took the time to get high at my bedroom window.

I thought about Diesel and the good few times we shared. It was cool knowing his mother remembered me, and the fact that he was saving something for me. Maybe he hadn't forgotten me either.

He makes me write more poetry. Now that I've left club, if I want to get my extracurricular credits, I have to submit one of my best works by next Friday to make it in the school's poetry magazine. And if the thought of anyone would inspire me, it'd be him...

Dark and Diesel

I remember the night like yesterday
It was late but I saw your eyes vaguely
I felt your arms protecting me
You were a soldier seeming like an army
It was breezy out, it was pretty dark
I was in pain but you brought me out
You showed me life as simply as it should be
No drama, no fuss, you saw me for me
You let me in, gave me a comforted place
To lay my head, rest my heart at a moderate pace
No confusion and no games when you're around
Just puppy love and peace as we hit the ground
Softly, gently, you show me unconditional love
Bad boy, misunderstood girl, a match made from above

Living mi vida loco, living yours on the cutting edge
We got a crazy bond, wrapped inside our heads
Coming from homes we both wish we could change
Giving our all to fam, but still feeling estranged
Fell in love then bounced out so quick
How'd you move on so easily while I'm sittin' here so sick?
Missin' you, wantin' you, cravin' your attention
Dreamin' of your body, the passion, our connection
Knowing your heart, understanding the life you live
Trying to get over you, but it's so hard to forgive
Life so complicated for both you and me
But in my heart you're still my Diesel, keepin' me company

Okay, I exaggerated a bit. I'm not sure if we're a "match made in heaven" or if we had the amazing connection I thought we did, but putting it down on paper sure made my feelings come to life. I hoped and prayed tonight for me and Diesel to reconnect. And if I could recall anything he said, it was that what's meant to be, will be. I had to believe that to be true.

VOLUME 17: THE BIG BEAT DOWN

Dear Diary,   *Sunday November 24ᵗʰ*

Today my mother took me to church again. With the roar of the music and the bass coming through the speakers, I was able to distract myself from the awful thoughts I had going through my mind. I didn't think about Deisel or Don, my absentee father, my tainted reputation at school, my falling grades, nor my fake ass friends.

I let the music take me to another place, somewhere uplifting and beautiful, like the heaven they sang of. I only wished that shit was real. There's gotta be a better place to be after you leave this world. Not that I felt I was worthy of getting in. But I needed to hold on to hope. How I'm feeling right now *can't* possibly last forever, right?

When the preacher started preaching, I started reflecting on something good from my past. The last happy memory I've ever had was with my grandparents. I remember when they used to pick me up on the weekends, back when mom and I were living across from the projects. Every Saturday, without fail, they'd come scoop me up and take me out. We'd go anywhere, flea markets, malls, birthday parties, restaurants. It was simple but it was significant. They showed me love like I'd never felt since. It was hard to imagine they raised my mother to be the complete opposite. If there was any a time for her to be a nurturing mother to me, it would've been after their passing. That's when I lost a piece of my soul that was much needed. But I felt empty and alone. I was too young to understand the concept of death and it angered me. I remember Saturdays rolling around and me waiting by my window on a Saturday morn, hoping and wishing for them to arrive. But instead, I witnessed the beginning of my mother's thrashings.

I didn't understand why I was being punished sometimes. I always did everything my mother asked of me. I pushed so hard in school and spent all my leisure time by her side. *Why wasn't it enough for her to just appreciate me?* I understand she lost two of the most precious people in her life but so did I. We could have been there for each other. But instead, she revoked the innocence and peace of my childhood. Taking away happy Saturday mornings and replacing them with terrifying ones.

I tried to focus on the positive elements of the sermon. "Searching for Love" was the theme. Pastor Clark spoke about love being in the least obvious of places... "Letting ourselves out of bad relationships and freeing ourselves from self doubt is the only way to make our hearts available for a genuine love to come flowing in."

But I, for one, feel like I been searching for love for waay too long and I'm still waiting for it to come my way.

Dear Diary,   *Monday November 25th*

Tonight was quite a relief! I was sitting up in my room writing a lil poetry while smoking up through my bedside window. Yea it's kinda what I've been doing lately. Those are the only things that take me out of this element and into another.

My mother bursts through my bedroom door without any kind of warning. I could have been doing a number of the private things that I do. And as I'm mid-puff she startled me causing me to cough uncontrollably. I quickly threw the bud out the window and hoped my mother wouldn't recognize the potent smell.

"What you doing up in here?" She huffed.

"Working on some poetry for the club, ma," I replied respectfully. I did not want a fight tonight. I was in my zone.

"Oh that stupid poetry thing?" She stared at me disgusted but I didn't dare answer. "I guess that's better than you being all in *my* space."

I definitely agreed. I was happy to finally have found something I loved. A hobby that was non judgmental and simple which actually helped me heal and feel free. Writing was my new world of dreams.

My mother gave me a rundown of this weeks chores she needed done. She told me my room smelled and I better clear up that awful stink that she (thank God!) didn't recognize in my room. But in the zone I was in at that moment, none of my mother's awful words could phase me right now.

Dear Diary,   *Tuesday November 26th*

I woke up this morning and got dressed and ready for school. I thought I heard the rummaging of clothes in my mother's closet but I knew she wasn't supposed to be home.

I put on my cutest clothes. I wore a belly length halter and high waisted jeans that exposed a bit of my navel. An outfit I'm sure my mother wouldn't approve of but I didn't care. I wanted attention and this was the only way I was gonna get it. All I had to do was wear my old gray sweater to cover my outfit up until I left the house.

As I was about to walk down our stairwell to make myself a quick bowl of cereal before leaving, I peeped out the staircase window and realized my mother's car was not parked in our driveway. Nor was it out on the street. I wondered what- or who- was in her room making all that noise. I know she wouldn't leave an unfamiliar man in our crib while I was still there. *Or would she?*

I tiptoed down the hall and into her wing, which I was mostly forbidden to enter. But I had to investigate the scene.

I peeked into her room through the crack of her door and saw a familiar image of a man- an unpleasant one, at that. He was big and burly and the way he sniffled his nose and reeked of cigarette smoke smelled weirdly familiar. I watched as he moved around my mother's room. He was searching for something, I could tell. *What?* Was the question in my mind.

He pulled open drawers and looked under her mattress. I was afraid to say anything but I knew it was my duty to do so at this point. If my mother was dealing with this guy, and he was going through her stuff so aggressively, she needed to know. But first, I would put a stop to it.

"Hey!" I exclaimed. "You looking for something?" I burst into the room ready to catch this man red-handed. But I was in for quite a surprise. I knew this man, I knew him well. His face was oddly and fearfully familiar. I couldn't put my finger on it until he spoke.

"Heeey, it's you. Diesel's supposed *girlfriend.*" He laughed uncontrollably. Was this strange man seriously in my house after the encounter I'd had with him outside of Diesel's. And was my mother *seriously* messing around with dude? It was all too much for me to take in.

"You- You're Diesel's father," I stammered out.

"Yup, that's what the damn DNA test says. And you are the little chick who stay poppin' up in my business."

"This is actually *my* house. And you're in my mother's room. What are you doing in here anyway?" I conjured up a bit of boldness and was determined to get answers.

"Look, you stop asking questions and I won't try to find out what you got under that oversized sweater. Ya hear me?"

he inched toward me. But I was not gonna let this man run me away again.

"I'm not scared of you," I started. "You running in and out of Diesel's life, now you wanna run up in ours. Get the hell out of here!"

"Oh, I guess you're not so much the coward your mother said you were!" he laughed. "Well don't go growing balls with *me* now. Cause I don't play that!" He stepped closer to me and pulled the gray sweater off my back.

"Step off!" I yelled. "Or you gon' see how big my balls are!"

"Does your mother know how you dressin' for school with that belly showing like you want all the wrong attention? Cause I'll tell her. And I'll *show* you its working too..." Drew, Diesel's father, reached his hand out and touched my stomach. This man was utterly disrespectful and I wasn't having it.

Not only was he going through my mother's stuff and putting his greasy hands on my body, but I had already built up some hate for him long before and that must've unleashed the beast in me!

I smacked his hands away and threw a few fast punches to his stomach. It's all I could reach on him with that height. But of course that wasn't enough to put him out.

The shock of my blows had him dazed for a moment. Then he came back at me so I hit him on the crotch where it really hurt and took off. I called my mom right away but she didn't answer so I hurriedly ran out the house.

Dear Diary,   *Wednesday November 27ᵗʰ*

I was on my last string with my mother this time. When I called her again to report what had happened when she left for work yesterday, she was not the least bit concerned about my fear or safety. She was much more concerned about her "man."

It wasn't about me or what I'd encountered waking up to a strange man rustling through her things. Here I was thinking I had done a great thing to defend my house and home, but no, my mother thought otherwise. I guess she was more disappointed having to come home to our huge empty house. And not because I wasn't there, but more because *he* wasn't.

She yelled and screamed at me through the phone. "How dare you even enter my room?! Who gave you the right to check up on me and my company?! I'm a grown ass woman and you keep forgetting who's boss! Wait 'til I get home this evening, I'm gonna tear your little butt to pieces!" I knew her words were to be taken literally. She despised me for intervening in her personal life. She rarely ever had one and now I screwed things up for her. *How could I make things right between me and my mother now?*

Dear Diary,   *Thursday November 28th*

I decided not to spend the Thanksgiving holiday home with my mother. Instead, I spent most of the day out at the North Fields mall, where most stores opened up in the afternoon. Not like I had enough money to get the things I needed but I had to stay away from home. Walking around, window shopping made me feel a little worse though. There were so many things in those stores that I wanted and couldn't have. Sneakers, clothes, and jewelry, they were all things that would change my life if I had them... right?

They were things that would help me feel better about myself, at least. No one could tease me about anything if I had the right gear.

All I needed to do was figure out how to get a little more cash so I could really step my game up. I knew there was no way my mother would give it to me but I knew for a fact she had it.

I figured taking a few extra $20s out her pocketbook would be the only way I was getting it.

Dear Diary,   *Friday November 29th*

I don't know what I was thinking! Why I came back home only a few days after I ran my mother's man away was not a good idea, especially with my stupid plan to take money from her. I should have known my mother wouldn't be having that.

So when I snuck in this evening and I saw her laying on the couch in our hardly-ever-lived-in living room, I should have known she would have one eye open and her ears ready and alert.

She caught me red-handed as I reached into her purse that was sitting on the glass coffee table beside the couch.

"Oh, you think you're slick, huh?" she arose from the couch like a mummy coming out of their casket. She shocked the life out of me and I froze in place.

"No," I replied reluctantly. "I needed something but I didn't wanna wake you."

"You tryna play me for a fool, huh? I'm sick and tired of your dumb ass!" She got up from the couch as I slowly started backing out of the living room.

"I wasn't tryna play you, ma. I just didn't want to inter-"

"Shut the hell up!" she barked. "You ain't been here in days 'cause you know I got an ass whooping wit your name on it waiting on you."

Yes, I did believe she was waiting until the day she could pay me back for running Diesel's father out of the house. But having been caught trying to steal from her certainly brought on more of her rage.

I was so scared. My mother and I had had some pretty gruesome fights. Even when I tried to defend myself, she wouldn't stop until she had beat me down to the lowest place I could go. As she lifted up a porcelain lamp my grandmother left behind for us, I thought about whether or not I had the strength to fight back this time.

I started to make a run for the door, but she wasn't allowing me to leave without a fight.

"Oh no, you're not getting away from me tonight!" My mother threw the lamp at my head, without a care in the world for her parents favorite lamp that was in pieces on our living room floor. Nor did she care that I was down and out on our marble floor.

"Get your ass up!" she pulled me by one arm. I was still conscious so I obeyed. She needed me to fight back so I did.

I swung my fist at her just like I did to Drew. "Is this what you want, ma? You wanna pick a fight? No doubt, I'll take you out just like I did your greasy little boyfriend!"

I was hoping to invoke a little fear in her. Not because I had the hate and anger she had, but because I wanted the fighting to stop. It seems she would never stop hurting me unless she realized she couldn't. If we were gonna fight tonight, I just had to win.

"You think you gon' take me out?! Ha, your weak ass sure knows how to run a man out the door but I ain't going anywhere!"

I thought about living this way forever, with a mother who was always looking for a reason to beat me down. The thought caused me to shiver and I blacked out for a moment.

Without a conscious mission, I threw my hands up and started swinging uncontrollably at my mother. I hated myself for doing this to her, but she left me no choice. As she pulled on my neck trying to choke me, I pushed her off me and into the staircase banister then ran out the door.

I had finally won. But I didn't feel like a winner. Of all the people who have tried to hurt me, I fought back and beat down my own *mother*. Tears began to fall down my cheeks for us both.

Mostly because I knew I couldn't return nor did I have anyplace else to go.

VOLUME 18: HITTING THE STREETS

Dear Diary,   *Sunday December 1st*

I've spent an entire 2 days out on my own. I been hanging out at this 24 hour snack shop on the corner of the main boulevard in our neighborhood. They have a bathroom I could use and plenty of food. Believe it or not, I got away with a few $20s from my mothers purse but of course the price I'm paying for these bills sure don't seem worth it now. I was just lucky to find shelter.

They had the most comfortable seats and one booth that I designated as my bed. I made good with the owner so he let me chill there as long as I needed. Especially because I bought all my meals from him.

I kept my ears to the streets, hoping to hear a mention of Diesel or his whereabouts. He was a pretty popular name and face in the area but it had been a long while since I heard anything of him.

I bet if he knew about these 2 awful experiences I'd had with his father, he would've handled it for me, or at least been here to console me during this horrible time. I wanted so badly to just stop by his house and check up on him, but the last couple times I'd been there, I wasn't even invited inside. I would look like a feign trying to go back.

So instead, I tried to make new friends over at the *Snack Shack* and today I met this delicious dude named Lonzo. He was tall and light skin, a different flavor for my liking but he was always coming in the store buying packs of gum and loosies and eventually introduced himself to me.

"What up, ma? You live here or something," he says to me.

"I could ask you the same thing, coming up in here five, six times a day," I joked with him.

"Oh, so you peeped the kid?" he said stroking his chin with pride. He was quite handsome, medium build, probably mixed with Spanish or something and was quite exotic. We had to be at least 10 years apart, but he looked good for his age and I was getting pretty mature myself.

"Maybe," I replied with a flirtatious smile. I didn't know what I was expecting from this encounter with dude but I was feeling lonely enough at the time to wanna find out.

Lonzo invited me to dinner, said I looked like I needed a good meal. He said he'd come back for me in a few hours and would take me shopping for an outfit to wear for our date. It all sounded like exactly what I needed to hear.

Dear Diary,   *Monday December 2nd*

Sure enough, Lonzo came back for me last night. He came rolling up in a brand new Dodge Charger and I got real comfortable sitting in the passenger seat of his ride.

He didn't exactly take me shopping in the way I thought he would though. He didn't take me to the mall or to a boutique or anything. Not only because it was too late, but also because the "store" was some underground shop in somebody's garage.

It looked kinda ghetto but I had no other options at this point but to go with his flow.

To my surprise, there was some official-looking stuff cramped in there on racks. Everything from Coach, to Fendi, Gucci, and Versace was laying there right before my eyes. Bags, clothes, accessories- it was all available for my picking and I was excited to dive and in and choose. I was like a kid in a candy shop. Never before could I for shop for such fine items without limits.

Lonzo was sweet in letting me pick out anything I wanted to wear for our dinner date. I sooo needed this. I was in the same clothes for days and they weren't exactly my Sunday best either.

I choose a casual 2 piece Burberry outfit, a button down top with matching fitted pants; a Versace body suit, and a Chanel bag to go with them. I didn't even care if it was real or not. Designers and names never mattered to me, fashion did though. And just having something fresh to put on my body was more than enough.

I saw Lonzo pull a couple stacks out to pay for it all and for a change, I was feeling like I was worth something.

We went back to his condo, a beautifully decorated home on the upper crust of our town. The spot was in the cut, one of those communities you wouldn't know about just by driving through. It's entrance was hidden and had security and a bellhop greeting you at the door.

I took a shower in his oversized bathroom. He made an appearance while I was in there and planted one steamy long kiss on me as I returned it. We got dressed and ready to leave but just before heading out, he pulled me close and started kissing me again. I returned the soft, tender kisses. I was happy to be shown a little affection.

Then, as we broke away from the kiss, he pulled my hand and asked me to go down on him. I couldn't believe this...

Once again, dude couldn't have done something nice just because. He had an agenda.

I definitely didn't wanna do it. I just met him and didn't know where he'd been or what he was about. I was fearful to find out what he would do if I refused though.

"I'm so hungry, can we go eat first and do that later?' I tried to stall. I even rubbed his leg to reassure him.

"I want it now," Lonzo said softly. "And I know we both have needs. I'll meet yours if you meet mine."

I couldn't fight it anymore. I was hungry as hell, I had no where to go, no one else who cared about me, and I was beginning to not give a damn about myself. So I just gave him what he wanted and went out to enjoy a 5 star dinner on him.

Dear Diary,   *Tuesday December 3rd*

I found out a great deal about Lonzo over dinner last night. He didn't have a job, he didn't have no family. His mother died when he was young, she overdosed on something. And his father was in jail. He said he spent most his teenage years on the streets, similar to how he found me. He said he had to fend for himself and make a living any which way he could.

"So exactly how *do* you make a living?" I had to ask. He was *loaded* and I damn sure was curious to know how.

"Hard work," was all he said.

"Care to go into detail?"

"I guess you can say I run a business. I keep my- workers- in line and stay in control. Long as they do what I say, they get paid which means I get paid."

I was still very unclear but I realized he wasn't gonna go into much more detail than that. So I dropped it and tried to live in the, otherwise, enjoyable moment.

Dear Diary,   *Wednesday December 4th*

Today was weird. After coming in from the gym downstairs of his condo, Lonzo kept ordering me around. He offered me a glass of wine which didn't seem like much of an option but like more of an order. I accepted, taking my first alcoholic drink. Then he asked me to do some strange things for him.

160

"Let me see how you move, girl." He walked toward his *Bose* stereo and was flipping through his music selection.

"What do you mean?"

"I'm gon' play a track and I wanna see how you move to it." So I obeyed. It was a poppin' beat, I couldn't help but move my body from side to side. I was feeling kinda sexy.

But that did not mean I wanted to have sex! And I must have been turning him on in the worst way. He started coming up close and moving with me. He even slipped me a $100 bill.

"Kiss me," he said and I did. "Lick me right here." He motioned toward his neck and chest. "Squeeze my-"

"Whoa!" I was taken aback when I saw where he going with this. "I'm actually feeling a little nauseous."

He allowed me to excuse myself but followed me into the bathroom. When he saw I was actually hovered over the toilet bowl, he got me some paper towels and held back my hair. It was actually very sweet.

But I knew I was gonna have to prove I was really sick or I'd be picking up right where he left off with me.

"Can you get me some water?" I asked.

In that minute he was gone, I stuck my fingers down my throat until a bit of my delicious lunch had left my body. *What a shame*, I thought.

"Damn girl, one hour of working out, a few minutes twerking and you're feeling it like that? Next time, you gon' eat after."

Next time? I thought. I didn't know what part of this would be repeated but I was truly disgusted by the whole ordeal. I wanted to be left alone which was gonna be hard with Lonzo breathing this hard down my back.

"I just need some rest," I said and slept right through dinner and late into the night.

Dear Diary,   *Thursday December 5th*

This morning started off like a dream, waking up in Lonzo's couch, which I was surprised he didn't try to creep up in with me.

Just as I thought about him, he came into the living room with breakfast. Waffles and eggs with strawberry glaze on top with a bowl of fruit on the side, all served on china dishes.

I loved living the good life up in there with him. But I knew at the back of my mind it had a price.

After we ate, Lonzo suggested we go down and take a dip in his condo's pool. I immediately thought about my hair and what it would look like if I got it wet and couldn't afford to hook it back up.

As I hesitated, Lonzo was busy getting undressed and started helping me do the same. His chiseled body was exposed and alluring but I tried not to stare. I had to stay focused as he began undressing me.

"Hold on, boo. I don't even have a swimsuit."

"I got you," he stepped away and returned with a stunning Burberry swimsuit I could not resist trying on. As soon as I had it on, he had a tall glass of wine waiting for me. "Drink up." And so I did. But I noticed he never had a glass for himself.

We headed down to the beautifully decorated pool space and I took a dip inside. The water was warm, the atmosphere was relaxing, and I was feeling the effects of the bitter tasting wine. We floated and splashed around making the most of the time we were spending together. I loved the serenity of being in the water. Life seemed good.

Lonzo started kissing me and before long, his hands were all over my body. He attempted to take off my swimsuit in that public arena but I resisted. He urged his hands under my garment anyhow and touched my privates like he owned my damn body. Although it gave me a familiar feeling, I grew very uncomfortable with this. The liquor in my system must have been the only reason I continued to let him take control. My mind and body were weak for him and I didn't want to fight his urge. I allowed him to have his way with me. At least he was gentle and discrete as we fooled around in the public but empty pool space. But although it felt good, I was feeling pretty bad about myself for allowing this.

"How about we ditch the pool and go skinny dipping in my Jacuzzi?"

"I don't think so. Actually, can I go get my clothes?" I got out the water, gathered our things and headed back to the room. He followed closely behind with his hands pressed on my backside, working its way down my thighs.

As I started getting dressed back in the apartment, he says, "You know what girl, I know other activities we can do that don't require no clothes at all." He smiled at me with that oh-so-charming smile, but I couldn't give in this time. He was already peeling through the dry clothes I was tryna put back on. If I let it happen like that again, it would always happen this way.

"Lonzo, I hardly know you. Can we get to know each other a bit better?" I thought it was a fair request.

But he did not. "You could wear my clothes, eat up my food, and sleep in my crib but all of a sudden, you don't know me?! Trick get the fuck outta here! Ain't nobody got time for you."

In that moment I saw Lonzo's true face. The sudden change in his tone was all too familiar to me. I finally realized what all the lavish living he provided was gonna cost. My body, my life, my freedom. I felt as though my life was flashing before my eyes.

If I left now, I would have to go back to nights spent alone in the corner store with limited food and possibly no clothing. Yes, I'd have back some control of my life, but what was actually left of it?

And if I stayed, I'd have quality meals, clothes, shelter, companionship, and comfort but I would have no control of my mind or body.

As easily as Lonzo gave me that one hundred bucks yesterday, I thought, *he would certainly take it away.* There seemed to be only one way of keeping it. *What did I value most though, money? Or myself?*

I had to make a decision quick that would change the course of my life forever.

VOLUME 19: LOST AND FOUND

Dear Diary,   *Friday December 6th*

I'm sure it sounds senseless to you but I chose to leave my designer clothes, my brand new Chanel bag, and that beautiful condo behind. Although Lonzo had given me "things" I had never had access to, I couldn't keep them. They were pretty things and comfortable things but they were *his* things. And I knew how it would've played out. He was gonna remind me I was using *his* things at every chance he got, not to mention every chance he wanted something from me.

And I was over being controlled. I left my mother's house to be free and Lonzo was planning to cage me in all over again. He wanted me where he could see me at all times and for me to do what he said when he said it. I just couldn't live that way.

Now more than ever before, I wanted to be the smart girl again. I wanted to learn things that would get me into a good college. I thought about someday having a great job and earning myself a decent living so I could afford to have the finer things all on my own. I was sick of living off my mother or even a guy that would provide me with a comfortable life but threaten to take it all away on the regular, just to keep reigns on me.

I had to work toward my own success. And going back to school would be the only way to do it.

Dear Diary,   *Monday December 9th*

I was on my way to school today in the same Burberry outfit I had left Lonzo's crib in. I kept it as clean as possible. My plans were to go see the guidance counselor and let her know I was ready to come back to school. I had been cutting for weeks and surely, I was behind.

165

It was not a good look for a freshman. But I hoped if I explained what I'd been through, she could help get me caught up. I wanted to join a another club and get back in the groove of the school thing, ignore the peers around me and succumb to the teasing if I had to. Just like I'd been forced to do in junior high.

This high school experience was supposed to be different. But just because this group was a little richer, and a lot fancier, that didn't change their ugly characters. They were just as bad as anyone else.

As I was nearing the block my school was on, passing a nearby deli, I was shouted out by my supposed friend, Tammy.

"Aye, Patricia, where you been girl?"

I neared her to chat for a bit. As much as seeing her brought that bitter taste back to my mouth, I didn't wanna walk right past her and start more drama for myself. Besides, she's quite the gossip and I probably needed the scoop from her before I walked back in that building.

"What's been goin' on Tammy? I've missed you and the girls," I lied.

"Sooo much!" she cooed. "We made it to the cheerleading semi-finals and I was chosen to be the tip of the pyramid! Being the lightest and all."

Of course, there was always good news for Tammy. I tried not to hate.

"That's what's up, girl. I'm happy for you." I hoped it sounded sincere. "So, have you seen 'you know who' around?" I referred to Don.

"Hell yea, Don has been the talk of the town since that *Socialface* scandal. Other girls have actually stepped up accusing him of other questionable stuff. Thanks to you, dude got real humble. He even got kicked out the poetry club!"

That was excellent news for me. I was soooo happy to hear that. I could possibly re-join the club again and continue doing what I do best.

"Word?" I was stunned but ecstatic.

"Nice outfit, by the way girl." Tammy complimented. "What you had to give up to get into this fly gear?"

She did not want to know.

"Girl, please." I avoided any further questions and kept it moving now that I had the info I needed.

As I walked away, I heard her say, "It could use a wash and an ironing maybe but that's still some official shit. Nicee." It was cool that she confirmed the authenticity of my gear but still, I ignored her and kept it moving.

As I entered the building, I didn't feel as tense as I was feeling minutes before.

I went straight into the guidance counselor's office and truly hoped they could *guide* me back onto the right path.

"Patricia!" Ms. Kenton exclaimed when she saw me. "We have been hoping to see you back."

"Really?"

"Yes, your mother said you ran away from home. She's been pretty distraught and even suggested we un-enroll you from our school. Your therapist pulled some strings to get you in here so we were banking on you coming back within a certain matter of time before we made the decision to cut you."

"Wow," was all I could say. I knew for a fact my mother couldn't have actually been "distraught" over me leaving. She was probably shocked that I finally kicked her ass. But I know she didn't lose sleep over me. *Where were the police reports and the search team?* She didn't care where I was spending my time or how I was doing. I was alone out here on these streets and I know I was alone in this world.

"Yea, so how would you like to proceed with your academic standing? You've missed at least a month. You still need to fulfill extracurricular requirements and the holidays are coming up."

Damn, I had no recollection of what time of year it was. I was living aimlessly and praying just to make it through the damn day.

"I want to catch up, by any means necessary. And I'm a fast learner. I'll be back in class as soon as possible and I'll catch up on whatever I missed. If you would give me a chance to..."

"Sure, if you can have perfect attendance from here on out, I can grant you that. You have to make up any tests your teachers require and stick to an activity you can complete," she made the conditions of my return very clear.

"Sure. And I hear it may be safe to join the poetry club again since the rapist is gone," I put it bluntly.

"Rapist? Poetry club? Oh, Donald Quinn? Yes, he's under investigation right now. He's still attending school but he cannot take part in those activities until we get to the bottom of this. And I'm sorry about what happened, Patricia. Unfortunately, I had to find out about this through the web like everyone else. But if it's all proven true, he will be punished," she assured me.

I only hoped there was a way to prove it all true. But I'm sure the *Socialface* exposure was punishment enough for Don. It damn sure was for me.

As I got up to leave, she gave her final orders. "I also think it's best you return home, Patricia. Your mother misses you and you need to get a good meal. I can see you've lost weight. I'm sure you and your mother can bond some during the holiday. I'll give her a call and let her know you're back. I'll also be making an appointment for you to start seeing Dr. Graham again. You know, at least to discuss 'the incident'. I don't want it affecting your schoolwork in any way."

Ms. Kenton picked up the phone as I thanked her and walked out the office door.

I knew it was about time to head back home. We both had a good cooling off period. I definitely needed to get back into some clean clothes if I was gonna be going back to school.

Dear Diary,   *Tuesday December 10th*

Being back in the house was awkward but it wasn't nearly as scary as it was before. My mother wasn't as quick to start fights with me and it felt good knowing my mother had finally seen that ounce of strength in me. I couldn't tell if she was proud of me or resentful for it, but I'm sure either way she was not gonna mess with me the same way again.

I wondered to myself if she had actually missed me these past few days. She never showed any kind of concern before. I wished she loved me enough to care about my whereabouts and well-being. She didn't even ask where I'd been or if I was okay.

I'm sure most teenagers would rather their parents stay out of their business and leave them the hell alone. But if they actually experienced that, they would appreciate a nosy, overly involved parent over mine any day.

I was happy to be close by her though, no matter what our relationship was like this time around. I finally realized my mother was all I really had.

Dear Diary,   *Wednesday December 11th*

At school today, I was as focused as ever just like I'd promised myself. There was chatter all around me about everything from the incident with Christian, the incident with Don, my runaway, and my return. But I didn't lend my ear to all that drama. I needed to get back on track with my schoolwork.

But on my way home from school, after I had gotten off the bus that took me back on my side of town, I ran into trouble.

Just when I thought I was safely away from the nonsense I endured in my school with my evil colleagues, I realize I had been followed.

"Aye yo, Patricia!" some chick hollered at me. It was a strangely familiar voice but I was shocked hearing it in the middle of my neighborhood. No one around here really knew me, especially no girls.

I turned around to see that I was surrounded. It was Christian's girlfriend, Gina, and her pack of wolves.

"We thought we lost you when we heard you ran away," she started, inching closer to me. "But I'm glad we found your bum ass."

"Yea, 'cause you probably thought you could mess with an upperclassman's man, hers at that, and get away with it," one of her friends walked up to me. "What did you think you were gonna prove? Don't you know we run shit around here."

"I didn't wanna prove anything. People were callin' me names. I thought I could make it stop," I said with an ignorant defense.

"Ha! Now you're more of a punk, a whore, and loser now than ever. We'll make sure that's proven and it *sticks*!" she laughed.

"We warned you!"

The girls all circled me and started pounding on me. There were at least 6 bodies punching, kicking, and smacking me up. There was no way I could fight back or defend myself. I was taking the beating of my life... or at least another.

It was like the one I had during my last days of junior high. But this time, Diesel was not here to come to my rescue or so I thought.

That's when I heard the loud pop of gunfire being let out into the air.

I doubted this crew of girls came with loaded guns and so I was relieved when they backed away and scattered at the piercing sound.

"Yea, bounce up off her!" a female voice screamed out. "Or in about two seconds, I'm aiming this at one of y'all," she said. The girls each backed away one by one. There was pure fear in their eyes. "And don't ever come 'round here again," she finished.

The beat down crew quickly disappeared into the streets. They probably had a nearby ride or something. I doubt they would've been on this side of town so freely.

The girl who shot the gunfire came to my aide. She checked me for bruises and helped me up. It was very sweet of her but as this point in my life, I realized people don't do something nice for nothing.

Who was she? And what did she want? I pondered.

It didn't take long for her to identify herself and her connection to me.

"I'm one of Diesel's home girls, Sandy. And I know all about you and him. He had to skip town for a bit and he asked me to look out for you," she explained. She was red skinned and had sandy brown hair. She looked much older than I-possibly even 30. I wondered if this was the chick that Drew claimed Diesel had cheated on me with.

If she was, I don't think she would've saved me like she did. So I eluded his father's comments to being a lie.

"Really? Wow," I said. "Good looking out. Is he okay though?"

"Yea, now he is. He got caught up in a bad deal and he's been in hiding for a little while. I work for him so I gotta hold down the business while he's gone."

I was so relieved to hear these few details. This girl was just a worker and he was safe. On top of it all, he was still looking out for me. The love I had buried away for him came pouring back to the surfaces of my heart.

I continued to listen as she spoke.

"So here's the deal... We have to close out this deal tonight and we need an extra body. You think you can stand in for Diesel while he's away?"

I knew there was gonna be a price to pay for this rescue. And there it was. She saved my life so I'd have to risk mine.

"I dunno..." was all I could say. "I just got off the streets and back into my mother's house. I can't be getting in no more trouble. I'm really just tryna do the right thing..."

"Looks like trouble is gonna follow you either way girl," she replied, referring to the beat down that just took place. "At least if you help me out, I'm always gonna look out for you. And I know you know my word is bond." She grabbed hold of the weapon in her pocket, reassuring me she had power in these streets.

I needed protection at this point. And it's true, Diesel had saved me once and he had his people right there again when I needed them. The least I could do is return the favor.

"Aight bet, what you need me to do?"

VOLUME 20: ACCIDENTS HAPPEN

Dear Diary,   *Thursday December 12ᵗʰ*

Here I was on a school morning sitting up in the hospital. Only this time, it wasn't me laying on that hospital bed. It was Sandy.

I agreed to play my part in last night's operation. They only needed me as a lookout anyway.

But hey, accidents happen and I hope no one is pinning this as my fault. I did what I was told to do.

When Sandy and the gang walked into a seemingly abandoned crib on the dead end street up the road, I laid low in the whip. They had me play the music extra loud to distract anyone from hearing the sounds that might have been coming from inside. I had to watch the house and the streets and that's what I did.

There were a few passerby's that didn't strike me as suspicious though. They blended in with the streets with their baggy jeans, oversized sweatshirts, and fitted caps. I didn't think nothing of it when they passed by the car.

It's when I saw two guys walking up to the house Sandy was in that I panicked. This was not a part of the plan. There were to be no unfamiliar faces involved.

I put up my signal to the guys outside the car on the lookout and they started moving. But it didn't look like they were making moves of defense. Matter fact, they started confusing me when they walked in the crib wit the suspicious fellas. I knew something wasn't right but what could I do?

Next thing I knew, there was a huge commotion taking place on the inside. Shots were fired. Dudes came running out with bags probably filled with drugs and money. And me, trying to stick to the plan and not get myself too close to the danger- I froze. But after moments of observing, I saw everyone I knew who went in, come out. Everyone except Sandy- that is. And if there was anyone I had to protect, it was her.

The group rushed into the whip I was in. All shaken up and in a hurry.

"What happened?!" I yelled frantically. "And where's Sandy?!"

Nobody had a clear answer.

"Grease," one of them spoke to another. "Make an anonymous call to the police. Tell them you heard shots firing from the house. And let's be out."

I felt horrible riding away from the house without Sandy. I had to see what was up with her. But I could not be seen on the scene.

I asked to be let out. But the driver didn't pay me any mind. Someone from the team said, "That's your problem. You're too damn sensitive. She knows the risk she's taking out here. Just go home and meet her at the hospital on your own time."

"Yea, if you show your face tonight, you goin' down right along with her."

I had to obey. They said it clear and firm, like it was the law of the streets. And yes they were right, being sensitive and caring about people was a trait I always prided myself on but it certainly worked to my detriment at times like this.

So as I waited patiently in the waiting room for her today, I was fearful to hear the word on Sandy's recovery.

"You're the first visitor we've had for her," the doctor said as he approached me. "Are you family?" It was weird that nobody had come to visit this girl in the hospital. It had been hours!

Maybe she had no family. But no friends either? She must be worse off than me.

"Yes, doctor. I'm her cousin, Patricia. The only family she's got," I replied.

He led me to a private corridor and explained to me the damages done. The doctor asked me a few questions about our family medical history and about having any adult relatives. I made something up each time, hoping he wouldn't try and piece together what was all a lie.

"Two gunshot wounds to her forearm and waist. Possible nerve damages affecting her walking and mobility. There was quite a lot of external bleeding but not enough to cause a fatality. You're cousin will be fine with a few months of physical therapy I'm sure."

"That's great news," I smiled. "I'm sure she'll get through this. As long as she's alive and well. Can ya just patch her up and let her go free?"

"Well, Sandy is certainly alive but I don't know much about free. I understand that this injury resulted from a dangerous operation that took place last night," the doctor started. I knew about this all too well. But I gasped in pretend shock and let him finish so I could hear about what went down from a different point of view. "She was in the midst of a drug bust gone wrong. And she being the leading detective involved, she's now responsible for $50,000 worth of missing drugs & money."

Wait, she's a DT? Isn't that a cop? I thought. *And $50,000?! What really went down last night?* "Can I see her?" I asked. I needed answers.

"She hasn't woken in a while but I'll let you see her."

He led me into the hospital room and I stood by Sandy's bedside. I just met her but cared so much for her. She rescued me and I owed her my life. But I didn't know how I could help now.

She lay on the bed silently as I neared her bandaged body.

"Sandy, I'm so glad you're okay. I was so worried..."

After several moments, Sandy woke up and moved slowly as she tried whispering in my ear.

The doctor stood several feet away taking notes on his notepad about her development.

"Who did this to me?" she asked.

I didn't want to give names knowing Sandy had already lied to me about who she was, "I barely saw faces."

"You're gonna have to find them. Or better yet, find Diesel and make sure he finds them and gets that money back. Because if I have to take the heat for this, I'm coming for him, then you next."

I didn't have to ask any questions. I knew exactly what was going down. She was a crooked cop who had been working with Diesel to come up on some cash and Diesel's team crossed her. She had been hiding him and needed me, an unknowingly soul, to be her eyes and ears that night. But now, since his team either couldn't be trusted or didn't trust him, they double-crossed them both. Now Diesel's life would be on the line if he doesn't clear Sandy's name. "Gotcha," I said.

"Oh, and I'm giving you a week," Sandy spit out.

I backed away with fear but I knew that if I found Diesel, all would be well. Both in love and in war.

VOLUME 21: SEARCHING FOR LOVE

Dear Diary,   *Friday December 13th*

I had to go home and clear my head after the past few days of experiences I had. As much as I wanted to make my life right, I felt like I was digging myself deeper and deeper into trouble.

I was facing some of the worse consequences for decisions I haven't been able to make for myself.

Every time I wanted to do something my way, I was backed into a corner with no options for an out.

I just wanted to be free. But apparently freedom isn't free. I wanted to be loved but as much as I searched, love does *not* seem to want me.

Dear Diary,   *Monday December 16th*

I only had a few more days to find Diesel. So after school today, I planned to stake out by his house and demand answers. Babs would surely know where her son was. And this time, I wouldn't take no for answer. This was no longer just about my heart, it was also about our lives.

It was early afternoon when I first knocked on his door. Babs opened up immediately like she waiting on someone. By the way she rolled her eyes at me, she certainly wasn't expecting me. But I politely asked for Diesel anyway.

"Diesel's busy," she said.

"Well this is important. I'm not leaving until I talk to him or at least until you tell me where he's been."

"Ohmigod!" she exclaimed clearly annoyed. "Diesel!!" She yelled out his name through the house.

"Thank you," I replied. I couldn't believe he was right there in that house only a few doors away from where I rested my head and I was going crazy worrying about him.

Babs led me into their kitchen, which looked like it needed a good cleaning. It felt sticky and smelled like something had gotten burnt.

"I'm so sick of lying for him and hiding him away. His problems are taking over *my* damn life!"

"What do you mean?" I asked.

"Speak to him yourself," she said to me and turned away again. "Diesel, get your behind in here now! You got company."

In a few moments, Diesel's sexy dark frame was standing in the kitchen doorway. My heart skipped a couple beats after seeing him for the first time in months. I missed him so much, I wanted to embrace him with hugs and kisses but also to slap him in the face for disappearing from me for so long.

"Diesel?" was all I could say with utter shock.

"Patricia! Baby girl," he hurried over to me excitedly and gave me the huge embrace I was longing for. In that moment, my world stopped. I forgot why I was there and wanted to have an intimate moment with him.

After a few moments of this blissful moment, I jumped back into reality. "Nigga, where the hell you been?!" I pushed him off me. "I've been missin' your ass and handlin' your bullshit out in the streets while you right here chillin'."

"Whoa, whoa, girl you don't know the half!"

"Well, start talkin'."

Babs got up and I was hoping she was gonna excuse us. But instead she reached for a glass and poured some whiskey inside waiting to be entertained.

"First of all," Diesel started. "I was expecting a thank you for making sure my girl was being protected when bitches came after her again."

Word in the streets was always travelling. SMH.

"Oh, please, Diesel, 'your girl'? You really don't know what it means to have my back. And a 'thank you'? All I really needed was for you to be here. Would that have been so much to ask?"

"Actually, Patricia. It would. My life and my money was in danger. If I stuck around, you would be going down too."

"Well, guess what, Diesel, I *am* going down with you. You don't know what I've been through since you've been gone." Tears welled up in my eyes just at the thought. "Does the name Sandy ring a bell?"

As he opened his mouth to speak, a stunning young woman walked in the room. She was fair skinned, slim, and had long straight hair. And apparently she was there with my boo.

"Diesel, baby. What we eating?" She came up behind him and rubbed her hands on his shoulders. I felt so uncomfortable. The scene made me sick to my stomach.

Diesel stopped in his tracks. He kept his eyes on me though "I got some business to handle, can you go pick up something?" Diesel handed this beautiful broad $40. She counted the bills and was on her way. *Dumb broad.*

I was nearly in tears as I stood up to leave behind her. But Diesel wasn't letting me go.

He grabbed me by the waist and held me tight. "Girl, I'm sorry 'bout all this. I need you to understand this life I live, I ain't chose it. I'm in the game and I have to play by its rules. But you know how much I care about you. I've never been that far away. If anything I been protecting you from some craziness I got caught up in with the law and loving you from afar..."

Love?

"Really, Diesel. This is love? You're funny. I'm leaving," I said trying to free myself from his hold.

Diesel snuck a kiss on my neck. I couldn't fight it any longer. I loved him too.

Babs finally rolled her eyes and left the kitchen but not without her final words, "Diesel, you better not forget to handle that business she came for."

His mother was nosy and annoying and possibly also a drunk, but she was right. She made sure Diesel stayed focused on his money which was hard for both of us to do at times.

I kissed his cheek and waited for him to finally comfort my lips with his. All was well in our worlds. I forgot about Sandy and the accident and the threat she made. I didn't care to ask questions about the mysterious girl who came out touching on him. I was happy to have him to myself right now.

Diesel led me into his room, we hit a blunt, and crept into his bed where I felt all the safety I needed right there.

Dear Diary,   *Tuesday December 17th*

The next day I had to leave out for school from Diesel's house. As he walked me to the bus stop, we finally got a chance to discuss things.

Of course I forgave him for all the pain he caused me, because he really seemed sorry. And he was ready to be there for me now.

He asked me how my moms been treating me so of course I had to fill him in on the fight we had. I left out the experience I had while I was living on the streets and met that older dude, Lonzo. It didn't matter now that I was in Diesel's life again. Besides, we still had to stay focused on the Sandy situation.

"So she wants me to get her money or does she need the product?" Diesel asked me.

"Either or, I guess. Your boys got it and if it don't turn up, she's going down for it. And she has no plans of going down alone." I described the entire experience from beginning to end, giving as much detail as I could.

"That nigga, Grease. Always knew he'd be my weak link." Diesel shook his head with disappointment. "Well babygirl, don't worry your pretty little head about it. I'mma take care of this." He kissed me lightly on my forehead and I melted inside.

"Please do, babe."

We were at the bus stop and saw my bus coming our way when he said, "I gotta run though. I'll be here waiting for you at four o'clock."

And later that afternoon when I got off the bus, there he was.

Dear Diary,   *Thursday December 19th*

The week since I visited Sandy in the hospital was up. But I did as Diesel said and didn't worry myself about it. He was acting funny today though and I figured something was wrong.

He was quiet as we sat in his backyard this afternoon, smoking up.

I asked him straight up, "What's on your mind babe?"

"I don't wanna worry you, Pat."

"I'm already worried if you are. Just tell me what's up. Maybe I can help."

"Aiight, you wanna know?!" he hardened his whole demeanor. "I ain't get the money."

"What about the-?"

"I ain't get the drugs either." His head was down. He was feeling defeated. "My boys double-crossed me big time."

What did that mean? I pondered. *What were we gonna do?*

It was gonna be hard to reassure him things would be alright. Because I know Sandy had power and I- none. I didn't know how much weight Diesel held out here but I trusted him enough to find out.

"Babe, its alright though. I got your back and together, we'll get through this." I touched his face and gave him a reassuring kiss.

Dear Diary,   *Friday December 20ᵗʰ*

Today was cold and breezy. As I got off the bus afterschool to meet up with Diesel, I was hoping to tell him about the situation with his dad and my mom. It was time to confront that shit because it was killing me keeping it secret.

Our relationship was going so well though. It's like we picked up right where we left off and I was loving it. School days weren't nearly as bad as before because seeing

Diesel every afternoon made it all worth it. I breezed through it all and even started catching up on most of my schoolwork.

It was rewarding having a boyfriend again, someone I could be there for and he would be there for me. This feeling of love was a new feeling but I was getting very used to it.

I saw Diesel's silhouette from a far distance. My heart melted as it usually does when I see him. In his hoody and jeans, it turned me on to see his oh so familiar walk coming toward our spot- a park bench slightly hidden amongst a line of trees.

But as he neared me in the park, I noticed a rush of dudes creeping up behind him. He was instantly surrounded. I couldn't tell if they were gangstas, goons, or cops but my baby looked scared. And so was I.

He saw me running from the bench to his rescue and he discretely put up his hand to stop me.

His mouth read, "No. I got this."

I stopped in my tracks, still not knowing what to do. I reached out my hand as he signaled his eyes to stop me.

The D-boys pulled out the cuffs and I realized what was happening. The cops were taking away the love of my life and there was nothing I could do to save him.

My mind was racing as a million thoughts came to mind. *Who did this? Where were they taking him? And for how long? Would I be next?*

This was all my fault. *Why did I wanna meet in the park anyway? My selfish ass.* I wanted to get far away from his family and mine but I was forgetting the situation at hand.

As I backed away behind a tree, I saw Sandy sitting in one of the vehicles, in an unmarked car, with her window rolled halfway down. I saw her smile and this all began to make sense.

I wasn't sure if she saw me, but I knew one thing, she would be coming for me next.

Dear Diary,   *Sunday December 22nd*

I stayed home today. In fact, I hadn't left my house in the past few days. Diesel always told me if he got sent away, I should listen out for his call. But I hadn't heard anything and I was getting anxious.

It was time for me to hit up Babs.

When I did, she was not tryna hear me at all.

My days dragged on, trying to get through school and home life without my boo. There was nothing to look forward to at the beginning and end of each day.

And then my mother wanted to drag me to church with her today.

"I really don't feel like it, ma. I'm tired and I have some studying to do."

"Studying, huh? So you ready to take school more seriously now?"

"Yes, ma. I was off track for a minute but I'm back." I smiled at my mother, hoping we could keep a friendly convo going for a change.

"Okay," she bought it. "But if you staying in the house, you better wash them dishes. By the way, your cousin's coming back into town on Christmas Eve so tidy up the guest bedroom and put some fresh sheets on the bed."

I nodded with acknowledgement. I had only a few hours alone during my mother's church time. I hoped I had enough time to follow her orders and still be able to run out and find out what's up with Diesel. It was killing me being without him. After all we had been through, after all he did to protect me, I could not give up on him now.

So I headed over to his house and was greeted frantically by his mother.

"This is all your fault!" she screamed.

"What are you talking about, Babs?"

"You've done nothing but make our situation worse! Ever since you started coming around, my son's been distracted. You got him protecting you while he need to be worried bout his damn self, and his fam. You costin' him money and now you've damn near taken his life."

I couldn't believe what I was hearing. I couldn't let her break me down like this. Especially when she pushed Diesel into this world and I just happened to hop along for his ride. "Look, you really shouldn't point fingers when you're the one pimpin' out your teenage son to the streets."

"You watch your mouth little girl," Babs said sternly.

"I'm jus' sayin'. I love your son and I'm only here to help. But you forced him into this world and have no one else to blame for the consequences!"

"Get the fuck outta here wit that! My son don't love none of y'all hoes. And you damn sure can't help us unless you got the 5 Gs on his bail." I stood there shocked as ever as she continued to rant. "Matter fact, you probably set him up to save your damn self! Ya know what, you're not welcome here no more. Get the hell outta here and stay out of our damn lives!"

VOLUME 22: BRUISED AND BROKEN

Dear Diary,   *Monday December 23*

I knew Babs did not want me in her house but that was not going to stop me from trying to come through. After all, I needed to find my boo Diesel and she would know just where I can find him.

Today when I was knocking on the door, there was quite a surprise waiting for me there. It was Diesel's father, Drew, standing with his big burly ass staring at me like I was a piece of meat. I didn't know what to do now because all I felt for him was anger. I still hadn't told anyone else what I'd seen the day he was creeping up in the house in my mama's room. But he had hurt me, he's hurt Diesel, he's playing Babs, and I'm pretty certain he would someday hurt my mom.

"Well, well, well," he huffed at me. "Thought you got rid of me, huh? But here I am and I'm not going nowhere."

"You're the most disgusting man I've ever met. I bet if your family knew it, they'd be trying to *help* me get rid of you too."

"Is that a threat little lady?" he asked me. Yes this horrible guy read me right. I was going to out him if he did not give me the information I needed.

"Only if you don't tell me what's up with Diesel. Because I need to know. He's not the only one whose life is at stake right now, ya know."

"What you mean?" he asked.

"I mean, tell me what I need to know and maybe I'll tell you." I had really conjured up some boldness for this man I once feared. My heart raced as I awaited his reaction.

"Listen you are not about to come up in my crib telling me how things are gonna go down. You're on my turf. I make the rules around here."

"Oh so you don't like when people come up in *your* crib trying to run things, huh?" I replied.

"Listen you, I'm getting a little bit tired of your smart mouth and if you know what's good for you, you would run away and not come back. I thought Babs already warned you." He turned around and was getting ready to slam the door in my face.

I screamed out, "Please! I need to find him."

"Look if my son wants to find you he will. Stop searching. He don't wanna be found."

Those words cut me deep. It triggered a painful feeling in my heart that reminded me of my absentee father. Three and a half years ago when we were gearing up for the first annual 5th grade Father-Daughter dance, I was the only one who had no one to escort me. No big brother, no uncle, no stepfather, no male figure, and certainly no father.

I begged my mother to tell me something about him. I told her I needed him. "Everyone's gonna know I'm incomplete if I don't go," I'd said to her.

She didn't care what that meant to me. "You're incomplete because you're a punk, you're a wise ass, and you have no friends. Everyone knows that so showing up with or without a lousy father ain't gonna change nothing," she replied.

I lowered my head with more shame than I'd ever had before. She confirmed so many negative feelings I had for myself and brought me so much discomfort. Tears welled in my eyes as I asked once more, "Can you at least help me find him?"

"Do I look like I wanna find him?! Matter fact, does it seem like he wants to find you?! When are you gonna learn to stop annoying the hell outta me and realize he doesn't wanna be found?!"

It was years before I asked her anything about him again. Those words stung me bad. I knew at that moment that I wouldn't be worth anything to anyone if my own mother and father saw no value in me.

But hearing Diesel's father claim the same, I was hurt even more so. *Diesel actually told me he loved me. Could he have lied?*

I refused to except the emptiness I was feeling inside. I knew I couldn't push the issue with his fam, but instead I would have to take matters in my own hands. I had to find him, or at least find someone who would love me because the way I'm feeling inside is deadly. It almost made me not wanna live.

~

As I walked home in solitude, I was so very tempted to pick up another sharp object and cut into my skin to ease the emotional pain I was encountering. But I remembered the promise I made to myself never to do that again.

So instead, I went home and called my old friend James from summer camp. He certainly helped me fill a void when we used to fool around during breaks and after hours during the camp days. Boy was he shocked to receive my call. And when we met up, he was very pleased to see how much I'd grown up.

Oh, and he had no idea. But I intended to show him.

~

The night with James was amazing. I walked into his house feeling a little down but spending that much needed time in the arms of a guy was really curing.

Thank goodness we're on holiday break because I was in no rush to leave.

His parents weren't home when I first arrived. We curled up on the couch watching TV and he offered to make me some Hot Pockets. *Such a gentleman!* I thought.

He still had that acne issue going on but he was a little more built and his breath was on point for a change. I was actually kinda feeling him.

We started chatting about school and things. I told him about cheerleading tryouts and joining the poetry club. I told him I was having a hard time fitting in and how I'd dropped both. Although the cheerleading squad dropped *me*, he didn't need to know all that.

He was on a wrestling team and boy could I tell he was an athlete from the new muscles I felt when he put his arms around me. *Oh so sexy!*

We started to kiss and kissing turned to touching. I really didn't want to waste no time. His parents would be home at any moment and I didn't wanna risk getting caught. He didn't seem concerned about that though.

He took his time undressing me and then led me down to his crotch. I had been shy about going down in the past but now, I knew exactly what to do to please him.

Before long, he had his head down and was tasting my juices like I had never experienced before. He kissed me down low, bringing me to an ultimate level of unselfish pleasure.

"Ohh... Yesss..." I whispered out with passion.

"I'm glad you like that," he lifted his head and smiled. "I missed you, girl. And you know I always hoped I would get you back."

"Wow," was all I could respond. The lust he expressed for me was flattering and made me feel good.

To express my gratitude, I laid him down on the couch then gave him a ride like I'd never given before.

I was absolutely fulfilled by the touch of James' hands digging into my back and his rhythm moving with my body.

When we finished, we got dressed and continued watching TV. When his parents came home, we looked like we were just chillin' like we were supposed to be. They had no idea what they just missed.

We snickered to each other and eventually started playing video games.

His parents didn't kick me out when night came. I guess they trusted us. So after they went to sleep, we snuck up to his room and did it all over again.

Dear Diary,   *Tuesday December 24ᵗʰ*

Erica came over today! So I won't have much time to chat.

She and I have been catching up on everrrrrything we missed in each other's lives these past few months, including details about her new man.

My mother's taking us shopping later and tomorrow, we'll all be cooking dinner together. That will be a treat, I hope.

Maybe we'll even put up a tree! Whether or not, this Christmas will actually be a good one.

Happy Holidays!!

Dear Diary,   *Tuesday December 31ˢᵗ*

Me and Erica had been having the best week ever! There was hardly any drama or any sad thoughts about my dad, her parents, Diesel, Sandy, her adoptive household or any of that. But today, as she was packing to get ready to leave, she had a weird tantrum.

I had asked her if she loved her boyfriend and she began to cry.

"I think I do. But he will never know it."

"Why not?" I asked.

"Because I don't know how to show love anymore."

"What do you mean?" I didn't understand. As long as she and I been sought after love, we shouldn't have any problem accepting it when it comes.

"Every person I've ever loved has either left me or hurt me. For some reason, my heart won't allow me to love again," she said with sincerity. "It's like I'm-"

It was strange hearing this. I could only wish my heart would shutdown at times, just so I wouldn't feel the pain of love and loss. But she was here sad as ever because she wanted to love again and couldn't. It's like she is-

"Broken," we both said at the same time. We looked at each other and I too began to cry.

I knew all too well what it felt like. I was bruised and she was all the way broken. I tried to give her a hug but she pushed me away, threw all her things out the suitcase, and stormed out of my room.

I heard her in the bathroom, slamming down the toilet seat over and over again. When she finally came out all calm

192

and collected, I walked in after. She had cracked my ceramic toilet seat in several places. I did not fault her though. I knew what she was going through. I also knew it was my responsibility to replace it before my mother saw it that way and there was hell to pay.

I pondered about whether or not she did things like this often. We all had different ways of coping so I'm sure this had to be one way for her. I didn't bother to ask though. My cousin was feeling better and that's all that mattered to me. She probably just needed to take her meds.

When she did, all was well again. She resumed packing and continued to enjoy the rest of her stay.

Dear Diary,   *Friday January 3rd*

Diesel called today!!!!

Just as I walked in the door coming home from school, I heard the phone ringing. I missed the first call but it rang again and it was my boo! *His timing was on point!*

Diesel explained everything. He had been in protective custody and still is. He was forced to snitch on his whole squad- which I'm sure was hard for him to do... considering that's his whole business operation down the drain. Some of his closest friends and even some he considered fam would be going down with this case.

But he said he had to do it. To clear his name, my name, and to relieve him of that $50,000 debt. He would still be going to trial but he was only facing 6 months in juvenile jail, then he'd have to get back in school and try to change his whole life. That was all good news for me. He was currently free and it was only a matter of time until I'd have my baby all back!

He said he had been missing me just as much as I'd been missing him and nothing in the world could've made me happier. We agreed to meet up in a few days. He was waiting until all the guys he snitched on were arrested and in custody before he would be able to walk the streets.

I was so anxious to see him but I was willing to wait a little while longer.

VOLUME 23: SOMETHING OLD, NEW, BLACK & BLUE

Dear Diary,   *Wednesday January 15ᵗʰ*

Me and Diesel finally reunited today!

It was bittersweet though because he just wasn't the same. He urged me to stay home as often as I could because although the law was protecting us, the streets would soon have their eyes on us too.

I wasn't sure if he heard I was no longer allowed at his house so I invited him over here. I was taking a HUGE risk letting a guy come over my mother's house but Diesel was certainly worth it to me.

First things first, he wanted to light up. It had been weeks since he was able to, so I led him up to my room by the window I usually used.

His mind was in a distant place as he stared out the window intensely. His thoughts must have been deep and scattered because he hardly said a word to me. He looked a bit paranoid as his eyes searched the streets through my bedroom window.

"Everything okay, babe?" I asked, interrupting his thoughts.

"Yo," he motioned me to hush. "I'm good," he snapped.

I didn't like his tone but I took heed anyway. I stayed quiet until he was ready to speak to me.

"What you been gettin' into while I was gone though?" he asked grillin' me with distrustful eyes.

"Nothing, babe," I lied, knowing he wanted to know whether I had been with anyone else. "School and chores.

You already know!" Meanwhile, I knew he kept a close watch on me and would be able to find out whatever he needed to know... Although, that was before he went to the police and snitched on all his guys, so my secrets were probably safe.

"Why you stop coming by my crib then?"

"OMG! Your parents kicked me out! They told me this whole situation was my fault and that I should never come back."

"You let them tell you that shit?!" he huffed. I was taken aback. Diesel had never, *ever* spoken to me that way.

"Believe me, babe. I spit a little fire back at them but its their house, I had to respect that," I defended myself. *What was up?* I wondered. *What did he know? And why was he treating me this way?*

No matter what happened while he was gone, I was down for my man no matter what. I would fight his battles and support his wishes all the way through. *Didn't he know that by now?*

"Look, I'm under too much damn stress right now. I don't want to be worrying about what my girl's doing when I'm not around, you feel me?" I nodded. "You either gon' be down for me or you not. But you better let me know what it is."

It was a harsh way of putting it but I guess he's in an insecure state right now so I let him rock. "D, I got you." And I hoped for damn sure he believed me.

I leaned in real close hovering over his shoulder and comforted him with my slender arms. I needed him to know how much I loved him. I would give up anything to have his love. James was just a temporary fix but that's over. As long as my baby was by my side, I needed for nothing else.

"You holding me too damn tight." He pushed me off him. "Just rub my back a lil," he demanded. And so I did.

Dear Diary,   *Monday January 20th*

Today is Martin Luther King Day and that has always meant a whole lot to me. It meant strength, pride, overcoming, wisdom, and peace. It was a day I honored because Dr. King was everything I feel the world needs. But with him being gone, shit has certainly digressed.

Today was not just a day off for me to spend with Diesel, but it was a time of reflection for me. It was a day that inspired me never to change my frame of mind because at some point, I may have the power to inspire a transformation in our society.

Of course, I was waay far off from that ever happening. I have no power and no impact on anyone right now so there was no way I could see myself changing the world. But deep in my heart, I knew I'd someday try.

For a moment, I tried sharing my thoughts on that with Diesel but today he didn't wanna hear it.

"Yo, can you just keep quiet for a minute? You stay running your mouth about some silly dream." I was astonished by his words. "Don't you know this world is fucked up and there ain't nothing you can do about that?"

"Wow," I replied. "There were days when you and I thought we could change things together."

"Them days are over. The dream is dead. Look out for self and stop worrying bout everybody else."

His words hurt. Up until now, he was the only one I'd ever shared those seemingly impossible thoughts with. And he used to support me on it all. Now, I was back at square one, and no one saw my vision of brighter days ahead. Not even me.

Dear Diary,   *Thursday January 23rd*

Today was one of the better days I'd had with Diesel. He was more at ease after meeting with his lawyer today, but still he was a different D.

I was doing my homework when he gave me some much needed attention.

"Hold on, I'm almost done!" I squealed as he started kissing my neck and tickling me.

But he didn't care. When he wanted some, he had to have it.

He threw my book down and took full control. I was in my zone and was sooo close to finishing my homework but I decided not to fight him on it.

I was happy to have a playful piece of him back around.

When we made love today, it wasn't soft and sensual like it used to be though. It was rough and ruling. I felt a bit restraint as he held down my arms and deepened his thrusts into my body. It was pleasurable but uncomfortable.

I wanted to enjoy him as he kissed my body from head to waist but those kisses turned to nibbles and those nibbles turned to bites. He didn't go all the way down on me either though. It was as if he didn't trust me and was avoiding it. But I tried to reassure him it was all about us two as I gave *him* the full business.

I watched for him to scream out in ecstasy and felt exhausted after it all. I was beginning to put his needs and wants waay before mine and although I know that wasn't good, I had no intention of letting him go.

He needed me and I was gonna be right there.

Dear Diary,   *Monday January 27th*

You wouldn't believe this!!

Today at school Tammy and the girls came and approached me. Of course I thought they were coming to gang up on me about something but not even!

They came to deliver news about Christian's girl. Great news, at that.

Okay, I guess finding out she injured her arm in a skiing accident over the weekend isn't great news, but it was good enough news to me! (Sorry to say.)

Even better news was that, they were gearing up for the finals and needed a fill-in.

"Are you asking me to perform with you guys?!" I exclaimed.

Tammy answers for them all. "We just need someone to stand in for a while. I'm sure she'll be good as new by the time the finals come, but we can't practice without her position placed."

Leave it to Tammy, my so-called friend, to dampen the highest of my spirits.

"What if she doesn't recover in time though?"

"Then obviously *if* you can pick up her steps, you'd have to perform them!" Tiffany says sarcastically.

"Gotcha!" No one and their stank attitude could ruin my joy now. I would finally get my chance to prove I got skills. I was gonna be on the squad. Even if it may be temporary, I was gonna make the most of it. Things were starting to look up for me.

Dear Diary,   *Friday January 31st*

Today I was in a great mood after leaving cheerleading practice. I was focused and on point with my moves. I had every intention of doing the damn thing for those finals. Somehow, someway, I was gonna be seen doing it.

If I have to work my butt off from now until May to prove I was worthy of my spot, that's exactly what I'll do. I walked off the bus full of hope.

But upon coming home, my joy quickly turned sour as Diesel approached me at my door.

"Where the hell you been?!" he demanded an answer.

"I told you I have cheerleading practice twice a week, Tuesdays and Fridays."

"That's too much damn practice. You know I be here waiting for you and you taking your sweet time?"

"Babe, I got here as soon as I could." I casually tried to explain myself but he didn't appreciate my nonchalant tone.

"You think this is funny?" he grabbed my arm.

"No, I just think you're overreacting." Then he started squeezing my arm and wasn't letting me go. "Oww! That hurts!"

"I want it to hurt. So you can feel my damn fury." *Was he serious?*

"Diesel, stop!"

He eventually let me go but with a thrust that knocked me into a wall. Things were going too far.

"Now that you wearing makeup and you got your hair straightened out, you wanna play a brother?!" he said angrily. "You think because you on some dumbass cheerleading squad, you important now? Those bitches never cared about you and they never will. I'm the one who done had your back since day one and you wanna push me off to the side now that you think you some hot shit?"

He had it all wrong. There was no way I would ever treat him like second place. I just wanted to do a few things that would make me happy for a change. *It's taken me this long to find a little happiness and he couldn't enjoy it with me?* This was so unfair.

I was afraid to come any closer to him to try and ease his paranoid mind. I so badly wanted to embrace him with my love. I wanted him to feel my genuine care for him.

But he wouldn't hear any of that. He needed reassurance that I would put his needs first. Even before mine. And that was something I couldn't be sure I would do.

As I rubbed the black and blue wring around my arm where he tried squeezing the life out of me, I sat down and looked up at him with teary eyes. "I just want to love you, babe."

"Well, prove it," he said, taking my gym bag from my other hand and throwing it down on the ground.

Dear Diary,   *Saturday February 1st*

Diesel spent the night last night and I didn't give a damn about what my mother was gonna say or do about it. I had to do what I had to do to keep him in my life.

Besides, he was right. He was the only one who showed me any care or attention thus far and I was determined to show him how much I appreciated him. How much I *needed* him.

But in my desperate state of doing that, I had completely disregarded the fact that my mother would sometimes entertain his father in our house. And today, it all came to a head.

~

We sneaked out of my room extremely early and enjoyed our breakfast down in my basement, a place I only visited to do laundry and my mother's ironing. It was fairly dark down there and was filled with storage items. There wasn't much furniture but we sat on cushions on the floor and even made love on a heap of giant pillows.

As our relationship was starting to change, I still loved Diesel. Only now, the joy and comfort I once felt with him was replaced with fear and desperation. I was afraid of losing him either to the law or to the streets, to his family who now hated me, or to my own newfound happiness—cheerleading. I feared that his insecurity and distrust would turn him completely into a new person who would continue to bring me down. All while I was fighting to survive all my own troubles.

So I was desperately seeking ways to put my needs aside and keep him happy. Because as long as he was around, I would be good no matter what the sacrifice.

I massaged his back and kissed him everywhere imaginable. I whispered in his ear, "I love you so damn much, you better never forget that." I complimented his beautiful eyes and strong arms. After using that strength to do me wrong yesterday, he begged for forgiveness as we were laying down for pillow talk last night. And of course, I would forgive him and forget.

"I love you too, girl." Diesel must've known he had some making up to do as he responded softly, wrapping me in his arms and planting a passionate kiss on my forehead.

I was getting a little anxious having him in the house as I knew my mother would be waking up soon. "When are we gonna be able to go out and do stuff again, babe?"
"I'm not in no rush to be out and about, Patricia. So don't bug me about that. Just be patient."

He had a point. There was no reason why we had to be out there when he was in the heat of a most trying time. I was thinking too much about myself and what would happen to me if I got caught with him down there, but not enough about my man and his repercussions. So I left that thought alone.

When my mother woke up and called out to me, I simply replied, "I'm downstairs doing laundry, ma!" I wasn't nearly as afraid of her as I used to be. I just toughened up and actually threw some things in our washing machine.

"Good, take your time down there. I don't want you interrupting my breakfast anyway," she said. That's when it hit me that she had company. And Diesel still didn't know about the affair.

I thought this would be a better time than any to come clean about what I knew.

As the washer went into its spin cycle, I asked, "You know babe, you never speak about your dad. Are y'all close?"

"Why you wanna talk about my dad, all of a sudden?" he questioned. "He's just a no good man my mother happens to keep around just because they had me together."

Oh, so he knew his father had some ill intent. I felt relieved. But I still needed him to know the whole truth.

"I only asked because I keep bumping into him and it's always a bit awkward."

"I hope he's never disrespected you. I warned him about himself. Where you be seeing him?"

"A few times at your crib and even sometimes, I've seen him with my mom..."
"What?!"

"Yea, there was even an encounter we had when my mother wasn't home. He tried to attack me..."

"Wait a minute. Hold up," Diesel was shocked, angry, and confused all at once. "When was this? Why you ain't tell me about this?"

"This was months ago when you weren't around. In fact, when I came looking for you, he was the one who ran me away. I was scared."

"Months?! See that's what I can't stand about you. You stay punking out when shit gets rough. You don't know when to stand up and be about business. I don't even know why I fucks with you!"

He pulled away from our closeness. I saw him growing with rage. I felt horrible hearing him down me for having valid fear. I know I struggled with standing up for myself but I was building on that. At least I still came out and told him.

"You always knew my weaknesses, D. Why can't you be supportive about this right now?" I took his hand.

"Because you're starting to bring me down. And you've known some scandalous shit about my family all this time and you don't tell me?! I can't even trust you, yo." He threw my hand down and started moving toward the staircase.

"No!" I tried to stop him. "Please, let's talk about this." I didn't want my mother to see him nor did I want him to see his father up there. I pulled his arm as he took his first step up the stairs.

"I'm done talking to your wack lying ass. My mother was right about you bringing trouble all up in my life!" He threw me down and I landed on a row of boxes stacked against the wall.

I couldn't believe he was getting physical with me again, and now verbally attacking me. After I forgave him and he promised never to do anything like that again, he had fibbed.

We were both silent for a moment as I sat on the floor with my head down in defeat. I was certainly not going to fight his anger anymore. I needed him to realize what he's doing on his own.

He looked apologetic as he headed toward me. But we were quickly interrupted by striking sounds coming from upstairs.

We heard an argument blooming and soon after, a dish breaking.

Before long, we heard clarity in their voices. "Don't tell me to calm down," Drew snapped. "You're fucking up right now and I'm gon' let you know!"

"My daughter's in the house. Watch your mouth," my mother said.

"You think I give two shits about her?! She needs to be dealt with too!"

Diesel moved closer and closer to the upstairs door, finally recognizing whose voice he was listening to.

"Is that my dad?" he asked.

I just nodded.

"Oh hell no! This shit is crazy."

Diesel rushed upstairs and at this time, I didn't know what he would do. Who's side was he on? Mine, my mother's, or his father's?

The whole situation was messed up and I was most confused of us all.

I stayed in the basement afraid to witness a fight between any of the three of them. I, for one, was a target for them all and I was already beaten down emotionally. I couldn't take anymore of the violent banter.

I sat there and listened as Diesel confronted his father and defended me and my mother. His father didn't seem to have any remorse for what he was doing which caused Diesel to storm out.

I couldn't tell where my mother stood on the matter and knew it was only a matter of time until she had it out on me for bringing Diesel in the house and having him get involved in her business.

~

To my surprise, when we were in the house together and alone this evening, my mother didn't tear me down with her words as I expected. She dished out two dinner plates and sat down with me at the kitchen table.

"Who is that kid? He looked very familiar but I can't figure out where I've seen him."

It meant a lot for my mother to show concern about this guy who I obviously was hiding in her house. I wasn't sure if she asked because she was grateful for him stepping in on her heated argument or because she cared to know about my social interaction with him, but I was excited to let her in on my relationship with him either way.

"He's a good friend from down the block. And I really like him so we've been spending a lot of time together." There was no use telling her he was my man or anything. Less was more.

"How does he know Drew? And why did he care so much about us?"

"Diesel is his son," I replied.

"Ohhh…" my mother nodded. It all started making sense. "Is his mother in the picture?"

"Very much so," I confirmed. I thought my mother knew this. But it was comforting knowing that she didn't and she wasn't a straight up homewrecker on top of all her other character flaws.

"Damn," was all she said as she handed me her empty dinner plate. I wasn't sure if this information would change anything between them though. All I did know it was time for me to clean up the kitchen.

And so I did with ease.

Although I was a bit sad knowing Diesel left thinking so ill of me, I had a tinge of hope about my mother and I beginning to build a new, less combative relationship.

Dear Diary,   *Sunday February 2nd*

I called Diesel continuously today hoping we could make amends before more weeks flew by without him in my life.

I was hung up on and shut down by everyone in his family. I persevered until I got to speak to him myself.

"Listen, Pat," he said. "You need to leave me alone. We're not good for each other."

"Diesel, don't talk like that. You know we belong together."

"No we don't. Stop telling yourself that. You just go on and do your thing," he said casually. "Soon, I won't even be around for you at all so just get used to it from now."

I couldn't believe what I was hearing. He was breaking up with me. This was our end. *How would I go on?*

"But babe-" I opened my mouth to beg and plead with him for our relationship. But I heard the voice of a female call his name in the background.

"Look, I gotta go. You got your cheerleading and shit now. You don 't need me. And I damn sure don't need you."

I couldn't believe my ears. *Was he ending this?!! It was over? Really?* Then, he hung up on me. And I started balling out uncontrollably. Again, I wanted to die. I let the tears cascade out my eyes and down my face. *My life was officially over!!*

VOLUME 24: NOT GIVING UP

Dear Diary,   *Tuesday February 4th*

I had no choice but to get up out my bed up and get myself to school. It was a promise I made to my guidance counselor, my therapist, and myself not to miss anymore days. As my mother constantly reminded me, if I didn't use my brain for something, I pretty much had nothing.

I was extremely sad though. I was hurt and depressed thinking about Diesel and how hard I tried to make things right between us. I was there for him and even considered putting his needs before my own.

I put myself in so much danger for him and succumbed to the pressure of trying drugs just to fit in with his lifestyle. I was so disappointed in myself for going so hard and still failing. I was feeling empty knowing that all he needed was constant reassurance of my commitment and didn't find that with me. But instead, he sought it out in someone else.

Relationships suck! I thought. *It goes so wrong even when you're doing everything right.*

I could hardly concentrate on my moves at cheerleading rehearsal today. But I went through the motions and did my thing. In time, it became a great distraction from the destructive thoughts I had regarding the break-up.

When Gina's friends made sly and threatening comments toward me, it didn't even phase me. I knew they were under the impression that I could easily get back up if they ever touched me again. And without their leader around, they didn't take it that far anyway.

Of course they would throw jabs at me for making mistakes but I let their words roll over my head.

"Ohmigod, how hard is it to get on beat?!" one of the girls barked.

"Was she the only chick we could get?" I heard another girl say.

"Yes, Julie," I heard Tammy say. "Everyone else has curfews, boyfriends, and other activities. You're lucky we found someone with at least a little rhythm and absolutely *nothing* going on."

Another dig, I thought. But deep down I knew Tammy was doing me a solid favor in her eyes. I was probably the only person she'd let into the personal depths of her life and she in mine. I kept all the little secrets I learned about her and I'm sure she would forever be grateful. She was giving me a chance of a lifetime to live out a piece of my dream. It sucked that she had to still be a bitch in the process.

I had to stay focused on winning the championships. I was gonna prove myself as worthy and talented, despite the hostility I was experiencing from the group. I had no plans on giving up.

Dear Diary,   *Thursday February 6th*

I was feeling like shit all day. I couldn't get over what happened with Diesel and needed to fill that empty space in my heart.

To make matters worse, I bumped into Don in the cafeteria. And to my own surprise, I didn't run up to him and hit him, spit on him, or scream like I thought I would.

We locked eyes for a moment. Mine were filled rage and his of sorrow. I wondered if he had the balls to apologize to me for that awful sexual encounter. What he did unlocked a painful piece of me that will always sit in my soul. It was broken piece, a stolen piece, and a part of me I'll never get back.

But when I looked in his eyes, I could see he had pain too. Maybe it was guilt, or distress or shame, but he was going through it and I could tell. I wish I could ask him why he did that to me and those other girls. Why did a decent looking boy like him, with lyrical skills, and -up until lately- a great reputation; need to force himself on anyone?

But all I could do silently forgive him and move right on.

God would have to handle this one for me.

Dear Diary,   *Friday March 7th*

I've spent some time away from you because I've been writing a lot more in my poetry book. It's just as therapeutic for me to write in rhyme sometimes, especially because I'd feel much more comfortable sharing it someday.

Since I'm on the cheerleading squad now, I won't be rejoining the poetry club. But I'm still getting the extracurricular credits I need for submitting my work into the poetry magazine the school puts out every semester. That means I've gotta get back to work.

So, I'm off again! I just wanted to let you know I still love you, I haven't killed myself or anything, and I'm doing okay. LOL

Dear Diary,   *Tuesday March 18th*

Christian and the guys from the basketball team stopped in on our practice today. He paid special attention to me as I was dipping and turning to the music.

I had recently heard that he and his girl had broken up so I would have a little fun with him if he made any advances.

When he did approach me, of course he had his little entourage in tow. I wasn't too fond of these guys who encouraged taking that awful locker room pic that almost ruined my life. So I ignored the others and kept my focus on Chris.

Tammy, Morgan, and Tiffany stepped up behind me when they saw the attention I was getting.

"Patricia, when we gonna get up again?" Christian asked.

"I don't know. But I'm definitely kinda busy right now..."

Tammy cut in, "Don't act like you're too busy for him girl. You know you can leave a little early today."

"I dunno," I responded shyly.

"Me and the guys wanna take you and your girls out. You down?" Christian asked.

That was a different kind of offer. It would be a group of us. I wouldn't automatically be forced to be with one boy and do whatever he wanted me to do? For once in my life, I'd get a chance to go out in a social setting and enjoy some time amongst friends. Well, "friends", I'd say with air quotes.

"If all my girls go, I'm in," I said eagerly.

"I'll go let captain know," Morgan rushed away.

"Okay, so we out!" Christian said putting his arm around my neck and walking us toward the door. The other girls grabbed their things and followed behind with Christian's crew. *Look who was on top now?* I thought.

The other cheerleaders stared at us, being freshman leaving with upperclassmen, basketball players at that, had to earn us a little extra respect- or at least some jealous hateration. And I was now a cheerleader who messed with a baller and that gave me power like I never had before. We hung out at the pizza shop where I got to know everyone present in a whole new way. No one belittled me or threw digs at me. I was fitting in and it felt good.

But I couldn't forgot how this connection was made to begin with. I recalled the day when Gina first tried to fight me, and the girls were right there by my side. It's like they were always there when the ball players were involved. I guess they valued the boys and their reputations much more than they did our friendship. As much as that bothered me, I was happy to have their company at times like this, so I let it rock.

But the group setting was slowly dwindling though as each one of the guys took one of my girls out back or to their cars.

When Christian and I were left alone, I was filled with nervousness. I knew what he most likely wanted me to do.

But this time, I didn't want to do it his way. I wanted to be in control and this time, get what *I* wanted.

So when we slipped out to the men's room, and he started opening his pants in yet another bathroom stall, I stopped him.

I put my hands on it through the material of his jeans and felt the stiffness of his manhood. Meanwhile I took his hands and led them where I wanted it to go.

Into my shirt and under the bra my mother had recently bought me, I introduced his hands to my blossoming breasts. He carried out my wildest desires as he moved his hands and tongue around my chest.

But there was one more place I wanted his tongue to go. I had my hands in his hair and urged his head to move further down below. But he wouldn't budge. He would go as far as my bellybutton and come back up to my chest. "You not gon' go down?" I whispered to him.

"Hell nah, girl. I don't know where you been."

"I did it to you," I stopped to say.

213

"Yea, that's you. I'm not doing all that. I'll do this," he said inserting his finger into the moistness between my legs.

I was speechless for a moment as his motion brought me great pleasure. But I wanted more and he wasn't giving it to me.

"I'm done then," I stopped him, covered up, and got ready to leave.

"Oh no you not. You know what you need to do." He pulled me back in by my arm.

"I said, 'no'. If you want me going there, you're going there too."

"Fuck outta here. I'm not givin' no pop no head." He zipped up his pants and stormed out.

I was stunned by his comment. He thought I was a jumpoff!!

I'd never even given it up to anyone he knew! But the way I handled him must have been proof enough that I was easy. That's what I get for being so loose with my body lately. Giving myself to any ole body who would have me. All the while, I thought I was earning respect and gaining power. But I was giving everyone a reason to disrespect me and label me things less than what I deserved.

I left the pizza shop alone and made a decision never to sleep around again. I couldn't keep letting nonsense like this take my focus away from my schoolwork and activities ever again. Nor could I keep giving people a reason to disrespect my name. These dudes were not freakin' worth it. SMH!

VOLUME 25: HELP IS ON THE WAY

Dear Diary,   *Wednesday March 19ᵗʰ*

I was extremely itchy today. I couldn't make it through one period of the day without rushing to the bathroom and checking myself out. By 5th period, my underwear was filled with a yellow moistness I'd never seen before and I was frantic.

Did I catch something? And from who?

I caught up with Tammy after classes, who promised me she'd go to the clinic with me afterschool tomorrow.

Please pray for me. I have been wayyy too sexually active in the past few months and I know I haven't always been as protective as I should be. I can't trust these guys, not even Diesel, especially when he runs to a new girl every time we take a break. SMH! *How could I have been so stupid?*

This is the stuff they warned us about in health class. My dumbass probably missed the sessions about the importance of protecting yourself. I definitely missed the class where they handed out condoms. That could've saved me- especially if I have something permanent like herpes or HPV. Or even worse, a deadly disease like AIDS or HIV.

God, please give me another chance to make better choices. Please help me to be safe. I promise, I wont fall so weak to boys again. I'll find a new way to cope with my loneliness. I'll stop giving myself to loser guys who don't even respect me. I'll change for sure. Just please keep me clean.

I'm gon' have to say a lengthy, more sincere prayer tonight if I'm gonna get through this one.

Dear Diary,   *Thursday March 20*[th]

Tammy came with me to a *Planned Parenthood* far away from our houses and school. She had her driver pick us up and take us waaay out of our way so we could get tested in an isolated location.

She said she was gonna just get tested too because she'd had her first sexual encounter with Christian's friend, Kendrick, the other day and wanted to just know her status. That was her first experience with *a guy*, I'm sure is what she meant.

"I shouldn't have went that far with him," Tammy said. "I so didn't enjoy it as much as I thought I would. He was wack."

"Uhh, I don't think you'd enjoy yourself with *any* guy, Tammy," I tried to be honest with her.

"What do you mean?" she asked.

"I mean, you enjoyed yourself a whole damn lot when we played that little truth & dare game at your crib."

"Oh please, what are you talking about? Don't start bringing up your lies again, Patricia. I'll start spreading nasty rumors about you too," she threatened.

"It's just us, Tammy. And I'm not gonna tell anyone. But don't you think you may be more interested in girls?"

"Hell no, I was just experimenting," she folded her arms and turned away from me. "So just drop it!"

"Okie dokie," I said. "But if you wanna talk to someone about it, I'm sure the *Planned Parenthood* office can hook you up with someone who can help you figure things out."

She was silent the rest of the way.

Dear Diary,   *Tuesday March 25th*

After the long wait for our results from the *Planned Parenthood* office, to my relief, I learned, prayer really works!

I mean, I wasn't completely clean but I didn't have a permanent or deadly or transmittable disease like I thought. I just had an infection. Nothing a few days on antibiotics couldn't cure, I hoped. But I still had to be careful. That was a close call, for both me *and* all the guys I'd been with. Christian probably knew the risks and that's why he was so hesitant to give me what I wanted. SMH. Somebody shoulda warned *my* ass.

Lucky for the *always-lucky* Tammy, she was clean as a whistle. But she did mention that Morgan hadn't been feeling well since that day at the pizza shop and she was still waiting on her period. So we all needed to go back to *Planned Parenthood* with her to take a pregnancy test.

Uh oh! was all I kept thinking. *What would she do if her test turned up positive?*

I never got a chance to know Morgan very well but I know she was beautiful and talented and oh so loyal to Tammy. I didn't know how she would handle a situation like teen pregnancy nor did I want her to have to find out.

Dear Diary,   *Tuesday May 6th*

The week of the championships finally came. It was very disturbing to walk into practice today and see Gina.

I hope she wasn't thinking she was gonna come in here and take back her spot in our routine. I had been working my ass off for months and I was determined to do my thing in the big show. I had too much to prove not just to myself but to damn near everyone else.

With my growing boldness, I decided to approach her and see what's up.

"Hey Gina how are you feeling?"

"What's it to you?" she hissed with her nasty attitude. Even a broken arm couldn't humble a chick like her.

"I was just showing concern."

"First you go after my man, then you go for cheerleading spot, and now you think I'm gonna believe you're concerned. Beat it!"

"I didn't do any of that on purpose. I'm not like that," I affirmed.

"Whatever," she rolled her eyes at me. "I'm fine. But lucky for you, not well enough to perform."

I silently filled up with enthusiasm inside. *I was gonna live out my dream!*

But on the outside, I was calm. I wished her well and meant it- for after Friday of course.

Dear Diary,   *Thursday May 8th*

This evening, I invited my mother out to the championship performance tomorrow. I only hoped she would actually come out and support. She'd never been that involved parent who would ever put my passions before her work so it would mean so much if she showed up. This is what she wanted most of me- to see me in a social environment, looking good, and being admired. If I could give her any gift, this would be it. I felt bad giving her such short notice but I feared the entire time that something or someone would come between me and my moment.

But with it being just 1 day away, I was confident my time would finally come.

Dear Diary,   *Friday May 9th*

Today was showtime!!!!!!!!

There was so much adrenaline rushing through me as we arrived at the *Stoneybrook University Performing Arts Center* this evening. I was filled with joy and angst as I walked off the squad's coach bus and entered the large arena. I was anxious to know whether or not my mother was gonna come through.

But I also knew, either way, the show must go on.

Gina travelled with us and even wished me well as I was getting dressed into my costume. That was a shocker. I always knew her only to hate me.

When they called out, "Middlebrook High School Rockettes!", I was more excited to get out there than I ever had been about anything in my whole life.

When the music turned on, I got right in place and hoped to God one of these girls wouldn't try to embarrass me in front of this enormous crowd. I knew some of them really had it out for me.

But as the music blasted, I turned up and rocked out! It reminded me of performing in the acrobat recital as a child. The feeling was *amazing*!

I dipped, I twisted, I jumped, and I twirled. I danced on beat and with lots of sass. *Who knew I had it in me?!*

Now, everyone did.

All I could hope for was that my mother was there to witness me in action.

I searched the crowd that was roaring loudly around us for her. Hundreds of faces were before me and I couldn't point hers out. But as I looked by the doorway, I did see another very pleasant surprise.

It was Diesel. A *huge* surprise. Especially considering I hadn't told him about this, nor did he support my cheerleading in the first place.

I was anxious to get offstage and meet up with him to show some love.

As a group, we all cheered and hugged backstage. I finally felt like I belonged. But I couldn't stick around for long, I had to find Diesel. I wondered jealously if he was there for some other girl...

Just as I left the dressing area at back, I walked out and bumped right into him. He apparently *was* there looking for me.

But there was worry and concern written all over his face.

"What's wrong?" I exclaimed.

"It's your mother. She and my dad had a fight," he wasted no time filling me in. "She's on her way to the hospital. We have to meet them there."

My heart stopped. *This was supposed to be one of the best nights of my life and my mother was being rushed to the hospital??*

I didn't even turn back to get my change of clothes. I took Diesel's hand and rushed out.

Dear Diary,   *Saturday May 10th*

Diesel had taken the bus and the train out to Stoneybrook to get to me. It was a sweet gesture, showing he still cared.

But ain't nobody had time for that now, so we got a cab to rush us to the hospital.

He expressed how sorry he was that his father was the cause of this. My mother wanted him to attend the championship performance with her but he was intoxicated and wanted her to cook a meal for him first. (At least that's the version he was told.) They argued until they fought, which resulted in him pushing my mother down a flight of stairs.

I was astonished and afraid. I had been down a flight of stairs on account of my mother's own anger in the past. It was a memory I wouldn't want anyone to relive. Not even my mom. I prayed that she would survive this like I did.

When we got to the hospital, there was a social worker there waiting to question me.

"I must see my mother first," I insisted.

"Very well," this gentleman said. He waited outside the hospital door with Diesel and gave me a private moment with my mother.

I was the only one who would be showing up to be by her side.

When I walked in her hospital room, my mother was bruised and in bandages from the neck down. She had fractured her collarbone, broken her wrist and her tailbone, amongst other damages.

I could hardly believe my mother was laying there looking all lifeless and alone. It was an experience I'd encountered many times in my life but who knew the tables would turn on my biggest aggressor?

I had mixed feelings about all this. If it were a few months ago, it would have been hard for me to feel terribly awful about it. But since the big beat down between she and I, when I won that final fight, I actually found peace with her. I forgave her, just like our preacher said I should.

She didn't deserve this. Just because she didn't know how to express her love, and was an aggressive woman with lots of her own issues, it didn't give anyone the right to lash out and injure her this way. Besides, at the end the day, no one, especially not no woman, deserves to be beat down this way by a man.

Tears started to flutter out of my eyes and down my face. My mother's eyes were closed so she didn't witness my disdain. I took her hand and whispered, "I'm sorry, mom."

I stood there for several moments staring at my mom hoping for a smooth recovery. She looked like she had struggled and was about ready to give up.

But I couldn't let her do that. No matter what our issues have been over the years, there is still a chance we can rise above it all... Right?

My therapist always told me, if a person is willing and ready to change- a change will most definitely come. I have to believe there was some truth in that.

I was damn sure ready for *my* change. I was ready to live with peace and with joy. I only hoped my mother would survive this and share those moments with me. She was literally all I had.

When she eventually woke up, I was absolutely relieved. But it didn't take long for her to snatch my bliss away.

"You see what you caused me," she said. "I was trying to make it to your stupid show. And now I'm laying up in here with no man and a few broken bones."

"But ma, you're gonna be fine. The doctor said so. And you trying to come to my performance means everything to me."

"Child please," she rolled her eyes. "I don't need none of that. I need a warm body in my bed at night. Someone to share my life with. You've have consistently taken that away from me. I'm so over you!"

I lowered my head with shame. *Consistently though?* What was she talking about?

If my mother had any amount of hate for me before, she'd reached her capacity now.

"I still love you though, mom," was all I could say as I left the room and balled out in the waiting area.

Diesel was still out there waiting on me, along with the social worker, still on standby with his notepad in hand.

Diesel put his arms around me. "What's up? How's she doing?"

"She'll be okay. But me and her will not be."

"What you mean?"

"She's blaming me for this. She hates me. And she's never gonna let me live this down."

He was puzzled. "How can she blame you? My dad is the fucked up one, two-timing my moms and putting his hands on a lady. He's the only one to blame!"

"I know but you know how my mother is..."

"I'm gonna handle this for you, Pat. I'm tired of seeing you suffer," Diesel said with all sincerity. "Matter fact, I owe you an apology too. I'm sorry for how *I* been treating you, babe. You been about the best thing that ever happened to me and I been taking advantage. You ain't deserve the things I did or the things I said. I just ain't know how to handle you being all sweet and shit while I was scared and angry, going through all that. You deserve better from me and when all this legal mess is over, I'm gon' prove I can give it to you."

In the midst of the deep pain I was experiencing from my mother's disheartening words, I was filled with overwhelming joy. Diesel said everything I needed to hear from him and gave me the peace of mind I needed. "Wow," I replied. "That means so much."

We shared a long embrace, one that seemed to last forever. And again, I forgave him for all he's done and put me through.

I know we all have reasons for our ill actions but at least he came clean about his and promised to one day make it right. I only wished I could hear the same from my mom. But something was wrong in her heart and head, and it would take a lot more than a few broken bones for her to realize what good she had in me.

As I continued to vent to Diesel, the social worker approached us. He was probably running out of patience.

"I'm sorry to interrupt, but there's an urgent matter we need to discuss."

"What is it?" I looked up and asked him.

"We need to speak alone," he looked over at Diesel, clearly needing him to excuse us.

"I got some business to handle anyhow. I'mma dip out girl. I'll catch up with you later. Call me when you get home." He gave me a kiss on my forehead and was out.

The social worker introduced himself as Mr. Jeff Simmons. He explained why he was there.

"We have received an overwhelming number of hospital visits from your household over the years. These are never health related issues either, but instead have been

unexplained 'accidents'. I'm just here to find out if everything in your home is stable and safe."
Hmmm, what were his definitions of stable and safe? I thought. *I don't think I even know what that is.*

"Well, sir. You're a few hospital visits too late." I stated the truth with a bit of sarcasm.

"Can you tell me what has been going on?" He continued. "I want to help."

I really didn't feel like letting him in. I had already decided not to disclose it all with my therapist and already started writing out my problems like she suggested. *What else could this guy do to help?*

But I saw no more losses in this. We had already reached our rock bottom. And I did not wanna go down any further. Every time I even saw a glimmer of hope in my life, it was overshadowed by more pain, more tragedy, more sadness, and more self doubt. So I took one deep breathe and started sharing the ins and outs of my awful home life experience.

Dear Diary,   *Sunday May 11ᵗʰ*

Mr. Simmons and I spoke for hours. It was quite a relief letting it all out with a stranger who really couldn't judge or belittle me like some teachers, some friends, and some family did.

I told him about the shift in my mother's actions since my grandparents died, her attitude toward me ever bringing up my father, her anger toward my whole being, her secret affair with my boyfriend's father, our large but loveless home, and finally, the abuse.

"You talk a lot about the physical factors in your life," he said. "But what about the emotional impact and how this is all affecting you? What changes have you made to accommodate your mother's behavior and your father's absence?"

Hmmm, that was a good question. This past year had brought on many tumultuous changes for me. But I honestly didn't wanna tell him about my violent, jealous, rebellious, peer pressured, and promiscuous phases.

"I can't get to the root of the problem unless you take me there, Patricia." It was as if he'd just read my mind.

"Alright, alright," I gave in.

So I shared with him a brief synopsis of my past few years of pain. I purposely left out any mention of Diesel and the illegal lifestyle his family lived. I didn't want him any deeper in trouble.

Mr. Simmons seemed to understand what I was dealing with. He closed his notepad and simply stated, "thanks for sharing, Patricia. Your actions are not abnormal. You have been through a lot and you're still growing and becoming a stronger young lady everyday. I don't want you to think you have to go at it alone though. Believe me when I tell you, help is on the way."

I wasn't sure what kind of help he spoke of or if it was actually close to the help I needed but anything was better than nothing at this point.

VOLUME 26: FINALLY FULFILLED

Dear Diary,   *Monday May 12th*

It was my third day in the hospital, waiting on my mothers recovery. No one had come to visit her at all. It was just me.

I decided to head home, make a call to Diesel and get some much needed time alone. I was definitely getting another few days of excused absences so I was in no rush to return to school.

The streets were busy as I made my way down the block. But I didn't pay it no mind and hurried myself home.

I checked the mail and actually had something come in my name. "Forestdale Inc." it read. Never heard of them. I threw it to the side, thinking it was some of that junk mail I always hear adults complaining about. I would check it later.

I was too excited to speak to Diesel about my return home and my mother's slow but sure recovery. The phone rang several times and no one answered. I was determined to get in touch with him so I tried and tried again. When Babs finally picked up and I announced myself, she hung up. I was getting annoyed.

Maybe she'd heard about my mother & Diesels dad but I had nothing to do with that. I needed her to forgive me if ever she thought I did. I at least wanted to apologize for not telling anyone sooner.

So I showered and changed my clothes then walked through the lively crowds that surrounded the block and went straight for Diesels back door. There was some big bouncer looking dude outside their gate screening their visitors.

"Look I'm a good, good friend of Diesel's. I need to see either him or his mother," I insisted.

"If you such good friends, how come you don't know he got shot last night?"

"Huh?" My heart skipped a beat, as I hoped this news was untrue.

"You ain't hear? Diesel was gunned down right at that corner yesterday." He pointed to the lamp post at the corner that was now caution-taped off.

I was too confused and my heart was beating frantically. "Tell me he's okay, though."

"Nah, I even can't even tell you that." Dude was dead serious. "He and his father was there arguing and someone got in the middle, just shot D in the chest."

"What?!" This wasn't making any sense to me. *Why oh why in this fancifully decorated neighborhood was all this going down and no one to protect the people who walked among them? Why couldn't the cops be called before things got taken that far? And why of all people did it have to be my heart, my love, my Diesel who'd undergo such a causality?*

"Tell me he's alive at least??!!"

"He might be alive now but he lost so much blood laying out here, his survival ain't even anticipated. He's in a coma now but it ain't looking too good, sweetie."

"No! No way!" I could not believe my ears. My heart was shattering to pieces. My knees got exceptionally weak. I was ready to ball out uncontrollably, but I knew no one would be there to catch my fall. I was supposed to be coming home to my man, I was supposed to be by his side throughout his trial and long after. I was gonna wait for him while he did his time and now, I may have to face the fact that he'd be gone forever? Life sooo isn't fair. *Why him? Why me? Why us?!*

We belonged together. Without him, I just didn't belong. *After his longwinded apology, pouring out his heart to me and admitting his wrongs and fears, how could he leave me now?*

I knew he was involved in a dangerous game though. Drugs, girls, and all that unexplained cash certainly came at a cost. I was taking a huge risk even stepping into his world and I had done so hoping to at least gain his love in the end.

Taking drugs was hardly a pastime that helped fix anything for us. It was just a temporary distraction, but a permanent drawback in our lives. Knowing where it led Diesel, I knew it was finally time to quit.

I needed him to survive this or I wanted more than ever before to just die.

If I couldn't have him here with me, there was officially nothing left to live for. So I ran home, without a second thought and conjured up a plan to end it all.

Dear Diary,   *Tuesday May 13th*

I woke up this morning feeling extremely sick. I was mad as hell though because I wasn't supposed to have woken up at all.

I spent hours gathering all the meds I could find in the house and when I realized they weren't enough, I checked under the bathroom sink for all the deadly chemicals I could find.

I decided to consume some glass cleaner and see what that would do.

Its potent smell and awful taste did enough damage to me. I was anticipating much worse for my insides. But to my disappointment, I still woke up today- just dazed and ill.

I was hallucinating a bit, even thought I was home with a father and mother, happily and calmly. Only thing was, this father I dreamt of didn't have a face. He was tall, dark, and handy around the house but he didn't have a voice.

I thought I was speaking to my two loving parents until the poison wore off and I realized I was still alone and depressed.

Even as my stomach felt as if it was burning and corroding inside, my heart felt exactly the same. *Why was I still here?* I thought sadly. *Why wouldn't God just take me away, simply and smoothly?* No one would care. Not even me.

My eyes drifted closed again and I continued to dream about how my life would be if it were ever to be complete.

~

The loud ringing of the front bell startled me in this deep sleep I'd fallen into. That was a sound I hardly heard up in here.

Who the hell could this be? If it was Diesels father, I would surely try to kill him. His no good, piece of shit actions were to blame for all my recent woes. The bell continued to ring. It was difficult for me to get out of bed with the excruciating pain I had in my body and the lack of motivation to see anyone.

Ring! Ring!

I slowly moved through the house as I realized the person at the door wasn't gonna give up.

At the door were several unrecognizable faces. All except my therapist, Dr. Graham.

"Patricia!" she exclaimed excitedly. "I'm so glad you're okay."

I wasn't though, I thought.

She came at me with open arms and gave me a huge hug. Her loving embrace felt great. For the past few days I felt as though no one loved or cared about me and it was comforting to receive her visit.

But I looked around at the 3 others who surrounded her and realized they were here for something else. This group meant business.

"Who are they?" I asked pointing at the others.

"This is Mary from Child Protective Services. And Johan and Roberta are from a family care organization." They each stuck out their hand for a shake. I unenthusiastically shook back.

"May we come inside and talk?" Mary asked. I was tired of talking really but I could tell by the persistent ringing of my bell, they weren't gonna take no for answer.

"Sure," I widened the front door allowing them all to step inside. I led them to our living room and we all took a seat. It was awkward entertaining these strange guests in my mothers house. We hardly ever did that. I don't even think I was allowed.

I was still feeling a little woozy but I tried to remain stable amongst this serious looking group.

Dr. Graham spoke up first. "We received a lengthy report on you from Mr. Simmons. Some things were even a huge shock to me. But it was all very valuable information and I want you to know we are all here to help."

"Okay," I slouched back. I wondered how.

"We want you to know we have preventative services that can protect you while your mother is recovering physically and from her unhealthy mental state," Mary stated.

"What's that supposed to mean?" I was confused.

"We can temporarily remove you from your home or send someone here while she's in treatment and recovery," Johan cleared up.

"I'm not leaving my home, that's for damn sure," I affirmed.

I remembered everything Erica told me about that temporary housing situation. It was no good and certainly not a better option for me or my mother. If she needed help, I would have to be here every step of the way to make sure she gets it.

Surely they could work that out, right? The group looked around at each other.

"We will work that out," Dr. Graham said.

Roberta spoke up next. "Aside from that, we came across some information from an 'incarcerated parents' program that might be of interest to you..."

"What the hell would interest me about that?" I snapped getting more and more annoyed. "You wanna put my mother in jail now too?! I knew I couldn't trust you, Dr. Graham!"

"Patricia, please listen. It's good news. You must hear this..."

I started feeling light headed and the room started to spin.

"We found your father, Patricia. He's been at the Stoneridge County Correctional Facility for the past 14 years." And that must have been when I passed out.

Dear Diary,   *Wednesday May 14th*

I woke up comfortably in my bed. My stomach wasn't aching as much but it felt empty now.

No one was around and I started to believe the last memory I had of the group of social services coming to my house was all a hallucinated dream.

Did someone want to separate me from my mother? I hoped not. And did someone actually find my father? I so badly hoped so.

I started to hear faint voices echoing through my house. I tried to lift my arms and feet to move about and find them but I was frozen in place.

I then started to scream out but only jibberish came out. I must have truly done a number on myself with those chemicals.

I shouldn't have even been alive. But I was and I'm sure it was for a reason.

~

I began to hear the faint sound of voices rise.

"I think she's up!" someone said peeking through my room door. "We revived her."

"Thank goodness we were here to get help!" another stated.

As they all surrounded me, they'd revealed I had to have my stomach pumped because I had consumed a deadly chemical. *Poison Control* was there, an internal medicine doctor, the whole nine.
It felt good actually having these people there fighting for my life even when I had long since given up. My blurry

233

vision was clearing up and my senses were returning to normal.

I conjured up the strength to ask, "Where's my mother?"

"She's still in the hospital. Recovering from the accident. Then she will be under psychiatric care," Dr. Graham answered. That sounded about right.

"And what about my dad?" If all these folks were here, surely what I heard about them finding him had to have some truth in it.

"Well," Mary started. "We located him at the Stonebridge County jail. He's been there your whole life and we contacted him. He would love to meet you, if you would be interested."

Would I?! I was as excited as ever. I'd waited my whole life to meet this man. Know him. Speak to him. Touch him. Any information about him would have been sufficient and here they were offering me a chance to see him. *Wow, I actually had a dad.*

"When do I meet him?" was all I could muster out. The surrounding group looked around and smiled. They were happy to help me make this long awaited connection with my father. Joy, fulfillment, and hopefully peace of mind was near.

Dear Diary,   *Friday May 16th*

I went back to school today. I had tests to make up and assignments to hand in. Believe it or not, I had been keeping up while I was home- up until the suicide attempt-that is.

And my teachers were unbelievably understanding, especially after hearing about my mother's accident and finding out I performed for the cheerleading championships which resulted in our school's victory. They allowed me to do take home tests and my English teacher gave me a week to write a 5 page essay about my goals and dreams. That would be easy. All I ever do is sit and think about that.

Although I haven't decided on a career path, this assignment would definitely help me reflect on that. And lastly, my Social Studies teacher asked me to do a research project about one of the religious groups we studied and define how it shaped society as we know it.

I would really have to dig deep into my heart, mind, and soul to complete these assignments and I truly needed to do so anyway. I needed to dissect my relationship with God. He actually came through for me when I least expected him to. I was more than grateful.

Things were looking good for me. I couldn't wait to get to cheerleading practice to find out what the girls thought of my performance last week. *Would they finally give me my props? Would they respect me? Would they treat me like I belonged?*

I quickly found out the answer to my questions were no, no, and no. Christian's ex, Gina, was back on the squad and greeted me with her entourage as I walked into the cafeteria where practice is held afterschool.

"What are you doing here?" she said with her attitude back in full swing.

"I'm here to practice. Don't we have a rally coming up?" I replied.

"Didn't you know you were just a fill-in? I'm back. So be gone. We don't need you anymore," she said shutting me down.

"But you saw the championships. I did my thing up there. Can't I stay?" I begged.

The girls all laughed. "Did you not hear her? We don't need your little ass anymore," one of the girls snickered. "You were crampin' our style anyway."

I was torn up inside. It took everything in me to keep from weeping out the agony I felt in front of the entire squad. I thought I had finally proved myself to this crew. After I busted my tail working toward the big championship performance (and contributing to the big win), I thought I had proven I was worthy and talented enough to belong.

But apparently it wasn't about talent and skill. It wasn't about how much determination and hard work I put in. It was only about who fit the bill, who would follow the captain's lead, and who could tear others down when the time was right. At that moment, I no longer wanted to be a part of this group.

I searched the room for Tammy, wondering if she would have my back for once. But she was far behind in the crowd. Our eyes met and she turned away shyly.

I knew now, I had to make my exit. I was still alone here. Nothing I did would ever change the way people saw me. Just as my mother has always said, I'm a worthless loser and no amount of smarts or skill will ever change that.

I turned around, put my head down, and walked out with shame.

~

When I was safely outside that God-awful building, I wanted never to return. There was just too much pain to be experienced there. In fact there was pain everywhere. Every time I thought I had conquered one issue, another would come about. I was so empty inside. I couldn't wait the few days more to meet my father. If that doesn't go well, I'm throwing in the towel for real.

That's when I heard someone call my name. "Patricia! Wait!"

I turned around to see who could possibly want to have anything to do with me.

I saw Tammy running after me. And even as I continued to keep it moving, she didn't give up.

"What is it?" I gave in skeptically. "You came to kick me while I'm down?"

"No, Patricia. I didn't. And you know what, that's you're damn problem. You so busy believing you're the loser everyone says you are, you can't even see when you're winning." Tammy continued. "I actually came to tell you I'm sorry for the way the girls treated you. You definitely didn't deserve it."

"Oh now you want to say all that. You couldn't defend me in there?"

"I'm not an idiot, Pat. I'm not gonna check those girls in front of everyone and become their new target. I told them about themselves *after* you left. I quit their stupid squad and I came out here to ask if we can still be friends."

"Whatever," I said with disbelief.

"There you go again. I'm telling you the truth and it's not good enough now?"

"Why now, Tammy? This whole year you treated me like garbage."

"That's why I'm apologizing. I'm sorry for lying on you to the girls too. I just wanted to fit in like everyone else. And you know damn well it's not easy," she spoke honestly. "But you're the only one who's actually been there for me. You have always been honest, you kept all my secrets, and I know you mean well. I don't wanna lose someone like that in my life."

I smiled, hoping she wasn't tryna pull my leg or something. "Seriously?"

"Yes, Patricia. I'm not as superficial as you think."

"And you sure this is not just a little crush?" I joked with her about her questionable sexuality.

"No, silly!" she hit me playfully. "You're so not my type! Although I do gotta tell you who is!"

I was shocked she was finally ready to talk about this. I guess she actually trusted me and wanted a real friendship. It was something I had never had the chance to experience before and it meant so much to me now. I finally had a friend.

I smiled at her as we started walking and she locked arms with me, ready for some girl talk.

"So listen up, girl! I got an exclusive invite to Kendrick's year end pool party. You down?"

"Kendrick from the basketball team?" I knew him all to well from the day he accused me of being a dike to that evening out with his boys and my girls. Not to mention he was voted MVP of the team this year.

"Hell yea!" she answered excited. "So you know it's gonna be off the chains! But Tiffany doesn't wanna go because she refuses to wear a bathing suit and Morgan most likely isn't making it due to the baby situation, so you in?"

"Most definitely! But wait. Morgan's actually pregnant?" I was shocked as Tammy nodded yes. "And she's keeping it?"

"That, she hasn't decided yet," Tammy explained. "But either way, we gotta be there for her. She's always been there for us."

That was true. Morgan was a bit of a follower but she was the one of stopped me from getting my hair pulled in the boy's locker room that dreadful day. It was good to know Tammy recognized things like that and would at least be a loyal friend when she needed to be.

Dear Diary,   *Monday May 19*[th]

Today's the day!!

I was going to meet my father at last! I was more than ready to make this distant dream come to life. All my life, I've been incomplete without the other half of my DNA there to guide me, love me, and support me. I needed to know why.

A million questions stored up over the years came to the forefront of my mind.

Why were you missing from my life? Why does my mother hate you? What did you do to warrant 14+ years in jail? When will you be able to come out? When will you be able to hug me the way I always imagined a father should his daughter? Why are boys so immature? How will I ever know when a boy really cares for me? Will you ever be able to protect me from harm?

It was time for me to get answers.

I waited outside afterschool for Dr. Graham to come pick me up for the jail visit. I wouldn't have wanted anyone else by my side when I made this encounter with my dad. She had learned enough about me over the past year to stand strong and supportive beside me no matter what the outcome of today was. I grew to trust her and realized she had the very best of intentions for me. She had proved it in so many ways, this being the very best of them.

As I entered her burgundy colored Acura RDX, she greeted me with a hug.

"Here we go, Patricia. Are you ready?" she asked.

"Ready as I'll ever be," I spoke up confidently.

"Great, and when we leave there, we'll go visit your mom."

"Have you heard anything about her recovery, doc?"

"She's not in great condition, to be honest with you. She's not fighting hard enough to get through her therapy and exercises, so its hard to say how long it'll take for her to get better and come home."

"So, what's gonna happen to me if she stays in there a long time?" I asked, afraid to be taken into the foster care system for any amount of time.

"Well, there are plenty of great people would love to take you in temporarily..." she started.

"Hell no, no way! I don't want any 'temporary' situations. Why can't you fix this doctor? Can't you bring my family together once and for all?"

"It isn't that simple, Patricia. Each one of your family members are battling their own demons and if they can't get right with themselves, they can't do much for anyone else. It's best each of you get help separately so when you come together, you'll be a stronger unit. Don't you think?"

"I guess," I said, saddened by the thought of that although I knew Dr. Graham was right. Who knew how long that would take though? "I'll never belong to a real family, will I?"

"Well that all depends on what a 'real family' means to you," she replied. "If you mean someone who loves and care for you unconditionally, who will always support you, and protect you no matter what; I'm willing to be a part of your family... If you would have me, of course."

I looked up at Dr. Graham. *Was she offering to take care of me while my parents get right?* I was confused and taken aback by the thought of that. "Would you really want to be *my family?*" I asked, feeling a bit undeserving of such an honor.

"I already feel like we've become family, honey. And I filed the paperwork to take temporary custody over you until either of your parents are willing and able. If it all clears, you will officially have me in your life- full time. And no matter how short or long a time it takes for you to go back home, I'll be here for you long after."

"Wow, that's great news!" I could hardly believe someone gave a damn about me enough to do such a thing. "Why'd you choose me, though doctor?"

"Believe it or not, I went through most of what you're going through. It took years for me realize I had any value to the world until I was adopted by a great family who showed *me* a change. I got into this field to help others realize their value when they can't see if for themselves. And when I met you, I felt as if I met my younger self."

"Wow. I can't imagine a smart, beautiful, sweet lady like you ever going through what I've been through."

"Why not? You're a smart, beautiful, sweet girl yourself and you've been through it."

I put my head down, "I'm different though. You just don't seem like the type."

"Trust me, what you see on the outside of people cannot begin to tell their stories of struggle. Because everyone's been through something- whether mental, physical, emotional, you never really know. But it's how they choose to deal with it that makes them who they are. I'm committed to using my pain to uplift and inspire others. So understand this, as much as you believe I'm helping you, you are helping me."

"Thanks, Dr. Graham. I'll love you forever for this!" I turned and gave her a big smile.

"Just call me Sharon, now."

"*Auntie* Sharon feels more appropriate," I smiled at her. The afternoon was already off to a great start. "Just promise me you won't ever give up on me."

"I promise."

~

After the hour and a half drive, we arrived at Stoneridge County Bridge and as we crossed it to enter the jail, I knew there was no turning back. Today I would find out about the other half of me.

We got to bypass most of the intake at the prison. All Dr. Graham had to do was flash her badge or whatever and we were good to go. They still made us go through detectors and searched our belongings but we didn't wait on no lines, get body searched, or fill out strenuous paperwork.

I was able to speak to my father in a private room where only a wooden table separated us. A guard stood in the room and Dr. Graham stood right outside the door.

When Patrick Thomas walked in the room, I instantly felt connected to the tall, thin, dark man who stood before me. We had very similar features, same complexion, and those infamous pointy ears.

"Ohmigod, you're beautiful!" he said his first words to me. That was the first time in my entire life anyone had ever called me that. This moment felt too good to be true.

"Daddy?"

"That's a name I been waiting to be called my whole life." He spoke with a strong deep voice and smiled exposing two large front teeth similar to mine.

"If I knew you existed, you would've heard it a lot sooner," I replied. "What's up with that?"

"Baby girl, I'm not in here cause I want to be."

"That's what they all say. I wanna know *exactly* why you're here. And then I'll tell you why I'm here."

"Fair enough," he shook his head. "My baby girl know just what she want, just like her ole man."

That statement made me feel proud. He already considered me his.

I listened up as he revealed his and my mom's beginnings and how in love they were back in the 90's. He said my grandmother was strictly bougie and my mother was a bit of a rebel. She was intrigued when she met him as a recovering bad boy turned working man.

They were at the height of their 20s, she was just starting out at the hospital as a nurse, he was a contractor who often stopped in. He was previously in a gang and when he finally got out, he rushed into a marriage with a woman who had 2 kids and later found out she had a drug addiction. So the problem was, my dad was married with stepchildren, my mother was single and lonely, yet they still hooked up. I guess that was her thing.

My mother needed him much more than he thought she would. She was young and needy as he continuously dipped out of his marriage to have a little fun with her. "I really fell for her though," my father continued. "We had a lengthy relationship too. It was a quiet connection, it was real, and it was passionate. We would go out late at night, me risking everything I had at home to be with Pam. She just loved me so damn much. It was so good for my ego. She put up with anything from me. When I was absent, or upset, or broke, or even disrespectful, she kept loving me. It wasn't until she got pregnant when things went wrong..."

"Oh great. Blame the hardships on me..." I was growing resentful with every word he spoke. My father was nothing more than a lying, cheating bastard who hasn't yet taken responsibility for what he did. Some of what he said about his relationship with my mom even reminded me of mine with Diesel. The love between us was all so strong. But Diesel redeemed himself for his mistakes and as far as I knew, my father was just a coward who had given up on us.

"No, don't get me wrong," he cut off my thoughts to prove otherwise. "I loved you the minute I knew you existed. But I had just lost my job and I was scared out my mind. I already had a family to support and now I had to support you and your mother. So I got involved in some white collar crime bullshit."

"What's that?" I asked.

"Ya know, it's the kind of crime that takes real thought, a little skill, and lots of planning. An organized mission," he explained. "I partnered up with a guy who helped me embezzle thousands of dollars from the hospital funds. But I messed up telling your mother about this. She threatened to out me to the administrators if I didn't leave my wife for her. I told her I was doing this for her and the baby but she didn't believe me. She accused me of trying to abandon her, and even threatened to get rid of you. I knew then that she had serious issues. And that's when we *really* got into it."

"What do you mean?"

"I hate to tell you this Patricia, but when your mother was 7 months pregnant with you, we fought. I really let her have it when she said she was gonna give you up. I felt as if she was gonna hurt me by hurting you, so I would have to hurt her. And now I know that was wrong. I been waiting all these years for Pam to forgive me."

"What did you do to us?"

"I can't get too specific but... she eventually had to get treated at a doctor which is where she was convinced to press charges on me for attempted murder."

"What?! Attempted murder? That's awful, dad!"

"I'm sorry babygirl. I was desperate to make her feel my pain. But I didn't realize how much I had already hurt her. I didn't need to raise my fist or anything to her. I had already done so much damage to you both. And the fact that you survived that incident, I knew you were gonna be a strong little girl. I knew you would struggle but in my heart all these years, I knew you would overcome it all. I only wish I could've been there to help. But in just another year and a half, I will be."

As my eyes began to water, I fought to hold back tears. My father knew all too well what I was going through, without me having to say a word. He did understand what he set me up for and wanted to make it right.

"I wasn't half the man back then that I am now, Patricia. I was young and scared and lost. I was so damn selfish at the time, I didn't even recognize how much love I had surrounding me. Then me being prosecuted for both the attack on your mom and later on the embezzlement- I unknowingly ruined my entire life and everyone in it. I regret that everyday I'm sitting in this awful cell. I will never forgive myself for that. But I am begging that you someday forgive me."

I looked up into his eyes that so greatly resembled mine. I saw myself and the root of all my pain and suffering in his image. I was crushed to learn the truth beyond my existence but was also relieved to put the missing piece of my life in place.

It all made sense now. *This* is why my mother hated me. She saw this man who'd brought her so much physical and emotional trauma every time she looked at me. She thought my existence would have saved her relationship with my dad but I snatched it away. There was no denying this, my parents both needed help.

All I could do was forgive them both. They did their best for me and I just couldn't continue to let their pain live in me.

"I do, dad," I pronounced my forgiveness. I could no longer hold on to all my feelings of resentment, emptiness, and hurt. But he did owe me 14 years of wisdom, love, and support and I was determined to get it. "Now you need to hear *my* story."

I filled him in on my point of view of life without a father. The lack of love, understanding, peace, and completion in my heart that was keeping me from discovering true self worth. He listened carefully as I went into detail about the past and present encounters in my life. I asked my long awaited questions and he answered them openly and honestly.

"Tell me dad, why won't the bullying ever freakin' stop?"

"Girl, don't talk like that. That bullying is gon' stop and its gon' stop today."

"Yea right, " I replied.

"Don't you know bullies are just weak, hurt people themselves who try and take out their own troubles on others? I bet if you called them out on it, they would leave you alone."

"You think so?"

"Hell yea. Next time someone tries messin' wit you, you gon' say something like, 'What's the matter, you ain't getting' enough attention at home? You need mine?'" he came up with a few examples. Good stuff too.

"Once you expose their insecurities, I'm sure they won't wanna mess with you no more."

"What about when people talk about my clothes and my style, sometimes they're right and I could really step my game up."

"If you actually believe they're right, that's why they have so much power over you. The minute you stop givin' a damn about their opinions, they won't be able to hurt you. You have to learn to accept the things you can't change and change the things you can. It's simple."

Diesel once told me that. This was a confirmation. "That does sound simple. I could always up my gear game..."

"You sure can. With all the money your mother got when her parents passed, you better make sure you be going shopping on her dime every weekend!" he laughed.

"I will definitely start," I smiled, grateful for his wise advise.

"Then I have these issues with the cliques at my school. There's these groups of girls who just won't accept me, no matter what I do."

"Oh please, cliques are usually just a circle of people who don't feel comfortable enough about themselves to go at life alone. They need this whole group to validate themselves and once they find it, they not tryna let it go. Anyone at all who tries to step in and steal their shine is a threat to their position. As gorgeous as you are, it's no wonder you can't get in the mix. Those girls are probably hatin' on you, hoping you don't steal their boyfriends or take their spot on the squad or get into the schools they can't get into. Bump that girl. You don't need nobody's clique. And if you want one so bad, you might as well create your own!"

He was so on point! Maybe that's why I could never get on the squad. How did my father know all this? He was like dead on as he gave scenarios that almost exactly mirrored what I'd been going through with Christian's girlfriend. All the while I was feeling low and confused about being rejected from these groups when I was probably the biggest threat they had seen.

"Dad, I think you're right."

"I know I'm right! You were destined for greatness, honey. Don't believe for a moment that someone can rob you of that. There's a reason you're still here throughout all your challenges, throughout all your attempts at suicide, throughout all your beatings, and all your grief. As long as you don't give up, you are still in the running to succeed."

And he was damn sure right about that. I needed nothing else from my father that day but to live those powerful words he spoke. The bullying would have to stop here. I smiled and gave my father the long awaited hug we both needed.

The guard in the room moved aggressively close to us so we separated quickly.

"What about boys? Why are they so obsessed with sex?! And not enough with a good personality?"

"Uh oh, I was dreading having *this* convo..."

"Spill it, dad."

"Well..." he struggled to find the words. "There's level to this. The boys *your* age are all- experimenting. Just like you. Y'all are young and the only way to learn is to try things, that's why they gon' wanna sleep with as many girls as they can get. But you just better be careful if you gon' be out there *experimenting* 'cause I will break through these stone walls if I find out somebody done knocked you up or made you sick. Just get to know each of these horny little knuckleheads before you ever decide to be alone wit 'em. You never know their intentions and even when you think you do- you don't. Maybe- just maybe- when one of these little dudes puts a ring on it, he might be about something. But even then- you gotta remember not all things last forever. Just enjoy the moments, the good ones. And do away quickly with the bad."

I actually thought being with a guy would fill the void of not having a father. As much as I wanted- needed- and craved the touch of a dude, it didn't satisfy me for long. It wasn't the protection I needed nor was it the type of love I craved. They were temporary replacements for loneliness and the very worst kind. I was really looking for an agape love, a deep unconditional love, true admiration and respect; and most of those guys had no plans of giving that to me, especially because I hadn't yet found it in myself.

After finally meeting my father, I was ready to get to know him as he helped me get to know myself. Accept myself. *Love myself.* It didn't really matter now why he was there or how long anymore. It was a blessing just to put the broken pieces of my life back together.

I was so ready to build a relationship with him, his stepkids, my mother, Dr. Graham, and my newfound friendship with Tammy. I guess I just needed to know someone loved me. But I would have to stop looking for validation of myself in other people and things. I now had love flowing out from within. Starting with the love and loss of Diesel. I missed him dearly but knew he served his purpose in my life. Whether he survived his accident or not, he went out with a grand apology and I would continue to love him for that forever.

It was as if I finally found myself, and realized how much love and worth I had living inside my soul. I was no longer gonna allow anyone to take that away.

"I think I get it dad. You know how many times I didn't wanna live no more? But when I do continue on, I'd like actually see an upside."

"You gotta. Suicide is a permanent solution to a temporary lil problem. It's so dumb to give up without knowing how close you are to getting through."

"At the end of the day, all is well," he continued. "Life got challenges for every goddamn body. You ain't never alone so don't take it so personal," my father said. And for him to be sitting *jail* speaking all this positive talk, I knew I had to believe him. I would just have to be strong. "Things will *always* get better if you just believe in yourself and hang in there."

"You sure?"

"Positive, Patricia. I mean, look how far you've come without me," I listened attentively as he spoke. "Yea I know you may feel a little bruised but you ain't never broken. Life will go on, I *promise*."

The End

BONUS:

"THE SOUNDTRACK OF MY HEART"

My Collection of Poems

By: Patricia Thomas

I Heard It From The Basement

I sat in the basement and heard the loud noises,
I closed my eyes to block out the screaming voices
How bad it made me feel to hear the things I heard
All I felt to do was soar away like a bird
I ask myself "Did I do something to cause this?"
So why can't I be living in eternal bliss?
Everyone's shouting is bringing me great dismay
Do you know how it feels to go through this each day?
It has nothing to do with me, yet I feel their pain
Why do I hurt this way, am I going insane?
As the tears gently start to fall down my cheek,
All I do is listen, not a word can I speak
I shiver at the splitting sound of broken glass,
As each piece of my heart is being shattered so fast
It hurts just to hear the ones I love in such pain,
But whatever I do won't result in much gain
What I'm feeling right now is making me so weak
Sometimes I wanna fall into a never ending sleep
It pains my soul, it breaks me down
To know how they feel, to hear these sounds
But I must persist, I gotta fight
Overcome these battles with all my might
Stand by their side in the midst of stress
Find another way out of this crazy mess
I can't give up or ever give in
I must be strong, 'cause that's the only way to win

Loneliness Kills

She wasn't as beautiful as the other girls,
And didn't rock those expensive diamond and pearls
He hair wasn't long enough and wasn't as straight
She was seventeen, yet she never had a date

During lunch period she would always be alone
Wishing to be like everyone else, wishing to be known
She started to feel she wasn't as good as the others
She didn't think she compared to her only two brothers

One day someone made a comment that hit real hard
She felt so worthless, by hateful words she couldn't disregard
She ran home to her brothers as fast as she could
They were nowhere to be found, she wasn't feeling too good

So she wrote a note on how loneliness was too much to bear
And how being alone in the future was her greatest fear
Her brothers came home later that night to see,
Their little sister in the living room crouched on her knees

Scared to come closer and find out whether she'd died
They read her letter and realized she committed suicide
They cried out wondering, did this really happen to them?
They didn't even know their sister was having a problem

They slowly turned her over to see her still face,
Not knowing what to do in such a horrifying case
One brother questioned, "Could this truly be her end?"
The other shook his head and said, "It could have been
avoided if we had just been her friend"

My Ex

I was never unhappy when he was part of my world
The love he brought always had me wanting more
The way he got inside my soul and deep into my core
Before him I was hidden, he came and opened my door

Introduced me to things I had truly been longing for
There's no one else I could ever truly adore
Loving him made me feel like melting to the floor
My heart skipped a beat, my emotions would soar

His kiss, his touch, his voice did allure
The way he said my name was a sweet, tender lure
When we used to go out to eat or even to a store
He made me feel like I'd never felt before

The gentle touch of his lips on my smiling face,
Was like a magic spell that could not be erased
The way our eyes connected made my heart pace
Yet a feeling so perfect must have been a mistake

Because now that he's gone, my hearts in an awkward place
It hurts so freakin' bad that I cannot see his face
I'll be as strong as I wanna but he still makes my heart race
And I'll never forget the good times before he fell from grace

Empty

You left me so lonely, so empty inside
You didn't notice how bad you messed with my pride

I just wasn't able to figure you out
And you never understood what my love is about

I'd feel so defeated if this was a war
Your love so far gone, my heart you tore

How come you weren't able to simply understand?
Why'd you leave my side and let go of my hand?

I'm feeling so bare, so empty you know
So broken inside since you let me go

Don't you remember how good we used to feel?
You were the dessert of my every meal

But now I'm left hungry, starving for your love
And all I need is a miracle sending you back from above

Come back to me babe, show me the past was for true
Just never ever forget, I will always love you

Forgotten?

Maybe its me, but how come I am alone?
What happened to those convo's we had on the phone?

Don't you remember all of the things we've been through?
Remember when I helped you out and stuck by you?

And the times I forgave you over and over again
Have you forgotten how much I sacrificed back then?

How could you forget the good times we've had?
And the times I consoled you when you were sad?

I gave up so much for you and I'm not willing to stop
Because I need you to remember how I'd kept you on top

Please don't forget how much love I got for you
Maybe you've forgotten & you're acting like you never knew

I must ask again, did you really forget me?
You should have kept me in your heart, baby

Because you let me go with the memories we shared
And now you're acting like you never really cared

I can't seem to figure out exactly what went wrong
But I'm 'bout ready to forget you too, 'cause I've been puzzled
for too long

Understand, My Child

Understand my child, that you did nothing wrong
I don't want you to think it's been you all along
It's not your fault he didn't accept the love you gave
And don't feel upset that his love you still crave

Sometimes relationships work out that way
It leaves you in pain and your heart still wants to stay
You got to be strong, don't let it hurt you so bad
Don't sit pondering about the great times you had

He was wrong for not embracing your fruitful spirit within
Although you gave your all, and stayed close by him
He lost the most although it hurts you more
He doesn't see it now, but a great thing he's tore

They usually don't see the sacrifice they've made
'Til they've gone so far off and your love finally fades
I know you're still broken and torn up inside
But there's so much strength to be built where that pain now
resides

Just remember who you are & no man can change that fact
'Cause he won't be no different even if he take him back
You gave all you had and were so willing to give
All that's left to do is love, stay happy, and forgive

Build new beginnings and find greater memories to keep
Find a new love, not just in a man nor a late night creep
Recognize your values but don't let him take them away
See the love you possess and radiate it everyday

Enough

I've had enough of the yelling and all of your screams
It's about time you stop tryna influence my dreams
I've made up my mind and I know what I want
All these mean words you say are all that you've taught

Stop tryna turn my life into yours
I don't choose that path, I've already made my choice
I don't have your opinions, I don't share your goals
I don't think like you, I know things you don't know

You raised me, I know, and you did the best you could
But you don't own my mind, and I'm still gon' be good
I've had enough of your judgments, too much of your pain
You've made me feel like I'll be destroyed in the rain

But I'm stronger than that, that's something you should know
Of all the qualities you've reaped, that's one I did sow
We don't have much in common, you need to understand
That this is me and that's who I am

As my caregiver, my mother, you should know me really well
Just because we disagree, don't go sendin' me to hell
You need to start listening, please try to understand
I don't wanna fight no more, I just wanna take a stand

Lovely Loneliness

I am grateful for the strength of being independent and strong
But loneliness is a feeling that surrounds me when you're gone
It taunts me and leaves me longing for company
Though I wanna disregard it, seems like love don't love me
Once was close to a guy who had me feeling good inside
But he used and misused me 'til great feelings quickly died
There was another dude I loved but he didn't seem to care
Though I wanted to give my all, no way I'd be stripped bare
When a dude wasn't around, I'd indulge in my greatest craft
Drawing images in my mind, anything to make me laugh
Dreaming up the perfect man, but physical attributes don't
convey
One who'd fill my void and make me feel special in every way
At night, I lay my head down, wishing I wasn't on my own
Wanting to know what it'd feel like if my true love came along
I close my eyes and imagine I had him right there as I prayed
Yet I blink my eyes and the wondrous thought of him fades
I'm a strong young lady but I've still got my needs
I do what I gotta do, I wanna be where I wanna be
In the arms of a soldier who's got swag and some respect
Instead I'm ponderin' why I've dealt with so many guys I regret
I'm a smart single female, addicted to keepin' in real
Needin' a strong single male who knows how to make me feel
Who can entice me and delight me, always keep me smiling
I'll be his good luck charm and we can stay profiling
Who ain't tied down by seeds he chose to reap not sow
Who got an education along with a character I'd get to know
I have this grand vision of the joy I'll someday see
But today ain't that day and I'm still so lonely
Got my girls by my side and they've always helped me out
But that ain't what this empty feeling's all about
Its about having someone to hug, to kiss, to hold
To share this love in my heart, a love so gentle yet so bold
A hand to hold, a bond to share
Not even looking but I know he's out there
'Til we find each other out, 'til we meet face to face
I'm gon' embrace the love in me and do it at my own pace

Friend or Foe?

Friend of Foe? I really don't know
Thought you had my back, I turned around, where'd you go?
You were who I leaned on, and your secrets I'd never tell
But it was quite a shock that when I leaned, I had fell

Of all the times I stood by the very best of my friends
I thought we made a deal that forever had no end
I was always right there when they had been attacked
I took hits for 'em, felt the painful stabs up in my back

Never did I question if they'd do the same for me
I had enough faith not to doubt the obvious you see
I love them like sisters and some like a brother
I was loyal to you all, never placed one above another

My heart goes out to friendships, no matter what the cost
But in this game of friendship, I feel like I have lost
Those who took advantage, have surely hurt me to the core
But now I know my friends from foe, I won't be hurt no more

Closer

Wanting more than your voice whispering from a distance
I await a touch that travels far lengths to be experienced
You're far and I'm here yearning for your presence
Craving that great feeling that eases me when I'm tense

You don't seem to know how much I desire you here
I miss you, wanna kiss you, just want you to know I care
But my tears start falling from the ache of my loneliness
I reach out to capture the thought of you nonetheless

Needing you here to confirm these feelings are for real
Waiting patiently for the day I can finally exhale
I don't want none of these onlookers passing by
I'm lost and confused, 'cause I need you by my side

I want to be touched, please lay your hands on me
Step a little closer, reminisce on how we used to be
Reflect on the days I tickled you to tears
Then rolled over and let you scare away my fears

All I ask is that you love me like you did from the start,
Please come a little closer to my heart

Beauty

Beauty to me isn't judged but just what the eyes will see
Beauty is as beauty does, it's joy, love, and positivity
Beauty isn't a color, a size, a name or price
It's not always a certain look and isn't always looked at twice

Beauty goes beyond a surface to the depths of ones soul
It's constant sense of giving is beauty's ultimate goal
Beauty isn't just portrayed on someone's fair skinned face
Nor is it determined by ones height, weight, or race

The media leads us to think there's just one set type to be
But truly we must know, it's simply beautiful to be free
Beauty is a state of mind, loving yourself and others
It's beautiful to have the support of fellow brothers

Beauty is knowing what makes you happy and why
Beauty is finding things in life that with strength, gets you by
Your smile is so beautiful, not because of straight, white teeth
But for the joy it brings when you're sinking down beneath

Finding good amongst bad is worth experiencing it all
The lesson you learned is beautiful and will guide your next fall
Beauty to me is an attitude, a persona and a mood
These things are all unchanging as true beauty never should

Most of what we believe is beauty will fade over time
We all know our grandfolks were once considered a dime
But even still, I see nana's beauty because I know her heart
She's had that peaceful spirit 'til the end from the very start

That's all I want to be, gorgeous from within
Attractive for my heart and mind, never for my skin
So when you say I'm beautiful, I hope you truly see
The beauty I possess lies deep inside of me

Who Am I ?

While you're over there looking at me
Look into my eyes, what you see?
You see my dark eyes and my brown skin
But can you see the me within?

You see my clothes, my hairstyle too
Did you know I have something to say to you?
While you look on my surface and fail to see
The fascinating things I hold inside of me

The love I have for enemies and friends
Will go on loving, it has no end
I cannot change the past or take back the pain I caused
Just wanna get better and put negative things on pause

My family I appreciate but I guess not enough
There are just some times when they make it real tough
I fight and struggle keeping up with my school grades
While others think I have it all made

All my life, I have only wanted to succeed
To keep up in the world but it's difficult indeed
I fail and stumble, I digress and I fall
But people often forget, I cannot do it all

We all mistakes but not all can forgive
I realized that, in this life that I've lived
But I do my part, tryna make things right
Share my greatest gifts, because that's actually worth a fight

I may have loads of pain buried deep inside
They're buried down below 'cause those thoughts have died
I'm still moving on up, I'll reach the top
To become a better person, I'll never stop

So look into me a little deeper, as deep as you can go
There's so much more I'd like for you to know
I've been prejudged and misjudged so many times
Next time, look a little deeper, read between my lines

Start Your Own Diary Now...

Dear Diary,

I am (name) _____ a
(relationship status, sexual orientation, gender)
_____.
I have (siblings, children, & pets) _____
_____.
I love (significant other[s], family member[s])
_____
_____.
I am usually feeling _____.
Today specifically, I am feeling _____.
I enjoy (hobbies, pastimes) _____.
What hurts me most is _____.
What angers me most is _____.
When I feel this, I _____.
When I need company, comfort, and support, I call on
(friends) _____.
I love to go (favorite places) _____.
I'm most afraid of _____.
I look forward to _____.
I aspire to _____.
I plan to change _____.
I like guys/girls who _____.
I also want you to know, (share an intimate story,
feeling, moment, or issue) _____
_____.
I relate most to _____ in this book because _____.

To Continue writing, Purchase a "Dear Diary," journal at DeliciaDavis.com

You have a juicy story to tell us all? Share it at DiaryDiscussions.com

About the Author

Delicia B. Davis serves as the creator and a lifestyle writer of DiaryDiscussions.com, author of the 'Dear Diary' book series, founder of the performing arts company, Precise Production Group Inc., and contributor of the popular parenting magazine, *Mommy Noire*. She received her Bachelor's Degree in Media Studies and Journalism and has since, gained resourceful experience in the business of arts & entertainment having worked for *BET News, Liberty Studios, Cox Enterprises*, and with *NYC Parks & Recreation*. Her writing, public speaking, and performance skills are evident in all her works.

As a young savvy businesswoman, Delicia has owned a performing arts company since 2008. Through programs, performances, & events, she has changed the lives of youth & young adults by administering dance, drama, music, writing, & mentorship workshops throughout New York City. She has been publicly recognized for outstanding leadership, community service, and performance by former Councilman Leroy Comrie, NY1 News, the Dr. Oz show, and the Queens Ledger Newspaper amongst others. As a mother, friend, and inspirational woman, she lives by the words of wisdom she offers as a life & relationship coach. Her mission is to share with the world that success is within reach and everyone has the power to achieve it.

Meet the Author at one of
many book tour dates listed
at **DeliciaDavis.com**

Receive your **free** bookmark
jewelry with book purchase at
a live event!

Book the Author for public
speaking engagements, special
events, performances, & **free**
youth arts workshops!

Check out other books by the author:

"Dear Diary, The Bullying Won't Stop"

CUT & EDITED for younger readers.

Available at: **DeliciaDavis.com**